Tough spiders here.

Giant Spider Cluster Lair

Dense cobwebs get in the
and visibility's bad. Not
hat, but also there are
giant spiders. They're
and poisonous besides, so
need to steel yourselves
going in.

igh concentration of
enemies here.

Stairway to
underground lake.

Rain of Arrows Corridor

The walls have cracks that
let arrows through. Skeleton
Archers are stationed in all
the passages, so mew can't
take your time fighting.

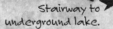

Deepest Part / Malicious Chapel

A chapel lined with
headless dog statues. This
is the altar-stronghold of
the Malicious Idol, the boss
of the left-hand route and
the strongest monster in
Forest Ragranda.

▲ Slime room with bad v

Yaaah! This feels great!

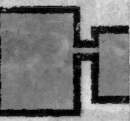

LOG HORIZON

Adventurer, you whose weight is borne by four winged soul! The mystical world of Theldesia
is home to dragons and giants, magical beasts and demihumans. Fragrant green winds...
across this new yet ancient land that opens below you...

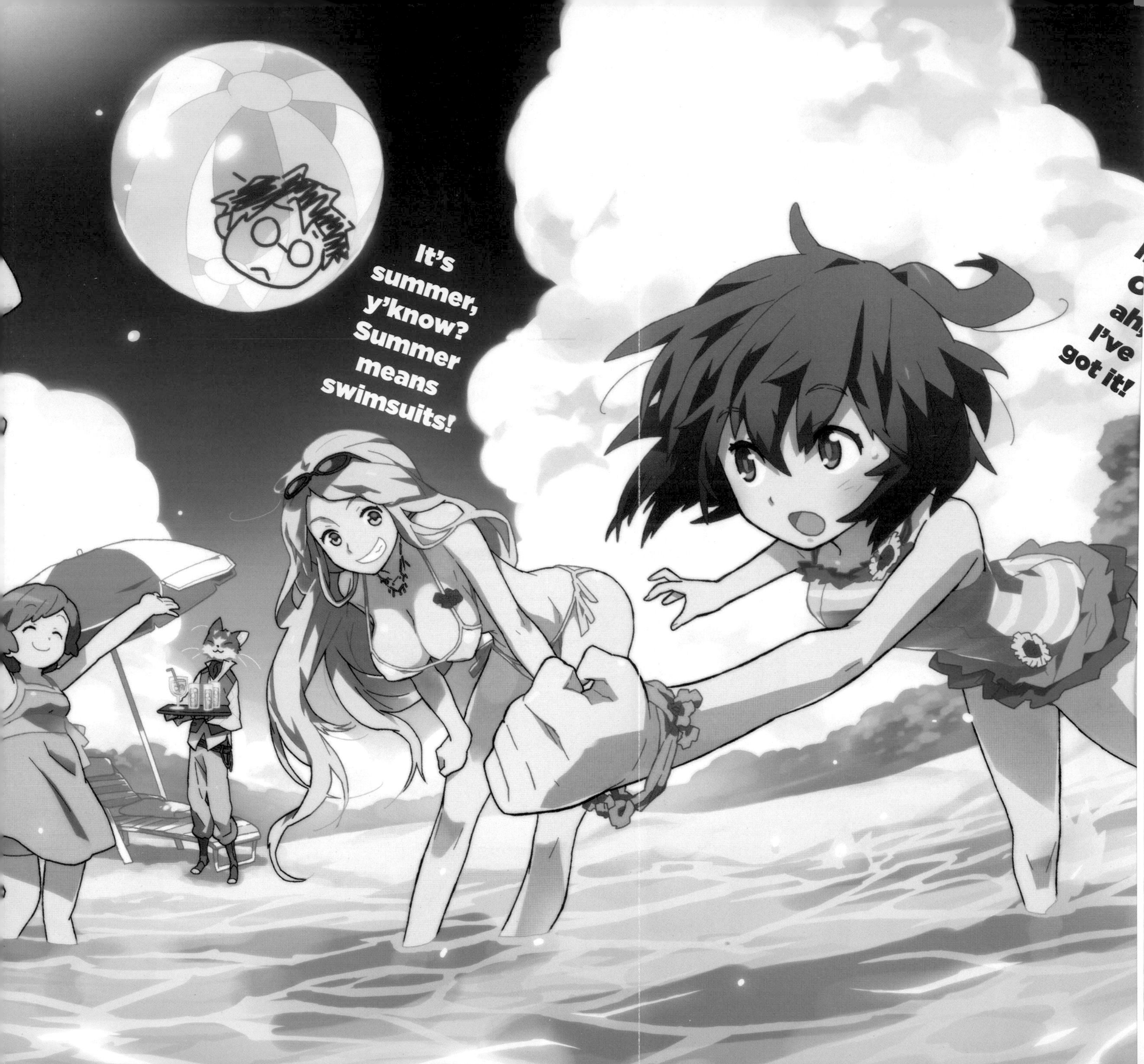
It's summer, y'know? Summer means swimsuits!
ah, I've got it!

Fragrant green winds blow across this new, yet somehow old land. The imaginary world of Theldesia is home to dragons and giants, monsters and demihumans. With a burden weighing upon your soul, go forth, O winged one <Adventurers> This land spreads out before you like a blank page; make your mark. In it!

L🜨G HORIZON

3 GAME'S END 【PART 1】

MAMARE TOUNO   ILLUSTRATION BY **KAZUHIRO HARA**

YEN ON
NEW YORK

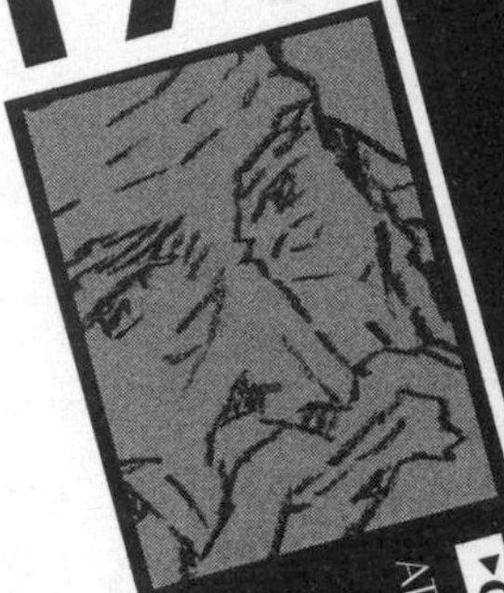

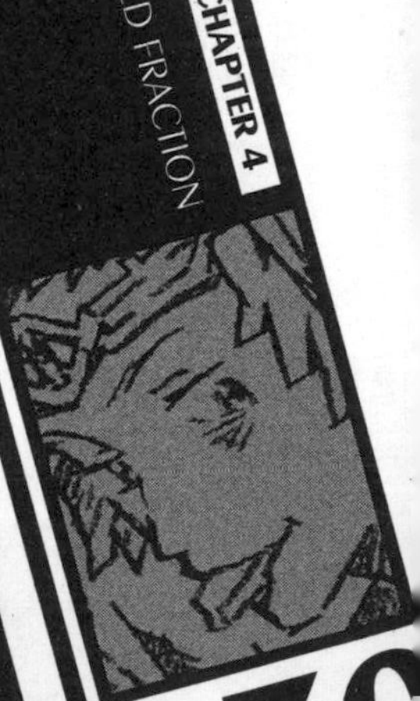

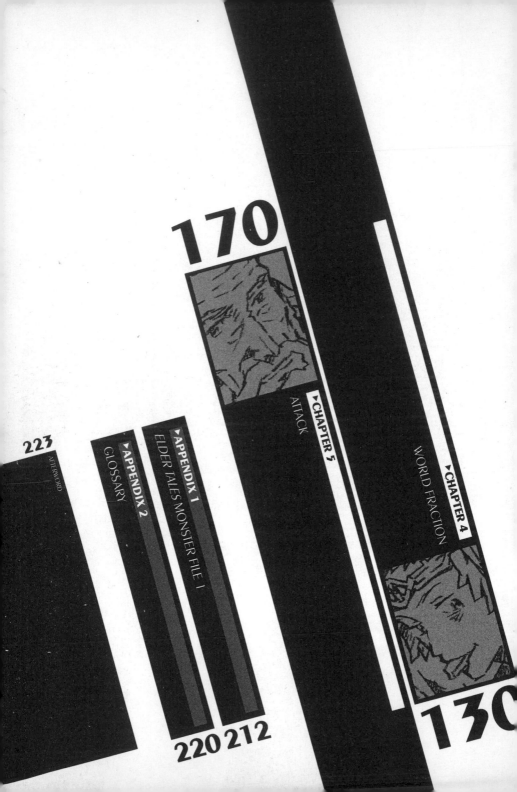

90

6

CONTENTS

1

▼ CHARACTER INTRODUCTIONS

▶ LOVELY ASSASSIN

AKATSUKI

▶ PANTIES WARRIOR

NAOTSU

▶ MACHIAVELLI-WITH-CLASSES

SHIRO

ALTHOUGH SHE FORMERLY HID THE FACT THAT SHE WAS FEMALE AND PLAYED AS A SILENT MAN, AFTER BEING SWALLOWED UP BY THE GAME, SHE CHANGED HER BODY TO MATCH HER REAL-WORLD SELF AND BEGAN PLAYING AS A SLENDER, BRILLIANT ASSASSIN.

A TRUSTY GUARDIAN AND SHIROE'S GOOD FRIEND: A CHEERFUL, TOUGH YOUNG GUY AND FORMER DEBAUCHERY TEA PARTY MEMBER. HE'D LEFT *ELDER TALES* TEMPORARILY, AND ON THE DAY HE RETURNED, HE GOT TRAPPED IN THE GAME WORLD.

AN INTELLECTUAL ENCHANTER WHO ONCE ACTED AS COUNSELOR FOR THE LEGENDARY BAND OF PLAYERS, THE DEBAUCHERY TEA PARTY. HE MAY BE A VETERAN PLAYER, BUT INSIDE HE'S A UNIVERSITY STUDENT AND HARD-CORE GAMER WITH HERMIT TENDENCIES.

▼ PLOT

IT WAS ONE MONTH AFTER BECOMING TRAPPED IN THE WORLD OF AN ONLINE GAME. THE TOWN OF AKIBA PERSISTENTLY CLUNG TO A ROUGH AND VIOLENT ATMOSPHERE.

SHIROE HAD INTENTIONALLY AVOIDED TAKING ACTION. BUT WHEN HE LEARNED THAT TOUYA AND MINORI—TWINS HE'D COACHED—HAD BEEN PULLED INTO A BAD SITUATION, HE FINALLY MADE UP HIS MIND: HE RESOLVED TO CHANGE THE TOWN OF AKIBA ITSELF.

LURING THEM IN WITH INFORMATION ABOUT FOOD, SHIROE ASSEMBLED TWELVE GUILDS THAT REPRESENTED AKIBA AND, USING A METHOD SO AUDACIOUS IT WAS PRACTICALLY A THREAT, INSISTED THAT THE TOWN NEEDED TO BE CHANGED.

AS A RESULT, ELEVEN GUILDS AGREED TO ESTABLISH LAW AND ORDER IN AKIBA AND FORMED THE ROUND TABLE COUNCIL TO GOVERN THE TOWN.

BY THE TIME THE TOWN BEGAN TO REGAIN ITS ENERGY, THE TWINS HAD JOINED SHIROE'S GROUP. SHIROE, NAOTSUGU, AKATSUKI, NYANTA, TOUYA, AND MINORI: THIS WAS THE BEGINNING OF THE GUILD LOG HORIZON.

NYANTA
▶ THE RETIREE COOK

A FELINOID SWASHBUCKLER AND FORMER DEBAUCHERY TEA PARTY MEMBER. ALTHOUGH HE'S A DAPPER GENTLEMAN, HE CALLS HIMSELF AN "OLD MAN." HIS CALM DEMEANOR MAKES HIM A CONFIDANT FOR THE YOUNGER PLAYERS.

TOHYA
▶ BOY SAMURAI

HE GOT CAUGHT UP IN THE CATASTROPHE RIGHT AFTER HE BEGAN PLAYING *ELDER TALES*. UNTIL BEING RESCUED BY SHIROE, HE WAS ABUSED BY A BRUTAL GUILD, BUT HE HAS ALWAYS BEEN A KID WITH A STRONG CORE. HE'S MINORI'S YOUNGER TWIN BROTHER.

MINORI
▶ MIDDLE SCHOOL MIKO

SHE'S A VERY RESPONSIBLE GIRL, AND SHE ACTIVELY LOOKS AFTER HER ENERGETIC, RECKLESS LITTLE BROTHER, TOUYA. AS TWINS, TOUYA THE WARRIOR AND MINORI THE HEALER ARE ABLE TO EXECUTE WELL-SYNCHRONIZED COMBINATION PLAYS.

【 ▲ THE GUILD MASTERS WHO ASSEMBLED FOR THE ROUND TABLE COUNCIL 】

PROLOGUE

Straining to hear the cry of a distant copper pheasant, the huntsman came to a stop.

Listening carefully to the sounds of the mountain, his ears were filled with the noise of approaching footsteps behind him.

It was nothing to worry about. The footsteps belonged to the huntsman's apprentice.

"…T-too fast… Haa, haa… You're too fast, master."

"Catch your breath."

His apprentice pleaded with him. His slight frame, not yet fully out of boyhood, was trembling.

He was fourteen. It hadn't been much more than a year since he'd begun training in earnest.

Compared to the huntsman—who'd devoted thirty years to trekking through the mountains—he was still wet behind the ears.

It wasn't that their physical strength was all that different. In fact, in terms of sheer strength, the boy might beat him. After all, the kid's beard still hadn't grown in yet, while he himself was going on fifty and his hair was graying.

Put simply, there was a knack to trekking through the mountains.

Ways of carrying your weight, ways of judging the stability of footholds, breadth of stride, posture: All were crucial. Without them, you'd end up wasting your strength.

Unlike the village, the mountains were a harsh world. Fundamentally, it wasn't a world that would tolerate humans. In the village, human laws were accepted, but in this green place, a human was just another animal. They were forced to fight on equal terms, the same as other living creatures.

Death was all that waited for those who spent their strength unwisely in this world. Deep in the mountains, simply surviving was a considerable ordeal.

…Or it was for the People of the Earth, at any rate.

For Adventurers, with their nearly inexhaustible strength, this wasn't the case. The huntsman had seen an Adventurer who looked younger than his apprentice *running through the mountains*, practically humming to himself as he went.

The sight had convinced him, to the depths of his soul, that they were different beings altogether.

Unlike people who lived in villages, the huntsman lived in the mountains. He was already well into middle age, but in the village to which he belonged, he was considered a skilled man.

His thick arms and legs, which seemed to have been polished red, and the solid line of his jaw gave him the unmistakable air of an expert. As a matter of fact, no one had ever gotten the better of him, even in drunken brawls.

The boy who panted and wheezed beside him, gasping for breath, had chosen to become a huntsman out of admiration for him. Once in the mountains, the huntsman used his skills with a bow to bag deer and boar, bringing precious meat back to the settlement, and he was a key figure in his small, impoverished village.

However, for that very reason, he knew his limits.

No matter what he did, he couldn't compete with an Adventurer. They might as well have been wind and thunder. Although he'd never met one personally, to him Adventurers were like dragons or other mighty monsters simply condensed into human form.

"Let's go."

With that brusque declaration, the huntsman set off.

Behind him came a pitiful wail, but he paid it no attention. He'd been put through grueling training like this by his own master, and in the process, he'd stolen the tricks of mountain trekking. If the boy broke this easily, he wouldn't learn a thing. Besides, the pack the boy carried wasn't even half the size of his own.

He detoured around a thicket, making for the ridge.

There was a regular rhythm to his pace, and he seemed nonchalant, but the huntsman was keeping a watchful eye on the undergrowth. The route they were traveling wasn't one of the trails that deer and boar used regularly. However, a man who let his guard down simply because that was the case would never last as a huntsman.

It was summer. The deep mountains were coming to life, and he knew bears would be out and about. He wanted to avoid a sudden encounter with one.

"M-master, where are we going?"

"The east ridge."

The mountain range they were hiking along was a vast region commonly known in Yamato as the Mountains of Ouu. Of course, the huntsman and his apprentice were from a nameless village up in the mountains; everything that surrounded them was "mountain," and they weren't particularly conscious of how far Ouu proper extended from where they were. To them, the mountains were just mountains.

The stream with monkeys. The great, craggy peak. Lone Cedar Ridge. If prominent landforms were referred to such that each party recognized them, that was enough.

The huntsman had planned to climb to Kite Rock Ridge by afternoon, then circle around toward its stream.

However, from the look of the boy, that might be overdoing it a little. Either way, once they were up in the mountains, he'd planned to stay for a week or so, and he'd prepared accordingly.

If today isn't going to be good for much, I might as well train him a bit.

Once he'd decided that all they had to do was reach the ridge, they had more leeway.

Although it was nothing compared to the man's tightly strung hunting bow, the boy did have his own short one. It wouldn't hurt to put him through the mill for a while on the ridge. It sounded as if he'd been practicing his shot in the village, but no matter how good an archer he was there, it was pointless if he couldn't shoot in the mountains.

Shooting at a straw post on level ground was just a game.

If he couldn't shoot up toward a ridge or down into a valley, bagging prey that had hidden itself in the shadows of thick grass or poked its face out of a thicket, his skills would be useless.

The sound of the huntsman's short exhalations; the sound of the boy's ragged breathing.

The occasional sound of a machete slashing through the undergrowth went on for a while.

In the mountains, they couldn't make straight for their destination. As long as they were limited by the abilities of human feet, they had to find and follow a walkable route if they wanted to go anywhere. Although they were *climbing* the ridge, sometimes their path meandered away from it, and in some places they had to go downhill.

Not only would an amateur have gotten sick of the repeated changes in direction, they probably would have lost their sense of direction. After all, the forest that surrounded them was dense, and its wild growth—undisturbed by human hands—nearly blotted out the sky.

However, with a certainty that came from long experience, the huntsman made his way steadily toward the ridge.

Struck by a sudden sense of wrongness, the huntsman lifted his eyes from the ground. The feeling was like an aura. In specific terms, it was probably trivial information—the smell of the wind, the soundless sounds of the songbirds and insects that filled the forest—and none of it was at a level where it could be put into words.

However, the middle-aged hunter did feel that something was different from the way it usually was, and he stopped.

"What's wrong, master?"

"Shh..."

Checking the boy with a hand, the huntsman began to make for the ridge. Up until now, he'd moved at a rather leisurely pace, but now his body rocked from side to side he moved so fast. He forced his way up, practically tunneling through the bases of thickets, and when he reached his destination, he could see all the way to the next two ridges.

The land was like a crumpled, gathered tablecloth. Even from high places it wasn't possible to see all that far, but from this vantage point, he had a good angle.

He could see the winding, rushing stream, and the direction of the forbidden land that lay at its upper reaches.

The swift mountain stream, the one the huntsman's people called "the monkey stream," stretched far beyond the limits of his vision. Compared to the other streams that ran through these valleys, it was broad, and with the dry, rocky riverbed at its edges, it formed a long rift in the greenery.

"That's…"

The boy's words trailed off.

He had no words to describe it.

That was only natural. The man was more than three times older than the boy, with thirty times more hunting experience, and even *he* had never seen anything like this before.

The stream was blotted out.

Blotted out by something dark, and rough, and crawling.

Living creatures.

The distance was too great and their numbers were too vast for him to really tell, but their movements were definitely those of living things. A huge horde of something alive—most likely some sort of demihuman—was making its way downstream. No, with numbers like that, they probably weren't just advancing along the stream. The trees hid it from view, but a group of such size that it provoked vague dread was advancing through the forest that spread below, rustling the trees as it passed.

The huntsman stared and stared at the scene, as if he'd lost his soul.

It was an overwhelming interruption. A premonition of the end.

No matter what sort of creatures they were, the huntsman was certain he wouldn't be able to do a thing about them.

That probably would have been true even if he'd been an Adventurer.

The horde stretched as far as he could see, deep into the mountains— Toward Seven Falls, which the huntsman's people called "the forbidden mountain." Their numbers were so enormous that, for a long time, the huntsman and the boy could do nothing but stare at the sight.

CHAPTER. 1

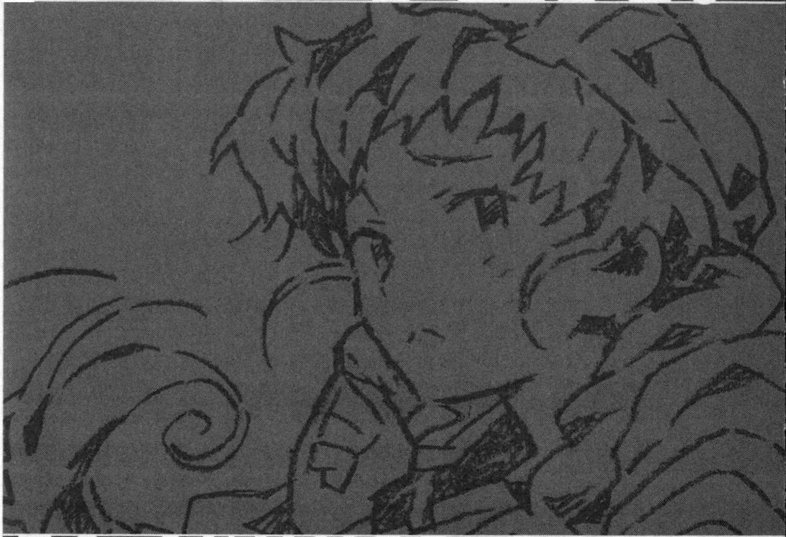

TO SUMMER CAMP

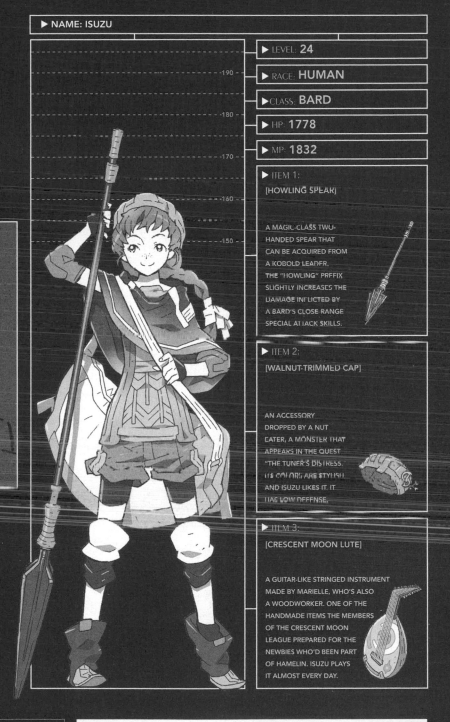

▶ NAME: ISUZU

▶ LEVEL: **24**

▶ RACE: **HUMAN**

▶CLASS: **BARD**

▶ HP: **1778**

▶ MP: **1832**

▶ ITEM 1:
[HOWLING SPEAR]

A MAGIC-CLASS TWO-HANDED SPEAR THAT CAN BE ACQUIRED FROM A KOBOLD LEADER. THE "HOWLING" PREFIX SLIGHTLY INCREASES THE DAMAGE INFLICTED BY A BARD'S CLOSE-RANGE SPECIAL ATTACK SKILLS.

▶ ITEM 2:
[WALNUT-TRIMMED CAP]

AN ACCESSORY DROPPED BY A NUT EATER, A MONSTER THAT APPEARS IN THE QUEST "THE TUNER'S DISTRESS." ITS COLORS ARE STYLISH, AND ISUZU LIKES IT. IT HAS LOW DEFENSE.

▶ ITEM 3:
[CRESCENT MOON LUTE]

A GUITAR-LIKE STRINGED INSTRUMENT MADE BY MARIELLE, WHO'S ALSO A WOODWORKER. ONE OF THE HANDMADE ITEMS THE MEMBERS OF THE CRESCENT MOON LEAGUE PREPARED FOR THE NEWBIES WHO'D BEEN PART OF HAMELIN. ISUZU PLAYS IT ALMOST EVERY DAY.

\<Fishing Pole\>
A magic stick that provides
both food and entertainment.

▶ 1

It was said that in the Age of Myth, many enormous cities had prospered in this region, covering the land's black skin. Perhaps that repression had spawned this backlash.

Although it was modeled after Japan, the plants in this world were lush and bursting with life. The undergrowth that covered the forest road seemed to spray up from the earth, and dense trees arched overhead, turning the road into a tunnel.

But black soil wasn't the only thing visible through the gaps in the undergrowth at their feet.

The asphalt that showed in places marked this forest road as something created in the Age of Myth.

Sunlight filtered down through the leaves, twigs became inky black shadows, and the tunnel stretched on and on.

For that very reason, the instant the greenery came to an end, the sight that leapt out at them was magnificent.

"Woooow..."

Minori gave an involuntary cheer.

The thirty or so companions that surrounded her seemed to feel just as she did.

"Yahaaah! Whoa! Dude-dude-*dude*!!"

Her little brother, Touya, promptly took the lead, spurring his horse from a walk to a trot and heading down the hill.

A strong wind that carried the smell of the sea raced up that same slope to blow over Minori and the others. The deep green road through the hills led from the pass they'd just crossed to the coast.

What was the name of the wide river that cut across the view?

On a hill that overlooked the seashore beyond, there stood a line of windmills several dozen meters tall. They couldn't tell whether the structures were ruined hulks or still in operation.

The coast was a brilliant white line.

They were still about ten kilometers away; from where they stood, it only sparkled and shone, and they couldn't make out any details.

"'Kay, folks! Save the celebratin' for when we're there. If we don't get there quick and find the campsite, no one's gettin' dinner!"

"You heard the lady. Skipping meals in the middle of a trip is *brutal*, guys~!" Naotsugu broke in, attaching his own joke to Marielle's words.

The newbies had dismounted on the forest road, but with a cheerful shout, they remounted their horses, formed two lines, and began to descend the hill.

The Zantleaf region.

In the real world, it was an area that consisted of the Bousou Peninsula and its surroundings.

In the world condensed by the Half-Gaia Project, it was a bit under fifty kilometers from Akiba as the crow flies. In this ruined world, where monsters lurked, the journey had taken three days.

"Are mew all right, Minoricchi?"

"Y-yes sir."

The slim, lanky figure that blocked the dappled light was Nyanta, a fellow member of Minori's guild, Log Horizon. His gaze was kind, his eyes narrowed in a smile, and Minori hastily answered in the affirmative.

When she looked, the Guardian Naotsugu, up near the head of the line, had also turned back to look her way. Minori gave a little wave to reassure him. It was soothing to be surrounded by friends from the same guild.

Although it had also been a guild, Minori realized once again that Hamelin had been nothing like this.

This party wasn't composed entirely of Log Horizon members, however. It was a large mixed group, made up of volunteers from many groups. There were about sixty members in all.

Akiba's foremost megaguilds, such as the Marine Organization, the Knights of the Black Sword, and the West Wind Brigade, had sent delegates as well.

There were around thirty-five people in this group—the main group—but she'd heard that a team of outriders had gone on ahead and had already arrived. The groups ultimately planned to join up at their destination.

Minori's group was on a camping trip which had, apparently, started with Marielle.

Minori hadn't been there herself, but according to Isuzu, a close friend of hers who was a bit older, it had happened this way:

I wanna go to the beach. I wanna eat shaved ice and curry rice and ramen at the beach. I'm tellin' you, I want 'em! I want 'em bad!! Can I? C'mon, please? I can, can't I? I wanna to go the beach! Let's go!!

...That proposal had come from Marielle, guild master of the Crescent Moon League.

I can sort of see it...

Minori was a member of Log Horizon, but for a short time before she'd joined, she'd stayed at the Crescent Moon League's guild house. It had been a confused few days, just after she'd been released from the corrupt guild Hamelin, which no longer existed.

Everyone at the Crescent Moon League had been kind to Minori during her time there, and she'd been in the care of Marielle, Henrietta, and Shouryuu. Marielle making a spoiled suggestion like that, and Henrietta looking troubled: That had been an everyday sight at that guild. Minori found it easy to imagine.

I bet she threw a temper tantrum on the sofa.

The thought brought a visual of Marielle hugging a big cushion and kicking her legs to mind, and it made her smile.

She couldn't blame her for feeling like that.

Even now, Minori knew that many players were doing everything they could to get back to their old world, but their efforts weren't likely to be rewarded overnight. She hadn't even heard rumors about the discovery of a clue to a solution.

In this world, it didn't take much money just to survive, and if there were no clues as to what sort of efforts would get them home, it wasn't hard to imagine that boredom would follow.

As a result, if someone had decided they wanted to take a summer vacation, there was nothing to stop them... Or there shouldn't have been.

However, Marielle and the Crescent Moon League were currently in a special position. That June, on Shiroe's suggestion, the Round Table Council—an organization designed to handle Akiba's self-government issues—had been established. The Crescent Moon League was one of the eleven guilds on the council, and Marielle, its guild master, was one of the councilors.

Since its establishment, the Round Table Council had been at the heart of conversations in Akiba, and it had also been in a position to lead the reforms.

Marielle was one of those select members. Wouldn't it look bad for her to leave on vacation for two or three days, let alone weeks at a time? After all, it had only been two months since the Round Table Council was created. Every day was a flurry of new information, and it was possible to feel the town of Akiba changing from moment to moment.

At the three big production guilds, particularly the Marine Organization, the steam engine experiment had reached its final stages. Changing the charcoal-fired engine they'd initially envisioned into a Salamander-fired engine operated by a Summoner had made the device compact at a stroke and led to a technological breakthrough.

In addition, ovens and waterworks had been designed for the new style of cooking, types of clothing (mostly underwear) that hadn't been seen before had been developed, and a huge hot spring had appeared in town. In the past two months, new discoveries and plans for more had been launched almost every day.

It would have been scandalous for a councilor to take a long absence (for a vacation, at that) during such an important time. ...Still, however true that was, Marielle hadn't given up. She'd talked Henrietta and Shouryuu around to the idea, and they'd worked out a plan.

The pretext they'd come up with had been, "A summer camp to train the newbies who have been entrusted to us."

"This area ap-*purrs* to be cultivated."

Just as Nyanta said, the slope that descended from the foothills soon became a country road bordered by terraced fields. Pumpkins, eggplants, tomatoes, cucumbers... The trees over there might be fruit trees. There was a sweet scent on the wind.

"Minoriii! Hey, Minori! These are pears! Awesome!"

"Oh, *honestly*, Touya!!"

Touya shouted cheerfully; he'd gone off the road and clambered up onto a simple stone wall built on the terraces. How long had it been since they'd eaten pears? She couldn't remember, but they really did look marvelously delicious.

"The People of the Earth are growing those! You mustn't pick them!"

Yet even as she scolded Touya, Minori's thoughts were otherwise occupied.

A summer camp to train the newbies.

Releasing the new players from Hamelin had been something Shiroe's group had done on their own initiative; it hadn't had anything to do with the Round Table Council. The official explanation had been that by the time the Round Table Council was established, Hamelin's punishment had already been meted out.

However, it had been a rather delicate time, and support for the newbies had been one of the issues taken up by the Round Table Council.

For that reason, the Council had readily agreed to the Crescent Moon League's proposal. The Crescent Moon League had accepted nineteen of the thirty-five newbies who'd left Hamelin, which made it a training guild for new players as well.

That said, there were newbies who'd left Hamelin and had not joined the Crescent Moon League. Most of them were players who'd been interested in the production classes and had entered highly specialized production guilds.

There were also newbies who were fortunate enough not to have been part of Hamelin in the first place. They belonged to all sorts of Akiba's guilds.

If they were conducting a summer camp officially endorsed by the

Round Table Council, it wouldn't be fair not to invite these other beginners. Coming to that natural decision, letters asking whether they wanted to participate had been sent to the newbies whose whereabouts were known. In addition, a notice to the effect that a summer camp was being held as part of the support measures for new players under level 40 had been posted in Akiba's plaza.

At that point, it became an issue of honor among the guilds.

Some had even felt that if the event had been approved by the Round Table Council, they couldn't shove the whole burden onto the Crescent Moon League.

There *were* some councilors who stated their positions wouldn't allow them to go with their newbies for training, and so refused the task of assisting the effort. Guilds with total memberships of ten were one thing, but if big guilds with one or two hundred members didn't send a leader or two, they'd look bad.

So in addition to leadership, support was provided in the form of food and clothing, and contributions of the new equipment that would automatically become necessary at higher levels were made on a large scale.

As they stared in blank amazement, the matter grew bigger and bigger, until it had become a large summer camp attended by more than sixty people... This was the full story of the summer camp's beginnings, as told by Isuzu to Minori.

Before they knew it, the slope became more gradual, and they entered the dense rubble of a ruined area said to have been a city in the Age of Myth. Back then, the hilly expanse had probably held many single-story houses. Compared to large concrete structures, wooden houses deteriorated rapidly, and there were no prominent remains of stone; only decayed timber homes here and there, many of them buried in weeds.

The city forgone, the peninsula of the Zantleaf region had become an area of forests, mountains, and gently rolling hills—an environment brimming with lush natural beauty.

The wide river they'd been able to see for a while now was apparently called the Great Zantleaf River. In the real world, the area where that river emptied into the blue ocean was called Choushi. It meant "the saké bottle," because the peninsula made by the river curved in and then out like the neck of one. Yet even in this other world, the Pacific in August was a bottomless azure so pure, it seemed to melt into the blue of the sky.

When they reached the edge of the river, they found several huts.

A look around showed that many similar huts were scattered all along the riverbank. According to her brother and his friends—who'd energetically gone on ahead and scouted—the huts were used for mooring small fishing boats or raising them out of the water.

With this area so close to the ocean, the boats probably went down the river to fish there. Storing the boats here, a little ways upriver, might have been a clever way to keep them from being damaged when the ocean grew rough.

According to Marielle, the People of the Earth who worked as fishermen lived along the river; there was a fair-sized town a bit closer to the river's mouth.

After leaving the bank of the great river and detouring around a dense forest of Japanese cedars, Minori and the others reached a reservoir that looked to be about five hundred meters across. Beside the reservoir stood a ruin made of reinforced concrete—unusual for the area—and it didn't seem all that old.

"Whoa! Hey, it's a school!"

As Touya said, it seemed to be a school building from the Age of Myth. Viewed in that light, the flat area that spread in front of the ruin had probably been the sports field. The chain-link fence and the school's gymnasium were mere shadows of what they'd once been, but definite traces still remained.

"Okay! Hey, kids! Startin' today, this is gonna be home for a while! Today, ya'll split into the teams we put ya'll in earlier and clean out three classrooms. That's three from the east end on the first floor. We'll be sleepin' twenty to a room. …If we end up wantin' a little more space, we'll clean tomorrow, too, and make the place comfortable somehow!"

At her words, the members from the big guilds who'd gone on ahead to scout came out of the school building, mingled with the newbies, and got to work.

"We'll be barbecuin' on the field for dinner tonight, so make do with box lunches and rolls for lunch, 'kay? And then, let's see, Team Three. You and anybody with Chef skills, come with me. We're goin' to the village to do some shoppin'! We'll be greetin' the village chief, too, so be polite. We'll head out in thirty minutes. All right: Man your stations!"

Responding to Marielle's voice, the group began busily preparing for the training camp.

▶ 2

Marielle and the rest of the provisions procurement unit walked down a country road in the midst of a raucous chorus of cicadas.

All the new players trailing after Marielle had summoning whistles hanging from their necks or waists, and they seemed very proud of them. These were items used to summon the horses they rode. That said, there were a variety of summoning whistles, and the items they had summoned rather low-performance mounts for just a few hours a day.

However, as far as the newbies were concerned, they were precious magic items. Each of them caressed the whistles with their fingertips, as if they were very important.

The whistles had been handed out to the newbies in advance, as support items for the summer camp.

Marielle and the others were making for the neighboring town on foot.

Along the way, they saw many People of the Earth working in the fields.

They hadn't wanted to appear suddenly in a large group and make everyone wary, so they were traveling to the town rather slowly, as if they were out for a stroll.

Of course, everyone had a summoning whistle, so they'd probably make their return trip on horseback. No doubt they'd have a lot to carry by then. However, it was only about three kilometers to the town. Walking would take less than an hour, and they'd wanted to get a feel for the surrounding area while they had the chance.

"Mmmm. Somethin' smells right good!"

The faint fragrance of pears hung in the air.

"It certainly does. If we find some good pears, I hope we can convince the growers to part with a few."

"Yes, I'd love some pears!"

Nyanta had come along to lead the provisions procurement team, and Serara stuck close beside him. Minori also nodded quietly. Several of the newbies who'd chosen to be Chefs seemed to be eyeing the fields and evaluating the quality of the vegetables as well.

Under the summer sun, the tomatoes and eggplants shone like jewels. The tomatoes were like garnets, the eggplants onyx. All sparkled with water droplets and hung heavy on their vines.

In the old cooking method, no one had cared about the quality of the ingredients. It hadn't mattered whether an ingredient was a bit small, or withered, or even—in extreme cases—nearly rotten. As long as a player could confirm the ingredient item on their menu, these things had had absolutely no effect on the finished dish.

Tomato salad made with fresh tomatoes had been exactly the same as tomato salad made with withered tomatoes (of course, both had tasted like soggy rice crackers), and there'd been no difference between the two.

However, in the new method, where Chefs used their own hands and real-life skills to cook, they couldn't be careless about choosing ingredients. A dish made with tomatoes that were just this side of rotten could never be anything more than food made with spoiled ingredients. Of course, the Chef's techniques were also important, but in order to make food that was really impressive, they had to use fresh, well-formed ingredients.

"I'd love to make pizza with those!"

"I bet tomato sauce would be good, too."

For all these reasons, as they walked along, the newbie Chefs gazed at the fields with interest.

It was only a little past noon, and they saw People of the Earth farmers resting or napping in the shade under the trees after their lunches. Occasionally one of them would wave, and they'd return the greeting, asking what sort of vegetables they were harvesting, and perhaps promising to buy some on their way back.

Earlier, Calasin of Shopping District 8 had stopped by the town they were about to visit to formally pay his respects, and possibly rumors about this had spread: The farmers were universally friendly.

"This is shapin' up to be one great vacation!" Marielle said in a sing-song voice.

Her tone was cheerful. Nonchalant, Nyanta corrected her: "Summer camp, mew mean." Rumors of Marielle's reasons for taking this trip had spread through the group, and everyone knew, but it was probably his duty as an elder to at least attempt to reprimand her.

However, there was very little gravity to his warning, and it was more of a comedic jab than anything.

The town was near the mouth of the Great Zantleaf River.

Possibly due to concerns about flooding, it had been built a little distance away from the riverbank.

The surrounding country was level, and the gently rolling landscape was divided into square, tile-like patches, with this one used as a field, that one for flooded rice paddies, and that one for an orchard. As the mosaic gradually grew more detailed, storehouses and sheds for storing farming tools appeared, and it seemed to them that before they knew it, they were in the town itself.

It was nothing like the fortified villages surrounded with fences and walls that appeared in medieval tales of chivalry.

The town's central avenue was a thick ribbon of asphalt that ran parallel to a canal. It had probably been modeled on a national highway from the old world. The road was lined on either side with many houses built of wood or stone. Unlike in Akiba, though, there were very few structures that used ruined buildings from the Age of Myth; as far as the eye could see, the only ones were the cluster of gigantic storehouses near the river.

Along the avenue, they saw five or six shops with signs hung out.

Shiroe had told Marielle that he hadn't seen any shops in the villages they'd passed on their way to Susukino.

In farming villages that were designed to be self-sustaining, and in larger settlements that combined animal husbandry and agriculture, the general rule was that the villagers helped one another.

As long as they lived there, there was no real need for money. For that reason, specialized facilities such as shops probably weren't necessary. At least, that was how Henrietta had explained it.

However, this place, the village of Choushi, was more of a small town than a village. In a town of this size, there might be some meaning in having shops.

"Well, well. This is quite… It's far finer than what I'd imagined," Nyanta commented.

Of course it couldn't compare to the town of Akiba, but it was large enough that it made them wonder if it wasn't home to several thousand People of the Earth.

They stopped in the center of the wide avenue, and the rest of the group surrounded Marielle. People had always said that Marielle was good at looking after others. It made her feel a bit like everyone's big sister, and she didn't find it at all unpleasant.

"Let's see, now. Hmm. What'll we do…? All this shoppin'… I think I'll leave that to you, Captain Nyanta. Then, you're Lukisea, right? I'll give you money, too, so split up into two groups. Talk among yourselves and settle on what to buy. You've got memos, right?"

"Of course," Nyanta said, accepting the task.

Marielle nodded, then checked her own magic bag, just once. Having made sure the gifts she'd brought along were there, she looked around the group. As a formality, she planned to go call on the town's mayor.

Since it was just a social visit, she wouldn't need many people, but it was probably best to take at least one companion along for appearances' sake.

As she thought about who to take, her eyes met Minori's.

Why not? She looks like she's got a good head on her shoulders.

As she thought this and began to open her mouth, Minori spoke first: "I'll go with you."

She's sharp, too.

With that, the party split up to run their errands.

It sounded as though Nyanta's group planned to head toward the harbor. Apparently coastal fish were sold from the cluster of storehouses on the riverbank. Come to think of it, fresh meat was a common food for Marielle and the other Adventurers, but they hadn't had fresh *fish* lately. If there were delicacies around, it would be nice to try them.

"All right, then. You an' me will…"

"Yes, let's go pay our visit."

Minori might be a practical person, but, as she'd heard, she was probably still in middle school. She was so nervous her back was stiff and ramrod straight, and she walked as if she was marching. Marielle ruffled her hair.

I lost her to Shiro's place, but she really is a good kid, isn't she. … Hmm, I may've let a bargain run off on me.

"U-um."

"Hm? What, Minori?"

"Why are you patting my head?"

"Well, because I wanted to, obviously!" she sang out.

Minori was looking a little cross, but she won her over with a smile, and they walked down the avenue like a couple of sisters with only a large age difference between them.

On the way, they asked a Person of the Earth who had an armful of parcels and seemed to be a housewife, and were told that the mayor lived in a big, two-story mansion at the intersection just ahead. She said he was an old man over seventy, and that, although he governed the area, he was a sociable person, so there was no need to worry.

"All we need to do is pay our respects?"

"Yep, greet him, then give him what we brought for him…"

Marielle made a mental list of the things she'd talk about.

In her pack, she had a barrel of cherry liqueur she'd brought from Akiba. It weighed nearly one hundred kilos, and ordinarily, Marielle wouldn't even have been able to lift it, but thanks to her incredibly convenient magic-laced rucksack, she was able to walk around as if she were carrying nothing at all.

Other than that… She'd say that they'd be using the ruin for about two weeks. That they were about five kilometers away from the town, so they shouldn't cause too much trouble. That, however, they'd like to come into town to buy provisions once every few days.

"That's right. We'll pay our respects, exchange courtesies. We'll have to sound him out about layin' in provisions, too. If we buy too much from one farmer, people might start fightin' here in town..."

"Oh, that's right."

"Well, I guess all we have to do is listen to the mayor. Then we'll make some small talk... If there's any info around here, I'd like to get that, too."

"Information...?"

"Right."

Marielle nodded.

After the Catastrophe, this world had changed. The non-player characters were People of the Earth now, and, strictly speaking, they weren't sure whether they still performed the functions they'd had in the days of *Elder Tales*.

The People of the Earth who worked at the Market and the Bank seemed to be carrying out their duties as usual, but some, like the new clerks who had been hired by the Round Table Council, had begun to choose new lines of work.

Setting up a hypothesis based on that fact, they didn't know whether the quest system, which had been an important part of *Elder Tales*, was still functioning normally.

Quests were a type of mission, and the story component of the *Elder Tales* game had depended heavily on the quest system. For example, a place like the village of Choushi should have had quests such as "A ghost appears in a field outside the village. Please exorcise it," or "We're going to an island off the coast to catch fish. Come along and guard us."

Quests sometimes began with an item or place that seemed significant, but more commonly, the beginning took the form of a request from a non-player character.

This provoked doubts: Now that the non-player characters at the heart of the system had become People of the Earth, wasn't that function gradually being lost? Even if a certain quest was operational at this very moment, if that Person of the Earth lost their life, from that point on, the quest might not begin.

...This had been Shiroe's worry, anyway. However, Marielle could understand the sense of impending danger.

*　　*　　*

For example, in the days of the *Elder Tales* game, there had been "standard quests" that everyone completed. One of these quests had had a magic rucksack with a gravity-negating effect as its reward. Marielle and every other veteran player had this bag, and they used it all the time. It was just convenient. If, by some chance, it became impossible to undertake this quest, the new players wouldn't be able to get this magic bag. The effect that would have was probably greater than they imagined.

"Shiro thinks about all sorts of stuff, and he wants me to bring home as much info as I can. About Choushi, and about the People of the Earth. We think we know 'bout them, but we don't really understand."

"I see... Yes, you're right."

Minori nodded meekly, as though she'd been convinced. "What do you suppose Shiroe is doing now?" she continued.

"Kiddo? He's probably collectin' information, too. Or... Well." Marielle giggled, as if she'd just realized something. "He may not be gettin' to do much of that, actually."

▶ **3**

The bright, elegant melody came from a string quartet.

The vast hall was decorated magnificently and filled with the laughter of ladies and the murmurs of gentlemen. Even then, it was likely that only 40 percent of the guests were here.

They chatted in small groups scattered around the room, gathering at the sofas set along the walls and at the round refreshment tables, leaving the center of the hall deserted.

The official start time hadn't yet arrived.

Apparently, at parties like these, guests were expected to arrive a little late, and the tendency was even more pronounced among royals and nobles. Shiroe had heard as much from a waiter he'd flagged down a moment ago. He gave a small sigh.

We've made ourselves look like country bumpkins, I guess...

With the tragedy of being so inexperienced they'd had no way of knowing about that aspect of the situation, they'd arrived a bit early, knowing they couldn't afford to be rude. Apparently it had backfired.

With no help for it, Shiroe's group gathered at the wall, moistening their lips with their drinks.

This was the Ancient Court of Eternal Ice.

Located just two hours away from Akiba, it was a palace that had been built by the ancient alv race. That was the castle's backstory, at any rate. In the world of *Elder Tales*, the ancient alvs were said to have been destroyed, and their race existed only in the past. They had had outstanding magical power and all sorts of techniques, but had been obliterated in the course of history. Faint traces of them remained in the half alvs, one of the eight playable races.

The Ancient Court of Eternal Ice—located on the southern side of Tokyo, in what would have been Minato-ku in the real world—was a giant, masterless structure. At present, it was collectively managed by the feudal lords of Eastal, the League of Free Cities.

—Eastal, the League of Free Cities.

It was an alliance that governed the area that was eastern Japan in the real world. In *Elder Tales*, the area under the jurisdiction of the Japanese server was roughly divided into five countries and cultural areas.

The area that would have been real-world Hokkaido was the Ezzo Empire.

Shikoku was the Duchy of Fourland.

Kyushu was the Nine-Tails Dominion.

The eastern half of Honshu was Eastal, the League of Free Cities.

The western region was the Holy Empire of Westlande.

In what might originally have been a ploy by the game operators to add plenty of variety to adventures, areas with their own unique races, customs, and artwork were gathered on the Japanese Archipelago, which had been condensed by the Half-Gaia Project.

Of these, Eastal, the League of Free Cities, whose territory was eastern Japan, was a league composed mostly of city-states. More than twenty forces known as "noble domains" or "noble cities" had formed an alliance that stood in opposition to the Holy Empire of Westlande in the west.

Compared to the real-world Japan Shiroe knew, the number of humans in this world was overwhelmingly small. This was true even if the People of the Earth, whose population had increased tenfold from what it had been in the game, were included in the reckoning.

Human territories didn't cover a large percentage of this monster-haunted world. When compared to all of eastern Japan, even the areas governed by the lords who belonged to the League of Free Cities were no more than bubbles of safe territory on the surface of the savage wilderness.

However, even if their numbers were small, there were probably about two million People of the Earth on the Japanese server.

And Eastal, the League of Free Cities, administered only eastern Japan; but even then, social rules and systems of government were necessary.

In Eastal, that system took the form of feudal rule by the nobility. In *Elder Tales*, whose basic worldview was based on medieval European fantasy, these lords all referred to themselves as nobles.

Each had their own castle or mansion, wore a crown and mantle or tiara and gown, and ruled over the People of the Earth as typical aristocrats.

The lords of Eastal gathered here, at the Ancient Court of Eternal Ice, once or twice each year for a conference at which they discussed various political issues. They also renewed old friendships, formally presented their sons and daughters as nobles, jousted, and formed relationships.

Seen from certain angles, it was an elegant culture, but on the other hand, the shape of the allies of Eastal desperately helping one another in the face of the threat of monsters showed through.

The Ancient Court, with its supports of magical ice, had been built in what would have been southern Tokyo in the old world, on the site of Hamarikyu, and for these and other reasons, it was used by the aristocracy of the People of the Earth as a venue for conferences and social occasions.

Shiroe's group was standing idly in the great hall of the Ancient Court of Eternal Ice.

"Huhn. That's quite a spectacle. Nerve-wracking."

It was Michitaka of the Marine Organization production guild who'd spoken, and he'd probably meant what he said. He was openly staring at the palace's furnishings and decorations.

"Pretend they're all monsters. That will calm you down."

The response came from "Berserker" Crusty, the leader of the combat guild D.D.D. Contrary to the image his byname evoked, to all appearances, Crusty was a pale, thoughtful, handsome youth, and today he was making a tuxedo look good.

"That's so very you," Michitaka cackled.

He was also wearing a tuxedo, and the impact wasn't at all inferior to Crusty's. In the first place, tuxedos were Western formal wear, and they were better suited to individuals who were rather stoutly built than to slender ones. For the two warriors, they were the perfect dress attire.

On the one hand, the head of Akiba's largest production guild. On the other, a man who was not only the representative of its largest fighting guild, D.D.D., but the representative of Akiba's self-governing organization, the Round Table Council.

Considering their reasons for attending this conference, making an impact was one of the best things they could have done.

"He's right. You're the only one who'd feel more relaxed surrounded by monsters, milord."

That said, Crusty's comment had probably been too bold. The tall woman who stood beside him admonished him as she handed him a small glass of sparkling liquor. From what Shiroe had heard, she was a member of D.D.D., and her name was Sansa Takayama.

He'd guessed as much on hearing the dress code, but this might as well have been a ball. Assuming that it might be necessary since they would be socializing, the three Round Table Council representatives had brought escorts as part of their entourages.

"...My liege."

For that reason, the slight girl who stood at Shiroe's side also wore a magnificent dress. As if she couldn't even hear the guild masters—two of the eleven on the Round Table Council—she spoke to Shiroe in a voice that was thoroughly forlorn.

Shiroe looked down at Akatsuki.

There was a difference of nearly thirty centimeters between their heights, so if she came too close, instead of her expression, all he could see was the top of her head. It was pretty inconvenient.

That said, if he crouched down so that he could look her in the eye when he talked to her, she'd say, "Don't treat me like a child, my liege!" so there was really nothing to be done.

"What's wrong?"

"I, um… I look…w-weird."

As she pleaded, Akatsuki's voice was like a mosquito's whine. It wouldn't have been possible to imagine this voice from her usual attitude.

Shiroe was perplexed; he had no idea what she was talking about.

There was nothing strange about Akatsuki's costume. On the contrary: It was arrestingly lovely.

Her beautiful black hair had been arranged, and her petite, slender body was sheathed in a gown. Its overall basic color was pearl, but the train of her light, flowing skirt was dyed turquoise to a point about halfway up, and as the color continued upward, it melted into the pearl white.

The clean color combination exquisitely complimented her black hair and eyes, lending her a dignified beauty. "Umm…"

"You don't look weird. As a matter of fact, you look adorable. You're lovely. A fluffy, sweet Lolita strawberry! You're so cute I want to take you home. No, I *will*!"

That was a declaration just now.

Henrietta, shrewd accountant and the pride of the Crescent Moon League, had cut in as Shiroe hesitated, bewildered. Her honey-colored hair was put up, exposing her neck, and her costume was unmistakably that of a noblewoman.

Her beauty was neat to the point where it seemed hard, and, in contrast to her looks, she always wore clothes that were rather reserved. They gave her an air of tidiness and were quite popular with some of her fans. However, seeing her in the evening dress she wore now, he had to admit that aristocratic clothes like these suited her best.

"A-are you sure? I can't relax. It makes it hard to hide weapons, too…"

"Honestly! Where did you pull that *kunai* from?!"

"My lieeeege."

Akatsuki ducked around behind Shiroe's back, as if she didn't know what to do.

She wanted to hide from his eyes, but she didn't seem prepared to put any distance between them.

Akatsuki's too conscientious about the word guard.

Even as she meddled with Akatsuki, Henrietta carried herself as if she was used to this. Shiroe had asked about her previous experience with fancy-dress balls, and had been told that she had none. She had said that her composure was all bluff, but from what Shiroe saw, he guessed she was so taken with Akatsuki that she simply hadn't noticed anything else.

Akatsuki was a small, lovely, black-haired girl with the air of a swallow about her.

Henrietta was an intellectual beauty with honey-colored hair.

This time, these were the two Shiroe had brought along as his staff.

Why were Shiroe and the others in the great hall of the Ancient Court of Eternal Ice in the first place? The circumstances made for a rather long story.

It had happened in July, about a month before, when the town of Akiba was nearly ready to burst like popcorn from the heat of the reforms.

The Round Table Council had received a letter jointly signed by the lords of Eastal, the League of Free Cities. Written in the name of Sergiad Cowen, the lord who headed the list, the letter was both a request for their participation in Eastal and an invitation to the conference and ball that would be held at the Ancient Court of Eternal Ice.

Eastal, the League of Free Cities, was an alliance of lords that controlled the area that had been eastern Japan in the old world. Needless to say, Akiba was one of the towns in their area.

Logically, now that Akiba had established self-government, it was perfectly natural for Eastal to contact them, and it was one of the developments Shiroe had anticipated.

The Round Table Council convened immediately.

It was probably the first time Shiroe and the other players had received this sort of invitation from the non-player characters. Although it was a situation they'd seen coming, the tension that ran through the Council was no small thing.

Eastal, the League of Free Cities, a part of this world's sociopolitical system, was actively acknowledging the Council as a member and attempting to clarify its position.

Even as the Round Table Council buzzed, its members carefully analyzed the situation.

What would happen if they agreed to this request?

No doubt the intent behind the request was to acknowledge the Round Table Council, Akiba's governing body, as a member of Eastal's council of lords. In that case, it was likely that the lord (in this case, probably Crusty, the Round Table Council's representative) would be given some sort of noble title.

In addition, they could assume that their continued participation in future conferences would be required. The merits were that they could collect vast amounts of information about the People of the Earth, and would gain negotiation channels. The demerits were that they'd be pulled into the People of the Earth's politics.

So what would happen if they refused the request?

In that event, they'd lose the merits they would have gained had they accepted, In other words, they'd lose a negotiation line with the People of the Earth, and they would be unable to participate in the lords' alliance. On the other hand, they wouldn't be dragged into the politics of the People of the Earth.

They also discussed specific demerits. For example, would they incur the lords' anger and trigger a war?

At this point in time, Shiroe and the others guessed that that possibility was a small one.

Akiba, after all, was a player town.

It had proportionate commercial facilities, and with this many Adventurers in one place, its martial power left nothing to be desired. In the real world, the development of modern firearms meant that the fighting abilities of individual soldiers had ceased to be a major factor in whether wars were won or lost. However, in this other, fantasy world, magic existed, and the differences among individuals' combat abilities could still have a marked influence on the outcomes of entire wars. It was a world in which victory in one-on-one battles and great victories in strategic sites would have a huge influence on a conflict.

Generally speaking, the combat abilities of the People of the Earth were much lower than those of the Adventurers. Even among settlers living in pioneer villages in remote, fairly dangerous regions, for regular farmers, a combat level of 20 would be considered quite high.

Most farmers and huntsmen had levels under 10, while the levels of merchants, women, and children ranged from 1 to 5.

Of course the People of the Earth also had martial power on their side.

No doubt the lords had soldiers, knights, and magic troops at their disposal. Their armies were fairly large, and from what Shiroe knew, their elite troops probably had levels ranging from 50 to 60.

There were also People of the Earth who had been given special abilities, like the town guards. Their levels weren't actually higher than the Adventurers'. Instead, they used special "mobile armor" to guard specific town zones. This mobile armor conducted magical energy from arrays placed around the entire town and granted high-output magic-combat abilities. It was elite, magical tactical weaponry.

In addition, there were non-player characters whose combat abilities far surpassed even these. In the world of *Elder Tales*, they were known as "the Ancients." Shiroe didn't know the detailed folklore, but it seemed that while the People of the Earth considered the Ancients to be like them, they also saw them as special.

The Ancients. Indigenous folklore aside, in terms of the game, their significance was clear.

In this world, the People of the Earth were designed to be inferior to Adventurers in many ways.

By battling over and over, Adventurers grew. Their levels rose, and their combat ability expanded to dozens of times its initial values.

Even lethal wounds weren't enough to destroy them: They returned to the temple and revived. They found, or retook, powerful items that had been left in ruins and with monsters all over the world, further developing their combat abilities.

To ordinary People of the Earth, Adventurers were a type of superhuman.

Of course, for a game, that was as it should have been. Under the RPG growth system, it would have been humiliating—and very stressful—if almost all the characters who appeared were stronger than the player.

There was significant meaning to the fact that the People of the Earth weren't strong in the game. However, on the other hand, when creating story scenarios, it was necessary to have "superhuman People of the Earth" in the cast as well.

When *Elder Tales* was a game, it had been studded with countless stories in the form of tales and legends, backgrounds for adventures, and quests. While there had been all kinds of stories, some of the plots had required heroes. One such plot might have been: "That hero is in dire straits! Go to his aid!"

Since this was a game, the players were the ones who did the rescuing, but if the level of the non-player character they were rescuing had been too low, it would have affected their motivation to play.

For example, if the story was that an Adventurer who could defeat level-90 dragons was going to save a hero who had gone to King of Evil Spirits Lich, and the hero was level 15, the story wouldn't look right.

In that case, players were likely to think, *A wuss like you shouldn't have shown up in a place like this to begin with! Just stay out of battles. Man, I don't even feel like saving you.*

At the very least, if the hero wasn't powerful enough to let players say, "I've come to back you up! Let's combine our strength and defeat the enemy!" the story wouldn't be exciting.

It was likely that the Ancients had been created in response to demands from the designers in charge of writing the stories.

Although it feels as though that idea is really being influenced by the situation on the game's side...

In any event, the People of the Earth did have martial strength of their own.

One type was the lords' armies. In terms of level, they might not be much of a threat, but they did have numbers. Another was special structures from the magic civilization that players couldn't use, such as the mobile armor. Finally, there were the Ancients.

If they refused to participate in Eastal, the League of Free Cities, they had to consider the possibility that some sort of fighting might break out. However, as they'd thought earlier, the possibility wasn't a large one.

The three forces of the People of the Earth all had their strengths and weaknesses. Each of these had points that warranted attention, but in terms of total combat power, Eastal couldn't match the Adventurers of Akiba.

Even so, the Round Table Council wavered between participating in Eastal and refusing.

The main argument of those in favor of participating was that there were no particular merits to refusing. If they participated, at the very least, they'd have established a formal channel of exchange with the People of the Earth. If they weren't worried about combat power, the possibility that they'd have unreasonable demands forced on them was low, and the demerits of participating seemed small.

The main argument of those who were against participating turned on the idea of being given a noble title. Emotionally, they couldn't stomach the idea of themselves, the players, being decorated by nonplayer characters and acknowledged as their companions.

By the time both arguments had been clarified, the majority of the council was leaning toward participation.

This was because the claim made by those who were against participation was obviously an emotional one. Of course, the emotion was rather problematic, and it was true that most of the players could sympathize to some extent.

Taking this into consideration, the Round Table Council posted a simple report in the town plaza. The paper held a notice to the effect that they had decided to participate in Eastal, the League of Free Cities in order to facilitate the exchange of information with each of Eastal's lords.

In this way, it had been decided that in August, selected members from the Round Table Council would go to the Ancient Court of Eternal Ice.

▶4

The group had arrived at the Ancient Court of Eternal Ice that morning. The journey from the town of Akiba to the palace had been a quiet one, with no trouble to speak of. In terms of time, it was only about two hours away, which put it even closer than the Shinjuku Imperial Gardens.

There were ten people in their delegation. Appearing as a large group would have provoked wariness, so the members had been selected carefully.

The one who absolutely had to attend, no matter what, was "Berserker" Crusty, the representative of the Round Table Council.

The League seemed to have an aristocratic culture. It wasn't clear how they would view the Round Table Council, a self-governing committee; and if they intended to talk on equal terms with the nobility, the Council would have to send a representative as well.

Next, they thought about the second member of the delegation.

Crusty was also the head of D.D.D., the largest combat guild, so it was decided that, for form's sake, they should choose a vice delegate from one of the production guilds.

The candidates were "Iron-Arm" Michitaka, general manager of the Marine Organization, Roderick of the Roderick Trading Company, and Calasin of Shopping District 8, and each tried to push the assignment onto the others.

After some squabbling, Michitaka of the Marine Organization was chosen.

The three production guilds weren't on bad terms with each other by any means. Each had its own distinguishing features, and all supported Akiba. However, for producers, this was a time when the town seethed with new discoveries. None of them wanted to leave it. This was what lay behind their reluctance.

Michitaka tried to get out of it by saying, "It's more fun chasing after news about inventions right now," but after losing eleven rounds of rock-paper-scissors, he couldn't even complain. He'd tried to shove everything off onto Calasin, but that seemed to have failed as well.

Michitaka was, after all, good at looking out for others. Ultimately, he came off splendidly, displaying the caliber of the largest guild by declaring, "Well, there's no help for it. Go ahead and leave it to me." However, the fact that he'd stubbornly followed up with the comment, "If anything happens, I'll sprint straight back here. It's only a two-hour trip, anyway," was a secret known only to the Round Table Council.

For the sake of balance, they decided it would be best to send a third delegate who could handle practical business and information analysis. When the Council had settled on that course, all eyes turned to Shiroe.

Of course the councilors who made up the Round Table Council were players in charge of the prominent guilds of Akiba. Each of their guilds held members who were particularly good at gathering and analyzing information.

However, the ingenuity Shiroe had shown was still fresh in their memories. In addition, they probably felt that as the mastermind who'd gotten the Round Table Council established, he needed to get out there and work more.

Personally, Shiroe had also been very interested in the summer camp, which was, unfortunately, being held at the exact same time.

Since it had been advertised as training for newbies, Minori and Touya were attending from Log Horizon, and he couldn't be negligent about gathering information from the farming villages in the Tokyo area. He'd taken every opportunity over the past two months to investigate, but he still felt that his contact with the People of the Earth was fundamentally lacking.

Shiroe didn't want to neglect either event, and he felt torn. Michitaka pressed him enthusiastically—"No, you need to come, too. I won't let you make me the only one to go with him"—and so, with no help for it, the tide was turned.

At the request of the Round Table Council, Shiroe joined the delegation as its third member. Akatsuki had declared from the beginning, "I will protect my liege," and so she accompanied Shiroe by default, joining the party as an attendant.

Meanwhile, the role of acting as leaders for the summer camp fell to Naotsugu and Nyanta. Both were good at looking after younger members, and both had a wealth of fighting experience in this postgame world. They'd be reliable in practical combat training and could be counted on to deal with any trouble that broke out.

One of Shiroe's miscalculations had been that, when Akatsuki's participation was determined, before anyone knew what was happening, it had been decided that Henrietta would join the delegation as an observer from the Crescent Moon League.

Henrietta was accompanying them as "Shiroe's attendant."

This was fine, but she would be sharing an anteroom with the other "Shiroe's attendant," Akatsuki, and Henrietta practically danced for joy.

She's clearly after Akatsuki.

Shiroe could do nothing but crease his brow.

It wasn't that he disliked Henrietta. She was beautiful, intelligent, and dependable. On the contrary, she was a woman you couldn't help but like. However, she seemed to have slightly eccentric passions, and they worried him.

Of course, to other members of the Round Table Council who didn't know the circumstances, Shiroe seemed to have managed to put himself between a lovely girl and a beautiful woman, to have "a flower in each hand," so to speak. Even if he told them that wasn't the case, they'd never believe him.

The delegation to the lords' conference of Eastal, the League of Free Cities, was determined through this selection process. The representative was Crusty, chairman of the Round Table Council. The first vice delegate was Michitaka of the Marine Organization. The second vice delegate was Shiroe of Log Horizon. Additional secretaries and attendants brought the total delegation to ten.

This is, what's the word… Uncomfortable.

Even as he thought back over the selection process, Shiroe was muttering to himself. He was trying to be inconspicuous in a corner of the great hall.

Although the number of people in the hall was gradually increasing, Akatsuki clung to Shiroe, hiding behind his back, and Henrietta smiled an enchanting smile, also leaning close to Shiroe.

"I'd expect no less from Shiroe. Look at that composure."

That was what Crusty said to Michitaka, but he had it wrong.

Shiroe wasn't composed. He was at his wits' end.

"Well, when you're a hero like this guy. *Snrk!* Even at a big scene like this one, being surrounded by two women is… Erm. It comes real easy to him. Right?"

"I *beg* your pardon. A ball like this is no more than a hunting ground for pitch-black Shiroe."

Even if he got back at Michitaka—who knew what was going on and was making fun of him—later, Henrietta's misguided overestimation pained Shiroe.

…This was how it was.

Ever since the uproar over the Round Table Council's establishment the other day, to Henrietta, Shiroe seemed to have become the owner of an incomparably black mind when it came to plotting intrigue.

If that had been all, he could have complained about it, but in addition, she expressed an overwhelming confidence in that blackness, and this made it impossible to frame a retort.

He didn't get it, but to Henrietta, *blackness* seemed to equal "highly esteemed." Shiroe was tormented, unable to flatly deny someone who was being kind enough to compliment him.

"I'm honored that you've joined us this evening."

Just as Shiroe was about to open his mouth to at least attempt to say a couple of words to Henrietta, it happened: A man who wore a silver, fur-trimmed mantle and was unmistakably a noble came to greet Shiroe's party.

Whoa, that's amazing… He's the real thing.

In line with Shiroe's impression, the middle-aged man seemed like a genuine aristocrat no matter how you looked at him. He had closely trimmed whiskers, and the eyes under his silver hair were keen. Age had made him sinewy, but his muscles seemed to belong to someone who'd stood on battlefields when he was young.

His deep blue suit, trimmed with umber, was meant for summer wear and didn't look that heavy. He wore a belt decorated with several medals, and a pair of tall, black leather boots polished to a high shine.

"It's a pleasure to meet you, and we thank you for your invitation. My name is Crusty. I represent the Round Table Council that governs the town of Akiba."

Crusty is seriously brave. He acts like a noble.

Crusty's response had been smooth, and he didn't look noticeably daunted.

Michitaka made his greeting next. He also didn't seem particularly tense. In terms of audacity, these two were outstanding even among the members of the Round Table Council. Shiroe was convinced that they'd chosen the right people for this job.

"My name is Shiroe. I look forward to our continued acquaintance."

Still deep in thought, Shiroe also gave a brief greeting. To a bystander, his simple attitude seemed to have no hint of tension about it, so they looked like an audacious trio, not an audacious duo. But Shiroe wasn't aware of this, preoccupied with other things:

We'll save the detailed introductions for later. I'm curious about this man's identity.

"My name is Sergiad Cowen. I act as facilitator for Eastal, the League of Free Cities."

Although there was no way of knowing whether he'd picked up on Shiroe's feelings, the middle-aged noble introduced himself. "Sergiad Cowen" had been the first name on the letter that had been sent to the Round Table Council.

So this is him... That means he's the most influential person in the east.

Akiba was the largest player town on the Japanese server. However, that didn't mean it was the largest town on the server, period.

The largest city on the Japanese server was the city of Maihama, which was built around Castle Cinderella.

In this other world, Tokyo no longer functioned as a single city.

This was because the world population was less than one-hundredth of real-world Japan's population, which was over one hundred million.

People created and lived in small settlements and havens here and there, surrounded by castle walls. This was true of the old Tokyo area as well. The region held relics of the advanced scientific and magic civilizations, such as the town of Akiba and this palace, and these had been put to use by several cities, but there were no longer enough people to manage and control the entire region.

In this world, the "good" human races—the eight available to play—had fallen so far from the protagonist's seat that they could no longer maintain the sphere of influence they'd held in the Age of Myth.

As a result, the old metropolitan area had split into several small cities with self-defense capabilities. Of these, the largest was the city of Maihama.

The next largest is Akiba. Then Shibuya, another player town. Ike-

bukuro is big thanks to the Tower of Sunlight. What would have been Shinjuku in the real world was completely destroyed by the Behemoth outbreak, so... After that, a little ways away, there's Yokohama, Asakusa... And that's about it.

That was the outline of the environment in which humans lived in the current Kanto region.

The middle-aged lord who stood before them was the ruler of Maihama, the largest city in the Kanto area. Unlike Akiba, Maihama had no temple, so it wasn't considered a player town. That aside, it had good commercial facilities and an abundant range of quests. It was a place that any player of average level or higher had probably visited at least once during the days of *Elder Tales.*

The city was known for its striking midair gardens and its elevated walkways made of intricately worked metal, and the white Castle Cinderella, the city's symbol, was said to be the most beautiful palace on the Japanese server.

Here in front of him, Crusty had promptly struck up a conversation.

He was saying, in brief, that the Round Table Council was a self-governing committee made up of citizen representatives. That he served as its chairman. That they had been delighted to receive the invitation and had taken them up on it.

"Hm. Hm... Yes, I see. In other words, these 'guild' groups are like landless nobles, and the influential guilds converse with each other and govern themselves? In form, you could say it resembles Eastal's method of convening lords and holding conferences to determine rules of conduct, only on a smaller scale."

"That's right."

Crusty nodded in response to Sergiad Cowen's words.

"But in that case... Hm."

Accepting a drink from an elf serving woman who'd appeared in the hall, Sergiad brooded.

"Even if you are its representative, will it cause needless friction for only one member to receive a noble title?"

"We believe it may. If possible, we would prefer to decline that particular offer."

"Hmmm. That would leave us with a bit of a problem."

"Could you maybe give the Round Table Council itself a quasi-noble title, then, or give it the right to attend by considering it a noble? That way we could join you at the same table."

It was Michitaka who'd spoken. With the easygoing attitude of a great man, he joined Crusty in persuading the old lord.

I don't think they're much older than I am, but... It doesn't look as if we'll have any trouble here.

Standing a short distance away, Shiroe watched the three discuss the matter.

It was likely that Crusty, and even Michitaka, hadn't yet turned thirty in the real world, but here they were, conversing with one of this world's nobles without giving an inch. Even watching from beside them, he couldn't sense any unease, and even if the two of them failed in their negotiations, it wasn't likely that a few words from Shiroe would be enough to turn the tide.

"As expected, we seem to be drawing quite a lot of attention."

Henrietta whispered in Shiroe's ear. When he looked up, the great hall was already filled with guests. According to his advance research, twenty-four cities and territories participated in Eastal, the League of Free Cities. Each had one representative, two counselors, and four or five attendants. If they'd also brought children or grandchildren to present, there would be a total of several hundred people here. Even a quick look around showed him that the vast hall was packed with more than a hundred guests.

The enormous hall had been decorated for the ball. It was awash in scarlet and gold, and even with this many people assembled in it, it didn't feel at all cramped. The groups that chatted here and there were sending furtive glances their way; Shiroe felt them, too.

Even then, no one's coming to speak with us, which means... Are they deferring to Duke Sergiad? Or has some sort of secret agreement already been made? If not those, is there some wild rumor we can't even begin to imagine going around?

Shiroe considered this.

It was likely that just as he and the other members of the Round Table Council didn't know everything there was to know about Eastal, the League of Free Cities, Eastal didn't know everything about the Round Table Council, either.

The invitation had been a good example.

Neither was sure whether it was all right to incorporate the other into their organization through what would amount to an order from above, or whether they would be met with severe retaliation if they failed to entertain them with the greatest care and courtesy.

Each wanted information on the other, but the conversations needed to acquire that information would be careful ones, as they took care not to let themselves be tripped up.

Inevitably, their exchanges would require a lot of time.

We may be heading into some tough negotiations.

Shiroe squeezed his eyes shut, pinching the bridge of his nose. Crusty and Michitaka were currently conducting the biggest of the negotiations with everything they had. In that case, it was probably Shiroe's job to find a way through this while he had the chance, but at this stage, he had no ideas.

Of course, he'd gathered as much information on Eastal as possible beforehand, but it was only knowledge from documents and the town's taverns. Undiluted information from aristocratic society didn't often find its way directly to the general public.

While Shiroe worried, the music abruptly stopped.

As the murmur of the guests receded like the tide, the throng near the arch of the great hall parted to reveal a shining procession. In the midst of a stir of goodwill and anticipation, three young girls and their partners had appeared.

▶ 5

"That's my granddaughter, Reinesia. She's fifteen this year."

Duke Sergiad smiled.

As he did so, his aristocratic dignity softened, and he wore the gentle expression of a grandfather.

"I expect you aren't familiar with it, but this is a tradition of ours. Once they have reached a suitable age, ladies make their society debuts at this ball. The ten-day conference that begins tomorrow is a place to work out Eastal's various problems, but it's also a place for us to interact with each other. In order to protect our territories, we nobles use martial and financial power that we accumulate constantly, but in this harsh world, it isn't enough. Well, and there's no guarantee we'll ever be able to prepare sufficiently, but even so. Sometimes friends and relations are better protection for us and our subjects than swords or money or castle walls."

Possibly having opened up to them a little, Sergiad thus explained the importance of their social circles to Crusty and Michitaka.

"I understand. We form groups known as guilds, too, and we work with our friends to support each other. It's a bit like being family. Sometimes we help each other across guild boundaries. That's also the mission of the Round Table Council," Michitaka answered.

"There are limits to individual strength." Crusty's answer built on Michitaka's.

It was lip service, but lip service was appropriate to the situation.

"I believe you're right."

Sergiad smiled back at them, as if their words had matched his own thoughts exactly.

Even as Michitaka and Sergiad talked, their eyes followed the three girls, who had just reached the center of the hall. The escorts—who supported their hands as if they were something very fragile—were probably knights who belonged to their territories. Each was very much a dandy.

"They're all beauties," Michitaka commented.

It was a merchant's patent compliment, but Michitaka was probably glad to be spared the trouble of lying. This time, there was no need for empty flattery.

The girl who'd advanced one step beyond the group looked a bit younger than fifteen, but she was lovely, with a slender neck and an air of fragility.

"The one in the center is Reinesia, my granddaughter. The one on the right with spring-green hair is Apretta, the daughter of Marquis Lester of Ouu. The fiery redhead is the granddaughter of Sugana, the lord of Iwafune. They're all making their first appearance in society this year."

I see... They're quite beautiful young ladies. They're currently being "presented," and this will act as their society debut.

As they looked on, the music began.

Considering the circumstances, this had to be their first time dancing in public, but they must have practiced and practiced: None of the three betrayed any inexperience in their motions. That said, their expressions were tense.

Woodwinds joined the stringed instruments, adding greater depth to the gentle waltz, and Shiroe realized that the music sounded familiar. It was the opening theme he'd heard every time the game loaded, back when *Elder Tales* was a game.

In this great hall, only the ten people in Shiroe's group shared that shock and nostalgia. They looked at each other sharply, as if they'd been stung, and soon felt flooded with the urge to smile wryly.

When their eyes met, they shared the bitter thought that they really had come to another world and had no idea how to get home. However, that didn't mean they were in any position to lose their composure, and they carried too much responsibility to do so.

Soon the sequence of phrases came to an end, and the princesses curtseyed in dainty expressions of thanks.

"Here comes the second piece. ... You should go dance as well."

"Huh?"

Michitaka answered old Sergiad with a question and an incredibly dull-witted expression.

"As I told you earlier, this ball is a social occasion that precedes the conference. Look around. Everyone's quite interested in you. I'm speaking to you in their place simply because no one knows how to interact with Adventurers, and they're wary. If things keep on this way, I shouldn't think you'll have an easy time exchanging information, let alone be able to trust one another."

As he spoke, a hint of mischief showed in the dignified profile of the old lord and representative of Eastal.

"They all want to see our guests dance. You there, the raven-haired young lady. What about you?"

Finding the conversation abruptly focused on her, Akatsuki gave a small jump as if she'd received an electric shock and hastily fled into Shiroe's shadow.

"I am my liege's ninja. Ninja are shadows and guards. I-I-I could never draw attention to myself in a public place like this."

His eyes then went to Michitaka, who shook his head from side to side, a rather strained expression plastered across his face. "No, no," he said, "I'm clumsy. I really couldn't!"

Although he might specialize in production, he did have the physical abilities of an Adventurer: He shook his head so fast it left a blurry afterimage. It was funny.

Well, of all of us, Crusty's the one with the best presence, Shiroe thought, chuckling to himself.

Crusty might have the fearsome "Berserker" as his subclass and byname, but to all appearances, he was a handsome, intellectual man.

He would have looked right at home on an American football team, and the phrase "a solidly built, brilliant, elite, handsome type with glasses" suited him perfectly. In terms of position, he'd be the quarterback, and he'd probably be the sort of leader who could execute a frontal breakthrough.

His powerful build meant he looked good in a tuxedo, and, conveniently, a lady from his guild was in attendance as his companion.

"This sounds like a job for Shiroe."

However, before Shiroe could speak to him, Crusty himself gravely opened his mouth. Shiroe was about to tell him to stop kidding around, but he was checked by Crusty's extremely serious expression.

"I'd like to speak with Lord Sergiad a little while longer. If you go, Shiroe... What was it? That's right. 'This ball is your hunting ground,' isn't it? I'd like you to use some of those brilliant techniques for the Round Table Council."

C-Crusty... You're saying that on purpose, aren't you?! D-dammit...

Shiroe felt the blood draining from his face.

He could face down high-level monsters and take a firm stand at major conferences, but Shiroe was a counselor type, a person who made meticulous plans and built battle lines with measures that were sure to succeed. If he'd had ten days' advance notice, no matter how tough the issue, he would probably have found a way to get through it, but when it was shoved at him abruptly like this, he could only stand there blinking.

However, Crusty, the representative of the Round Table Council, was asking him to take his place because he had matters to discuss with Duke Sergiad, the foremost lord of Eastal. Even Shiroe would have a hard time objecting.

All else aside, because Crusty and Michitaka had been dexterously handling the negotiations up until a moment ago, Shiroe had been standing around doing nothing. Of course, he'd been thinking about future plans, but since he hadn't been able to find any hint regarding those, once a task had been given to him, his feelings of guilt drove him to take it.

Haaah... I guess I'll just have to go embarrass myself.

Shiroe's shoulders were on the verge of drooping dejectedly when he felt someone watching him. He looked up and met Henrietta's beautiful smile.

"Master Shiroe. Sagging shoulders don't suit you."

"That's easy to say, but... I really can't help it."

More than half desperate, Shiroe sighed, but Henrietta had put up her index finger and was wagging it from side to side like a professor.

"Gentlemen must never betray a lack of confidence, even if all they can manage is a show of courage. That's doubly true for a guild master, you know. Mari's silly and foolish and thoughtless—and, while I'm at it, buxom—but that's one thing she knows perfectly well."

She couldn't have been more right. Marielle's smile encouraged her guild members most at the times when smiling should have been impossible. Shiroe felt remorse.

He was well aware that although he was clever, his weakness was a tendency to borrow trouble and brood over futures that hadn't yet arrived.

"All right. I'm sorry."

"Very good. Now, then... Since you're such a good boy, Master Shiroe, I'll give you a spell."

"Huh?"

Turning elegantly on her toes, Henrietta came to stand in front of Shiroe. She held out a hand sheathed in a silk glove.

"Akatsuki, my dear? Watch carefully."

When, overawed, Shiroe took her fingertips, Henrietta twined his arm around hers in a natural gesture and walked him out to the center of the hall.

Wait... Miss Henrietta!

As far as Shiroe was concerned, this was overdoing it.

Even if they had to dance, there were lots of places where they could blend into the crowd and get through a number relatively unnoticed. A corner at the back of the hall, say, or near the southern exit. The center of the hall was meant for the banquet's guests of honor, and for people who were really good at dancing.

"Master Shiroe. Smile, and stick out your chest."

"……"

He felt himself gulp. True, he'd been nervous at the conference that had launched the Round Table Council, and he'd had several heart-pounding experiences during PK battles and the earlier large-scale battles, but this was a unique sort of terror.

He couldn't shake the idea that the guests who filled the hall were watching him and snickering, evaluating him.

"That's good. Hold that posture, and put your hand on my waist… No, a little higher. …That's right, as if your hand is resting on the small of my back."

"I've got a confession to make. I have absolutely no dance skills whatsoever."

"My. Don't say 'confession' when we're standing like this. You'll make me blush."

Henrietta looked up at Shiroe and smiled.

She'd changed from her usual career woman's rimless glasses, possibly to match her ball gown, and her eyes looked larger than he'd expected. Being smiled at like that made Shiroe feel flustered.

"That's not what I meant. Seriously, please don't duck the issue."

"Master Shiroe? You do know what my class is, don't you?"

"You're an Accountant—Oh."

Henrietta lowered her eyes. Gazing at Shiroe's chest, she listened closely and began murmuring in a soft voice. She was singing, faintly, like a songbird's twitter, so quietly that it would have been easy to miss.

Even though she probably hadn't heard this waltz before, Henrietta predicted it in advance, marking time.

"All right, Master Shiroe. Let's begin."

The music filled the entire hall, like bubbles that rose from champagne and burst. The third song began. Henrietta stepped toward Shiroe, as if drawing closer to the elegant, classical melody.

Shiroe kept his chest out, continuing to support Henrietta's waist. Henrietta turned and twirled like a fluttering petal, guiding Shiroe, murmuring all the while.

That's right. Miss Henrietta...is a Bard.

"Bard" was one of the twelve classes in *Elder Tales*.

Although it was one of the three "weapon attack" classes—in contrast to Assassins and Swashbucklers, who used their own methods to inflict high damage—"Bard" was a support class.

"Support class" was the general term for classes that made battles unfold to their advantage by amplifying their companions' combat strength and lowering the enemy's. In *Elder Tales*, the only two support classes were Shiroe's Enchanter and Henrietta's Bard.

Bards' defining characteristic was that they controlled music. As stated in their name, Bards had music-related abilities, and they acquired many special skills with long effect times. In the world of *Elder Tales*, where most special skills had effect times that ranged from a mere instant to ten seconds, Bards were unique: Many of their special skills had effects that lasted minutes, or even permanently.

Henrietta said that she herself had never participated in one, but it was safe to say that these powers displayed their true worth in large-scale battles, where players had to withstand pressure for much longer than they did in normal battles.

In addition, although they were less skilled than Assassins and Swashbucklers, they also trained in hand-to-hand combat, and they were particularly good with lightweight weapons such as slender swords and bows.

Since weapon attacks didn't use MP, in long-term battles, they combined weapon attacks that didn't drain MP with long-term special skills that had good MP efficiency. Their energy-cost performance was outstanding, and they could maintain their combat abilities long-term.

On the other hand, precisely because the class was so specialized to long-term combat, they had extremely low instantaneous force in all elements of attack, recovery, and support. Their ability to find a way out of a situation with a sudden reflexive action was poor, and the fact that the class required deep insight and an eye for future developments made it difficult to break into.

*　　*　　*

And now here was Henrietta, in Shiroe's arms, twirling and turning at the center of the great hall.

Henrietta took the initiative and led, without forcing Shiroe into the steps. Before long, Shiroe grew used to the motions.

To begin with, their bodies in this other world were dozens of times more capable than their real-world bodies. Compared to his real, Internet-addict's body, even magic user Shiroe had agility and strength on par with an athlete.

About the time Shiroe was beginning to have a vague grasp of the way his own body was moving, a tiny eighth note sprang from the base of Henrietta's throat.

"Are you starting to understand, Master Shiroe?"

"Starting to."

Even as Henrietta whispered in a small voice, she didn't stop releasing the tiny eighth notes.

C was a sweet orange.

D was lemon yellow.

E was spring green, and F was a bright blue.

The G note was a blue as deep as the sea, and A was a magnificent purple.

B was a red that was halfway between raspberry and the middle of a sunset.

Shiroe didn't know how she was showing them to him, or how she was managing to do it even as they talked, but the multicolored notes that spilled from Henrietta's chest drifted around them like tiny fairies, then dissolved into the air.

It was probably a visual effect from one of the Bard's special skills, but wouldn't it require extraordinary instincts to match the music this closely? Or was it something anyone with a Bard's musical skills could do?

In other words… It's like a music game.

Shiroe hadn't been terribly good at them, but he'd had some experience with that game genre in the old world. In the real world, there had been games where you beat a drum or cut a rug while dancing on the foot panel of the large main unit.

Compared to those, the tempo of the music was slower, and the steps were far simpler. Shiroe focused his concentration, linking the melody he heard with the rainbow-colored notes that skimmed past Henrietta's smooth cheek.

"That's right. Right step. Right forward. …Half turn."

"Yes, *maestra*."

As Shiroe answered with a small chuckle, Henrietta looked taken aback for a moment. Then he saw her expression change to one of dissatisfaction, but, for some reason, even that was intensely fun.

Ahh, it's been so long since I heard music and enjoyed it. Since my body began to move on its own, Shiroe thought.

Web TV, Web radio, MP3s. Before, music had been everywhere. It had been free and so ubiquitous he'd forgotten just how special it actually was.

Music was special.

Something that didn't exist in nature. Something humans had created.

Like food, it was the sort of experience whose richness they'd only noticed once it was gone. He was grateful to the beautiful Bard before him who'd never stopped playing melodies in her heart, even during the time when they'd completely forgotten music.

"If you're able to relax now, straighten your spine. We're being watched by a crowd, you know. Your steps must be light as a feather. After all, Master Shiroe, you're our pitch-black counselor."

However, Henrietta herself lectured him like a schoolmistress. There was no telling how she'd interpreted his smile.

Shiroe concentrated on keeping his back ramrod straight. Solicitous toward Henrietta in his arms, he raised his left hand, being careful not to hamper her movements, leading her fingertips.

Shiroe and Henrietta danced, turning round and round.

The music sounded much clearer than it had just moments before. He heard the melody, rode it, and his body moved naturally. His toes and Henrietta's crossed the hall, stepping enchantingly, keeping perfect time.

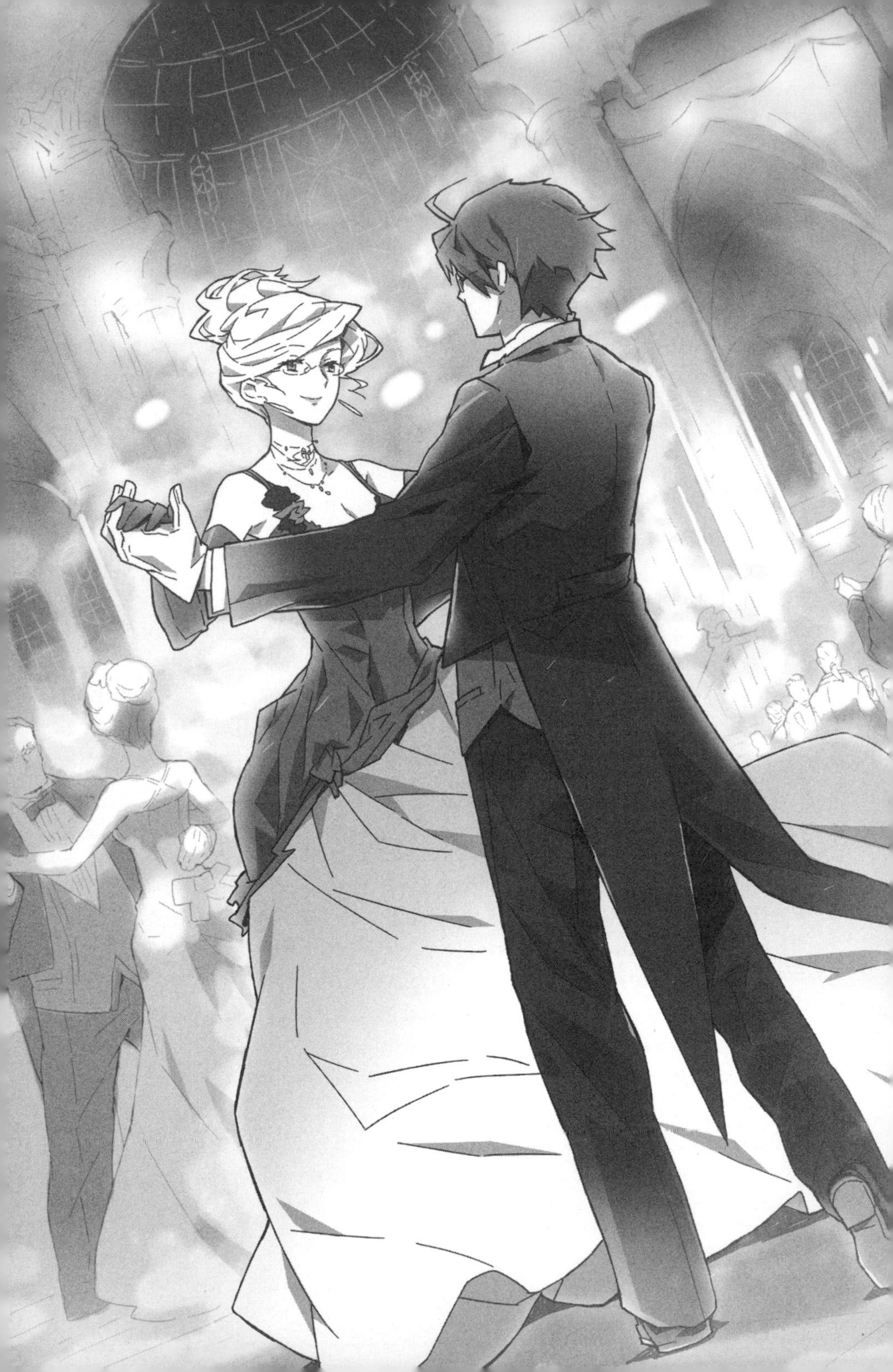

It must have been true that he'd relaxed a bit. Up until now, the great hall had been no more than a background, but now he could really see it.

Dancers spun around them like fluttering petals. The musicians performed their chamber song in perfect harmony, as if intoxicated.

Countless eyes watched the two of them. At this point, he could hear their quiet conversations clearly, even the spiteful whispers: *Apparently we can't write them off as mere backwater bumpkins.*

"Now then, one more dance. Let's leave every last one of those gossipmongers speechless."

"Understood. ...Milady."

As the next piece began, Shiroe and Henrietta took their first step into another dance.

CHAPTER.
2

FOREST RAGRANDA

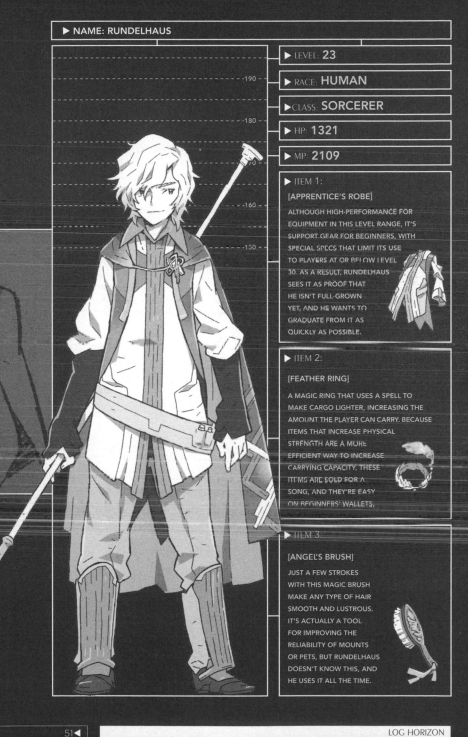

► NAME: RUNDELHAUS

► LEVEL: **23**

► RACE: **HUMAN**

► CLASS: **SORCERER**

► HP: **1321**

► MP: **2109**

► ITEM 1:

[APPRENTICE'S ROBE]

ALTHOUGH HIGH-PERFORMANCE FOR EQUIPMENT IN THIS LEVEL RANGE, IT'S SUPPORT GEAR FOR BEGINNERS, WITH SPECIAL SPECS THAT LIMIT ITS USE TO PLAYERS AT OR BELOW LEVEL 30. AS A RESULT, RUNDELHAUS SEES IT AS PROOF THAT HE ISN'T FULL-GROWN YET, AND HE WANTS TO GRADUATE FROM IT AS QUICKLY AS POSSIBLE.

► ITEM 2:

[FEATHER RING]

A MAGIC RING THAT USES A SPELL TO MAKE CARGO LIGHTER, INCREASING THE AMOUNT THE PLAYER CAN CARRY. BECAUSE ITEMS THAT INCREASE PHYSICAL STRENGTH ARE A MORE EFFICIENT WAY TO INCREASE CARRYING CAPACITY, THESE ITEMS ARE SOLD FOR A SONG, AND THEY'RE EASY ON BEGINNERS' WALLETS.

► ITEM 3:

[ANGEL'S BRUSH]

JUST A FEW STROKES WITH THIS MAGIC BRUSH MAKE ANY TYPE OF HAIR SMOOTH AND LUSTROUS. IT'S ACTUALLY A TOOL FOR IMPROVING THE RELIABILITY OF MOUNTS OR PETS, BUT RUNDELHAUS DOESN'T KNOW THIS, AND HE USES IT ALL THE TIME.

<MAID OUTFIT>
A MAGIC ITEM THAT
TRANSFORMS ANY HO-HUM
GIRL INTO A MAID
SUPER-BEING.

"Forest Ragranda?" Touya's voice pitched louder.

From the name, it sounded like a dungeon. When Touya hit him with that inevitable follow-up thought, Naotsugu told him, "It's not *like* a dungeon, it *is* a dungeon. Don't be dumb."

The sky had been lavender up until a little while ago, but now it was dyed deep indigo, and the field of the abandoned school where the group had decided to stay glowed red in the light of several bonfires.

Tonight, they were having a barbeque to celebrate their arrival at the base camp.

All the participants—around sixty, from what he'd heard—had gathered in the schoolyard and were noisily enjoying their meal.

It was August. The land had been scorched by the sun during the day, and it held on to that heat. However, the dry night wind felt good on their skin, and although they were sweaty, it wasn't that unpleasant.

Naturally, the food was superb.

Everything Captain Nyanta cooked was delicious, and when they ate in a big group this way, the atmosphere was indescribable. Touya had always loved this sort of thing. When he thought back, he seemed to remember pestering his sister, Minori, because he wanted to eat things served at the food stalls on festival days.

Minori had been bustling around handing out drinks, but when Touya waved her over, she came running. "What is it?"

"Hey. Minori. It sounds like we're going to a dungeon. Did you know that?"

"What? A dungeon?!"

Minori cried out in surprise, just as Touya had a moment earlier.

It was a three-week summer camp, after all. They'd naturally assumed there would be combat training, but they hadn't expected to go to a dungeon right off the bat.

"Me, too?" At her words, Naotsugu nodded.

"I know it's gonna be a stretch for you, Minori. You'll feel better being on a team with Touya than you would if you fought on different teams, though, right?"

"Well, yeah."

Touya nodded vigorously. Touya and Minori were twins.

In terms of exact birth times, Minori was technically older, but as far as Touya was concerned, just being older didn't make her his guardian. The feeling that he was a guy—and his big sister, a girl—was stronger. Since that was the case, although he wouldn't call himself her *guardian*, he did think he was the one who should do the protecting.

They'd be teaming up the whole time they were in this world anyway, so they might as well be together right from the start. More than that, Touya thought, if his sister got pulled into some kind of trouble, he couldn't even imagine not being able to be right there with her.

"Yes, that's…true."

Apparently his sister felt the same way. She nodded, meekly.

"Mew could go with the coast group if mew'd like, Minoricchi, but getting used to dungeons will put you mew in good standing later," Captain Nyanta said to her. He'd come up carrying a big, square platter piled high with grilled horse mackerel.

"The coast group…? What's that?"

Nyanta answered Minori's question with a courteous explanation:

Apparently, even though they were all newbies, there was quite a spread in their abilities. During the summer camp, there were plans to use this abandoned school building as a base camp, then split them into smaller groups by level, and put them through a variety of courses.

Players whose levels were extremely low—less than 20—would be fighting wild animals in the area around the school and giant crabs at the coast. They'd be accompanied by leaders and healers, so they'd be quite safe, and they should be able to accumulate experience nicely.

However, they'd be going up against solitary targets, and they wouldn't be forming parties. This was because, when working together as a party, if you didn't know what sort of special skills your main class had, what you could do with them, and which situations they were best used in, players couldn't combine their strengths. That was another reason for putting them through individual special training at this stage.

As a matter of fact, lots of the campers—Minori included—had gone down to the beach that afternoon, to "observe" it. True, Marielle had dragged them along with her, but they'd ended up playing at the shoreline in swimsuits. Minori felt a bit bad about that.

They had pushed all the work of setting up camp and carrying luggage onto the guys and had frolicked without a care in the world, as if this was vacation.

Marielle and some Crescent Moon League girls she was friends with had even had fun playing with a beach ball. "Wahoo! This is great! This's so much fun! It's summer, y'know? Summer means swimsuits! Talk about happy," she had proclaimed loudly. Her power to pull people in was truly fearsome.

Her bombshell figure was fearsome as well, and Minori had been just a little ashamed of her own childish swimsuit. However, if she'd overreached her style choice, that would have been embarrassing, too.

Adventurers whose levels were between 20 and 35 would undergo combat training in parties. There would be two types of battles: outdoor and indoor. The outdoor training would be held at the nearby Kaminasu Reservoir.

Meanwhile, the indoor training would be held in Forest Ragranda, the dungeon Touya had just heard about. It was located roughly half a day's journey from where they were, toward the peninsula's mountains. They'd be camping there during their dungeon expedition, and in a way, it was the hardest of the training courses.

Since there weren't many players whose levels were 36 and over, they'd be doing individual training. They'd be based out of the school building, and would receive instruction and tips on combat from high-level players. Every player was supposed to aim for level 40.

＊　　＊　　＊

Touya's combat level was 29. At Hamelin, he'd been made to work as vanguard for a hunting party, so he had passable skills.

Forest Ragranda, an underground ruin, reportedly held enemies with a wide range of levels. Players between levels 20 and 35 would be tackling this dungeon; Touya's level of 29 put him right in the middle, and it was likely that he had some difficult battles ahead of him.

When he imagined it, Touya felt the will to fight building inside him.

On the other hand, his sister Minori's Adventurer level was 21. Her level in her subclass—Tailor—was 32, which put her far ahead of Touya's subclass, but that wouldn't help her in combat. In terms of level, Minori would be forced to struggle hard. *I've got to protect her,* Touya thought.

"Well, we'll explain all that directly beforehand. If your levels are twenty-nine and twenty-one, your balance isn't that bad. All mew have to do is use your special twins' teamwork to fill in that gap."

Captain Nyanta squeezed *kabosu* citrus juice over the grilled, salted horse mackerel and began happily munching away. Possibly he'd been released from cooking duty for the day: He poured liquor from a jar into a bowl, which he then drained, looking truly satisfied.

"A dungeon, huh… I'm getting psyched!"

Touya couldn't stop the excitement from bubbling up inside him.

While he'd been Hamelin's captive, he'd gone hunting outside the town, but because of the round-trip distance and the balance of their skills, he'd never gone into a dungeon.

Dungeons in *Elder Tales* weren't necessarily underground prisons, as the name implied. *Dungeon* was the general term for enclosed structures in which monster battles were fought, such as ruins and castles, fortresses, towers, temples, and caverns.

Many dungeon zones were ruins from the Age of Myth, relics of the magic civilization, or simply natural caverns. Since these ruins had been turned into zones that were bases of activity in the wilderness, it was easy to identify invasion routes. There were many security advantages, they were sturdy, and therefore demand was high.

In this case, *demand* referred to demand from the monsters.

Many dungeons ended up being inhabited by monsters, regardless of the intent of their creators or those who had abandoned the space. Demihuman races who were intelligent after a fashion—such as orcs, goblins, and ratmen—settled in them and used them as fortified strongholds. Magical beasts such as Owlbears and Chimeras simply used these zones as dens, the way bears used caves.

Monsters with high intelligence, such as dragons and some high-level undead, were known to choose dungeons with high difficulty levels as places to hide their treasure.

Even though Touya had yet to invade a dungeon, he'd been part of Log Horizon for two months already. During his time at the guild house, he'd become great friends with Naotsugu and Nyanta, and they'd told him all sorts of things about battles in *Elder Tales*. Over the course of listening to them, he had accumulated a fair bit of dungeon knowledge.

Naotsugu said that battles in dungeons are way harder than field battles!

Touya was all fired up.

Naotsugu was Touya's current master.

Shiroe was Touya's benefactor and teacher, but when it came to weapon attack techniques and vanguard skills, he couldn't compare to Naotsugu. Yet even then, Shiroe had considerable knowledge, so he could probably have taught Touya what he was supposed to do.

However, Log Horizon currently had Naotsugu, and Naotsugu was an outstanding warrior. His history in *Elder Tales* rivaled Shiroe's, and even on the server, his experience was top-class. He was a Warrior, too, and Shiroe had recommended it, so at present, Naotsugu was teaching him.

Touya liked Naotsugu just as much as he liked Shiroe: He had a friendly personality that masked the age difference between them, and yet he was reliable, one of the good guys. Touya thought that men really needed to be about that, and tough.

Having been taught thus by Naotsugu, Touya was very conscious that battles were something to be challenged.

Someday I'll tackle my first dungeon and be on my way to becoming a full-fledged Adventurer. Saying the idea hadn't been on his mind would have been a lie.

"Okay, Minori! Let's do this! Starting tomorrow, we hit Forest Ragranda!!"

"Oh, Touya. …Honestly. I *will* catch up to your level, just you wait."

Minori seemed to have prepared herself; as she watched Touya, her expression was brave.

The two of them bumped their fists together in a greeting they'd shared since they were small.

The flames of the bonfires that crackled and snapped in the Zantleaf schoolyard that night seemed to give their blessing to newbies, and the resolve and determination they held that focused on the training set to begin on the morrow.

► **2**

The following morning. Minori and the others were making for the hills at the center of the Zantleaf peninsula.

There were no steep mountains on the peninsula. Instead, the whole area was covered with rolling hills. There were headsprings all through the countryside, ranging in size from puddles to ponds, and their pure waters flowed into the Great Zantleaf River, or directly into the ocean.

Even though it was only a few dozen kilometers away from Tokyo in the old world, in *Elder Tales*, it seemed like an untamed paradise.

In fact, even before they reached this place, they'd spotted lots of small, wild birds they'd seen before in the old world, such as bush warblers, Japanese tits, and crested kingfishers. They'd also seen deer. Wild animals like these could now be found all over the area controlled by the Japanese server.

The trees also reproduced vigorously. They didn't see any sacred, ancient trees like the ones in the town of Akiba, but Minori and Touya were deeply moved at the sight of several thousand magnificent Japanese cedars that stretched up into the sky, trees so thick they couldn't reach around them even if they linked hands.

Minori and Touya had been born and raised in Tokyo. Up until now, they had never felt the overwhelming power of nature.

The sight left Minori speechless, but Touya kept repeating the word "Awesome!" over and over, with his mouth hanging open.

How can my brother have such a tiny vocabulary? As his sister, it's a little embarrassing...

That was what she thought, and she meant it, but on the other hand, the fact that he was able to honestly express surprise and delight warmed her heart.

Their destination, which they reached after going up and down many, many hills, was a clearing where the trees had been cut away. When she kicked at the leaf mold that covered the ground with her toe, she exposed stone paving. At the edge of her field of vision she could see a huge, leaning *torii* gate, bleached nearly colorless by its long exposure to wind and rain.

Apparently this had once been the grounds of a shrine.

The fourteen members of the group who had journeyed here together dismounted from their horses, gathering in the center of the cleared square. They'd left the camp at the abandoned school before dawn and had reached their destination a little before noon.

They'd stopped to rest several times on the way Minori hadn't imagined that journeying through mountains would require so much time.

In the center of the group of newbies stood Naotsugu, Nyanta, and Lezarik, a male Cleric who'd been sent by the Knights of the Black Sword.

Nyanta pointed at the opening of a big stone cavern that they could all see.

"That's Forest Ragranda. The zone inside is quite extensive, but... Generally speaking, if mew turn right at the first T crossing, mew'll reach a slightly easier area, while if mew go left, mew'll find yourselves in a slightly more challenging area."

The newbies looked at the mouth of the cavern and gulped.

To tell the truth, Nyanta hadn't had to point it out to them. Their eyes had been riveted on the hut-like, underground entrance made of giant stones ever since they entered the small clearing.

Snakelike vines tangled around the opening, and although it was tattered, a ritual straw rope was strung across it. However, there was no hint of anything sacred in the air. All that was there was something rotten and poisonous, something that could only be called miasma.

"Oh, uh… You'll run into some small magical beasts in there, but most of the monsters are undead," Naotsugu commented, as if encouraging caution.

Undead.

It was the general term for monsters that, for various reasons, had been unable to die completely, or were driven by astral energy which had been bound to this world due to a curse or some other malicious reason.

Skeletons and Zombies were typical examples, but the term also included some monsters—such as Banshees—that didn't have physical bodies.

"This is a camp to hone your skills, and knowing your own limits is a skill. Always keep the way out in mind, and come back to the entrance when mew decide it's time."

"That's right. Take real good care of your lives."

Nyanta and Naotsugu both cautioned them.

"Naotsugu, Nyanta, and I will set up camp here and wait for you to return. We'll camp in this clearing, and you'll go into the dungeon every day. There's no need to capture it all in one day. I'll recover your health if you come back to camp, so don't worry about that." Lezarik was a stern-faced man, but apparently he was good at looking out for others, even so. He spoke as if to reassure them.

"Huh?! You're not coming in, master?!" Touya yelled.

In response, Naotsugu grinned at him and nodded.

"Well, duh. This is *a drill for newbies*, yeah? It wouldn't be much of a drill if you had a veteran along. You're a vanguard; you know this stuff. If I was the tank, you wouldn't get any practice."

This was true, come to think of it, but Minori still shrank back a bit.

It wasn't that she didn't trust Touya; not at all. On the contrary, she'd heard that Touya was an excellent tank (for a beginner, anyway). If anything, Minori was worried about her own recovery power.

Touya couldn't fully display his all-important stamina if the number of recovery spells he could get was limited, could he?

Still, since Naotsugu and Nyanta, their instructors, were saying this, she couldn't object. No doubt they were leaving it to them because they believed they could do it, and in that case, it was their duty to live up to those expectations.

The other newbies looked worried, too, but they were probably thinking the same thing. They all nodded.

Next, they split into teams.

Since the dungeon diverged into right and left sections inside, the eleven newbies were divided into two groups, one with higher skills, one with less advanced skills. Naturally, Minori and Touya were in the lower group. Their faces tense, Minori and the others split into two parties according to the list the Cleric read off.

The lower group, Minori's group, was made up of five people.

Since the maximum group size was six members, they were at a disadvantage in terms of combat strength. However, since there were only eleven members, one group would inevitably have five people.

The cornerstone of the vanguard, the one whose job it was to draw attacks and delay the enemy, was Touya. He was a Samurai and Minori's younger twin brother, and his level was 29.

The middle guard was Isuzu, a tall girl who was a Bard. She and Minori had been friends since their days in Hamelin, and now she belonged to the Crescent Moon League. She was a cheerful girl with freckled cheeks, and, unusually for a Bard, she used a two-handed spear. She was three years older than Minori, which meant she would have been in high school in the real world. Her level was 24.

There were three rearguard players.

First, a young male Sorcerer. Apparently his name was Rundelhaus Code. He wore a flashy robe, and his affected words and gestures made him stand out. It sounded as if he didn't belong to a guild. That probably meant he was a solo player. His level was 23.

Next was a Druid named Serara. She'd taken care of them on the day they escaped from Hamelin. When Minori had talked with her, she'd discovered that their levels were similar, and they had quickly become friends. She was also in high school, which meant she and Isuzu were close in age. Serara seemed to have a crush on Nyanta, and she'd ridden beside him for the entire journey here. Her level was 25.

Then there was Minori herself, a Kannagi. She was a healer, and her level was 21, which made her the weakest member of the party. Shiroe had taught her that actions in battle had nothing to do with level, but she couldn't help feeling uncomfortable.

The one bright spot was that the Druid Serara was also in her party. Even if Minori didn't have enough recovery strength, if she was with Serara, she knew they would get by somehow.

I wonder if Captain Nyanta arranged things this way because he knew that, too.

"All right, for the next fifteen minutes, I want mew to hold strategy meetings."

Nyanta clapped his hands and called "Go!" ending the orientation.

Minori and the others straggled into a group, still not entirely sure what was going on.

When she glanced up, the more advanced party—whose average level was about five levels higher than Minori's group—had also formed a huddle a short distance away.

"Umm, so… What are we supposed to talk about?" The moment the group was together, Touya spoke.

"Don't ask me." Isuzu looked around the circle, her eyebrows raised in incredulous confusion.

"Hmmm. I expect that's it. My friends: Shouldn't we simply build our enthusiasm?" Rundelhaus, who held a two-handed staff, spoke with what seemed to be complete confidence. The young man had blond hair and blue eyes, and it made him look like a picture-book prince, but as far as Minori was concerned, he seemed a bit too much like a pampered rich kid.

"Um…"

"Oh, yeah! That's gotta be it! We're heading into battle, after all. It's a dungeon, people! A *dungeon*!! Getting psyched up is key!!"

Interrupting Minori, Touya grabbed both of Rundelhaus's hands and shook them vigorously. "That's right! I see you understand! Enthusiasm is vital! Elegant grace is important as well, but the essence of men is enthusiasm and hot blood!"

Getting Touya's support seemed to have encouraged Rundelhaus. For some reason, they were really hitting it off.

Although I think we were supposed to discuss patrol file and formation...

"I see. Yes, let's do our best! It sounds like we'll be training in this dungeon for a week, plus we're teammates!"

Isuzu scrunched her freckled face into a cheerful smile. *I really can't say it now...*

When she sneaked a glance to the side, she saw that Serara looked slightly troubled, too. Still, there was no help for it, and when she smiled at her, Serara smiled back. That alone was enough to relieve Minori a little bit.

While Minori and the others were having their discussion, the advance party had gone straight into Forest Ragranda. Minori noticed only because Nyanta loudly called out, "Go give it your best!"

Unconsciously, Minori squeezed both hands into tight fists.

It had been two months since their escape from Hamelin, and Minori hadn't spent that time doing nothing. On the contrary, she hadn't really taken to being a Tailor, the subclass she'd been forced into at Hamelin, and she'd neglected it in favor of training under Shiroe, with Touya.

She had only been level 12 at first, and thanks to the training, her level had climbed to 21. However, Shiroe and the others had often lectured them about the ill effects of leveling up rapidly, and she thought that the pace of their practice had been relatively slow.

More than anything, Shiroe and the other high-level guild members had always been there to watch over them in battle.

This time, although a relief camp had been set up outside the dungeon, they would have to explore it—and fight in it—on their own. She couldn't have been anything but nervous.

She didn't think she was afraid of losing.

She was afraid to disgrace herself.

The thought that she might waste Shiroe's training seemed to turn her knees into sponges; they felt weak and shaky.

"What's wrong, Minoricchi?"

Finding herself addressed suddenly, she started and looked up. There was Nyanta's calm face, his eyes narrowed in their usual smile. His expression was inquisitive, and Minori shook her head vigorously. "It's nothing!" she told him.

Seeing her, Naotsugu chuckled. "Geez, Minori. You're such a worrywart.

"Listen up. If you run into trouble, step out in front. With your heart, not with your legs. Promise me, Micchi." Naotsugu dropped a hand lightly onto Minori's head, then walked away to speak to the other members.

Minori watched him go.

Naotsugu and Nyanta went around encouraging each member of the party and giving them advice. Serara was so moved she almost hugged them. Rundelhaus told them, magnanimously, that they could leave everything to him. Touya promised to bring back souvenirs. Isuzu gave an energetic bow of thanks.

"Okay, guys, there's probably enough distance between you and the first party by now. Get in there! Give it your best shot!!"

And so Minori and the others headed into their first dungeon.

▶ 3

The morning after the ball, Shiroe's group had breakfast on a spacious terrace.

The terrace balcony where Shiroe's delegation had gathered held a variety of ornamental plants, and the summer sun shone brightly through its crystal canopy.

The terrace itself was about the size of a small conservatory, and three tables were lined up on it. It was an astonishingly luxurious space.

The menu was orthodox, consisting of fresh bread and eggs sunny-side up, cheese and ham, jam, honey and butter. There was salad, an assortment of fruit, and several types of beverages. Each was presented beautifully.

Shiroe would have been perfectly happy with rice mixed with raw egg for breakfast, but this hotel-style breakfast held absolutely nothing to complain about. In the words of Michitaka, the production guild member: "Hmm, well, it'll do."

For the past two months, cooking techniques and the level of cooking in Akiba had been advancing by leaps and bounds. Although he had no idea what sort of tricks they were using, the other day a shop that served beef rice bowls had appeared, stunning Shiroe.

Processed seasonings that resembled soy sauce and miso were hitting the market one after another. From what he had heard, factors related to fermentation and maturation meant it would take years for their flavors to improve, but the taste was so welcome to tongues that had grown accustomed to awful food that it brought tears to their eyes.

"Nn. Pass the jam, my liege."

Akatsuki spoke to Shiroe; her tiny mouth was full of bread. Apparently her idea of "ninja loyalty" was a bit different from the rest of the world's, and aside from her calling him "my liege," their relationship was a very candid one.

"If you don't eat some salad, too, your skin will get rough, Akatsuki."

Henrietta was itching to meddle with Akatsuki, but Akatsuki seemed poised for flight on her chair.

"What a fine morning this is, eh?!" Michitaka interjected.

As he said, the sky was a particularly beautiful blue that morning.

No wind blew on the glass-enclosed terrace, but the canals that ran here and there kept it cool, and the summer made itself known, not by its heat but by its bright, sparkling light.

"Indeed it is."

"Berserker" Crusty was calmly drinking tea with milk. His attendants were also eating their preferred breakfasts. When they'd first arrived on the terrace, the three tables had been farther apart, and the caliber of the breakfasts laid out on them had clearly been different.

It probably mirrored the difference between "nobles and their families" and "servants" in the eyes of aristocratic society.

However, the party hadn't paid any attention to that. They'd moved the tables closer together, passed the basket of bread around equally and were eating whatever they liked. If there wasn't enough to go around, all they'd have to do was take some of their travel rations out of their packs. As a matter of fact, some attendants were drinking special thick, green drinks, even though (or because?) it was morning.

"This certainly is elegant. I assumed they'd prepare lodgings for us, of course, but I never dreamed…"

Henrietta's words trailed off.

The previous night, after the ball, the lodgings they'd been shown to had been more of "a wing" than "rooms."

One wing in the southeast corner of this floor of the palace held twenty rooms. In addition, it was equipped with small conference rooms, this terrace, a dedicated bath, a game room, a common room, and several reception rooms.

"Still, this is…hm."

"What, Shiroe?" Michitaka asked.

"Michitaka. Is anyone who came with you a Chef?"

"Well, yeah. What about it?"

"It would be a good idea to have supporting Chefs and service supervisors, and we should have ingredients brought in. The group brought in for support should be no fewer than three and no more than six, and they'll have to be skilled."

"True," Crusty said, responding to Shiroe's words.

"What are you talking about? I don't think they're gonna poison us."

Michitaka sounded perplexed. Shiroe answered him.

"No, I meant that all this space is probably intentional. …They're assuming we'll be receiving guests. The conference lasts about ten days, and I thought that was long, but various things are beginning to make sense. No doubt they will hold a big conference of sorts, but before that, there are probably going to be a lot of separate conferences or requests to chat—tea parties, if you will."

"That's probably true. As a matter of fact, I did get a number of invitations to tea during the ball yesterday."

"Come to think of it, yeah."

"I kept my responses vague, though."

As Crusty finished speaking, his expression was as cool as could be. Still, under the circumstances, it wasn't likely that the invitations would stop, and depending on the situation, some might be practically forced on them. Shiroe suspected they would need to prepare for it.

* * *

"I wonder what's going on with today's conference. …Hey, Caille."

"Aye-aye, General Manager, sir."

Michitaka called to one of the members he'd brought from his own guild. He ordered the young man he had called Caille to discern the schedule for the day's conference events. He also reminded him not to forget to gather information.

Caille left energetically, and Shiroe, Michitaka, and Crusty returned to their tea. The three of them were seated at the same table. The others were at tables near enough that they would hear right away if spoken to, and it was safe to say they were sharing the same conversation.

"…Looks like the situation's more complicated than I thought."

Crusty and Shiroe nodded, agreeing with Michitaka.

Eastal, the League of Free Cities, was composed of twenty-four noble houses. The addition of the Round Table Council would make it twenty-five. Their territories were scattered all across eastern Japan. Each regent noble had their own territory; most controlled only one fortified city, the farmland that surrounded it, and several smaller villages.

The largest of these was the City of Maihama, under the control of Duke Sergiad. Even then, its population was only about thirty thousand.

Of the three girls who had debuted at yesterday's ball, the remaining two were the daughter of Marquis Lester of Ouu and the granddaughter of Sugana, Lord of the Free City of Iwafune. The populations of both cities were around ten thousand each, which meant they were about average as far as nobles went.

Akiba had a total population of twenty thousand, of which fifteen thousand were Adventurers. Viewed in that light, it was easy to see how great a force it was. Setting aside the combat abilities of individual Adventurers, in terms of population alone, the town of Akiba was one of the five biggest cities in Eastal.

In addition, in this world, even in eastern Japan, there were countless tiny villages that weren't under the protection of a specific noble or territory.

It wasn't that these independent villages had objected to the rule of a lord and rebelled. On the contrary: In this world filled with monsters, they would have liked to be protected as citizens if possible. Apparently the lords were unable to send soldiers from their central cities due to distance and other reasons.

The role of a lord was to protect the safety of his citizens and territory. In some cases, in exchange for that safety, they collected taxes.

Of course, crimes occurred even within territories, and monster attacks probably happened as well. However, these unforeseen situations were completely different from not being able to muster an army large enough to provide protection.

If a village was less than a day's journey on horseback from the lord's castle, it could probably be protected, but it would require a constant military presence to protect villages that were farther than that.

Journeys and travel in this fantasy world took more time than one would think. In practice, rapidly mobilizing small units and using them to protect a wide area was an impossible feat.

Viewed the other way, there were lots of farming people living in this world who were not under the protection of a noble. If the lords could only obtain sufficient military power at low cost, they would be able to collect far more taxes.

Well, just knowing the general circumstances means all the information gathering was worth it.

To that end, the nobles had set their sights on the Adventurers.

This was why, even in the days when *Elder Tales* was a game, a huge number of quests had involved guarding villages or travelers and wiping out monsters.

Even if they had been rather like mercenaries, with a one-time payment, they could commission tasks that they didn't have enough regular soldiers to perform. They could even take it a step further and contract out duties that normally belonged to regular soldiers. If they did, their regular soldiers would be able to go to a different region or fight on a different battlefield.

In fact, it hadn't been at all unusual for lords to rely on Adventurers when an independent settlement that wasn't under their protection was attacked by demons or demihumans.

Ever since the Catastrophe, Shiroe and most of the other players had been very busy trying to understand the circumstances, survive and retrain themselves. Naturally, the demand for Adventurers in these independent settlements was probably growing. In addition, it was likely that the lords were aware that the Adventurers had touched off a technological revolution in Akiba and elsewhere.

"It looks like this lot wants to curry favor with us. Not that I can't see why."

As he added honey to his hot tea, Michitaka spoke for all of them.

"Now I understand what you meant, Shiroe. 'Our relationship with the People of the Earth'… We really did need to put measures in place here. If Akiba had stayed confused under these circumstances, there's no telling how they would have tried to undermine us."

"It's still too early to let our guard down," Shiroe responded, sounding glum. "There's a good possibility that they'll begin trying to undermine us now."

His insight, although it erred a bit on the side of the fantastic, was showing him several bad scenarios.

"For now, let's leave the talk about undermining for later. We can't do anything unless we know the other guys' basic action plans and what approaches they're going to take."

"True… What do you think, Shiroe?"

Responding to Michitaka and Crusty, choosing his words carefully, Shiroe began to speak of the situation he'd been processing since the previous night.

"I think it's already fairly clear what the nobles are after. Initially, they came to gauge how ambitious the Round Table Council and those of us in Akiba were. That and, although this isn't a nice way to put it, they wanted to see how barbaric we were. However, I think we can probably assume that these were resolved to a certain extent at yesterday's ball. At the very least, they know we're intelligent enough to hold a conversation, and that we seem to have common sense.

"Given that, their next goal will be to curry favor with us. Naturally, they're likely to give Crusty or the Round Table Council a noble title. As far as they're concerned, there aren't many disadvantages to that. If there's a cat, it should be belled. I think we can assume that all the nobles are in agreement on that point. Of course, there are probably many nobles who are jealous or feel rebellious. Still, they'll put that off as a decision that's already been made, and in the stages before that, they're likely to begin making individual attempts to win us over."

When Shiroe had gotten that far, the crystal door to the terrace opened and Caille, the young man from the Marine Organization, returned. He seemed to have managed to find the information: When Michitaka nodded to him, he made his report.

"They say we'll be officially contacted about it after noon, but apparently the lords' conference for today has been cancelled."

Hm, nodded Crusty. When Michitaka urged him to go on, Caille continued.

"From what I heard from the palace's servants—and apparently the servants take care of this palace year-round—the lords' conference is like this every year. It begins with a ball, and then there are lunches and tea parties, soirées and dinner parties each day. That's why they bring so many attendants. Apparently our party is relatively small, and so is the amount of luggage we brought. That's why we have all those rooms left over. Then, for a few days right before the final day, the lords' conference is held, the matters everyone laid the groundwork for earlier are discussed, and they wind things up quickly with the majority in favor."

Shiroe nodded.

Come to think of it, even though there were twenty-four participants, there were large differences in their power and the size of their territories. Rather than holding repeated lords' conferences and fielding majority votes and objections, factional maneuvering built around individual interviews and separate deals would make for a much smarter discussion. In Japanese terms, this was known as "laying groundwork," and it wasn't at all unusual.

"Since that's the case, beginning today, the schedule for the next few days is pretty clear. Of course, Akiba has high combat capabilities. Every lord knows that if they fought us one-on-one, they're the ones who'd be destroyed. As that's true, although they'll be very careful about approaching us, anyone who manages to secure the Round Table Council as an ally will be able to reap a huge return in this world as it is today. As Crusty and Michitaka said earlier, we'll probably get more invitations and requests for separate interviews. I'm sure we'll see scores of attempts to attract or employ Akiba's military power, financial strength, and people, as well as the products and items we've invented. For now, we'll have to get through these negotiations."

"And we'll need a basic action plan for that… Hm."

At Shiroe's words, Michitaka scowled. This was quite a knotty problem in its own right.

"As the Round Table Council, we can kick every offer to the curb, turn down every last thing. However, there are probably combat and production guilds who will want to take advantage of those commissions, and some guilds will. Guilds aside, players could even undertake jobs as individuals. It won't be possible for us to be vigilant down to the details. For example, buying something from Akiba's Market and selling it off in another town isn't the sort of thing we can stop by forbidding it. The same goes for combat-related requests. If they ask us to supply five thousand mercenaries, we can tell them it's impossible and can probably refuse, but if someone asks to hire a few Adventurers, even if we veto it, if there are players who will undertake the job, that's that."

"I expect that's true," Crusty agreed.

Akiba's new system was finally settling into place. Over this two-month maturation period, many Adventurers had begun to get used to combat in this other world. The backup systems, with a focus on food, were also falling into place.

The next wave would be the exploration of the world. Discussions of investigating the Fairy Rings would also begin to take shape. When that happened, the opportunities for every guild to accept quests and commissions would increase. That freedom should be guaranteed.

"If distribution seems likely to happen on too large a scale, we may have to consider tariffs… What do you think, Miss Henrietta?"

"…Well… Economics isn't my specialty, so I can't declare anything with confidence. I'm just an ordinary accountant, you know. However, at this point in time, what strikes me is that Akiba is not a town of primary industry. It isn't a place where we can harvest abundant crops or marine products. If distribution is going to cause any sort of trouble, it will probably be in processed exports. If we limit ourselves to imports, there won't be any trouble. On the contrary, we'll be in trouble if we *stop* importing.

"Regarding exports though, considering the transportation in this world, I think we'll need to be most careful with items that are relatively scarce but have great influence. Something that may cause larger issues than those is an outflow of techniques, or of people who know those techniques."

As Henrietta commented, she adjusted her glasses.

After thinking about her words for a little while, Shiroe continued the conversation. "You're right; for the moment, that's also... Well, we should probably have the Round Table Council discuss it and decide how to handle it after the conference ends. However, I don't think we should completely refuse to speak with the lords.

"To that end, tell them there are plans for the Round Table Council to establish a contact for discussions of dispatching military force, technology provision, and exports, and that it's going to happen soon. If they deal with that dispatch contact, their requests will be considered and they'll receive an answer. ...That should be a safe response. Of course, after the conference ends, we'll need to create the contact. If there's no more than a certain amount of routine work, it should be possible to create a system to handle requests practically. For example, if it's a request to exterminate one hundred goblins in the mountains, the job can be assigned to suitable combat guilds under the contact's supervision. ...That sort of workflow. With regard to commerce, an order for two hundred sets of dishes can be handled by the contact as well. If we get a request the small and midsized guilds can't handle, *then* we can convene the Round Table Council and take it under consideration."

The idea Shiroe had worked out was to coordinate the former quest system through the contact-point person.

"Sounds doable to me."

"I think it's reasonable as well. There shouldn't be any issue with us advancing matters at our own discretion up to that point. I'll report in via telechat."

Michitaka and Crusty both agreed.

"However, I don't think the nobles will be satisfied with something like that. If they can't get the Round Table Council to move as a whole, they'll probably try to conclude secret pacts during the period of the lords' conference, even if it's only for commissions directed at the

Marine Organization or D.D.D. In order to deal with that... We'll just have to handle things on a case-by-case basis. Just make sure not to give them any way to trip us up."

Shiroe's words ended there.

He couldn't set up any specific countermeasures for this. Decisions would have to be made on the spot, so although he could propose guidelines, he couldn't issue tactical instructions.

"I suppose that's our job," Crusty agreed generously.

His calm and sense of reassurance were everything you'd expect from the leader of a big guild. His natural charisma was showing through.

"You mean get information out of the other guy, but be careful not to make contracts by mistake when we do it?"

"Yes, I think that's the best line to take."

Henrietta also agreed with Michitaka.

After that, the staff who'd accompanied them joined them in brainstorming countermeasures for several foreseeable situations. After they confirmed with each other that they could anticipate bribes and backroom deals, and that information should be exchanged as secretly as possible, the delegation's breakfast came to an end.

▶ **4**

Reinesia's mood was flying low.

"Flying low" was a figure of speech; in reality, her mood was very close to rock bottom. She couldn't actually be at "rock bottom" in the usual way, because she was the granddaughter of Duke Sergiad, the greatest noble in the east.

In other words, her station didn't allow her to hole up in her room by herself and be depressed.

The expression "rock-bottom depressed" evokes images of being in such low spirits that moving is impossible, but she had dedicated ladies-in-waiting who were with her constantly, and every morning they dressed her and sent her off to all sorts of functions. What she wanted didn't come into it.

In that sense, rather than being "rock-bottom" depressed in a fixed location, she was "flying low": depressed, but on the move. Privately, she thought this wasn't very different from being dragged around.

Haaah...

She sighed.

She was in one of the many midair gardens of the Ancient Court of Eternal Ice. She'd forced her ladies-in-waiting to leave her alone there. It was just past noon.

...She didn't think there were any tea parties during the day today, but after sunset, there'd be a dinner party. She would have to join her grandfather, Duke Sergiad; her father, Phenel; and her mother, Saraliya, as they greeted several nobles and showed them every courtesy. It wasn't a very difficult thing, and it wouldn't require much work, but it made her heart terribly heavy.

She drooped limply, resting her forehead on the summerhouse table.

It wasn't that anything particularly painful had happened.

She'd been born with this temperament. She was timid and shy, she worried over silly little things, she was pessimistic and apathetic. That was how she thought of herself.

She was the sort of person who, if left alone, would stay in a corner of her room counting the stains on the wall and find it soothing. You might say she was gloomy, or that the cheerful aspect of her personality was tragically lacking. She knew it was strange to say it herself, but seen from a human perspective, she thought she was the sort of girl people really wouldn't want to be around.

In terms of appearance, Reinesia had long, silver hair and a delicate neck. She was a slender, lovely girl. In particular, her eyes, which tilted down at the outer corners, were a deep blue-gray that seemed filled with a mysterious melancholy. Her bust and the other key areas of her figure were modest but substantial enough to assert her femininity. She was well within the preferred range, and not many men would have denied that she was beautiful.

Ahh...

That said, the shape that slumped over the table in the summerhouse looked for all the world like a dismal failure of a human being.

Even she had heard her beauty praised by those around her, and she was aware that it happened rather a lot.

However, she assumed that 50 percent of the praise was said out of consideration for her grandfather, Duke Sergiad, and that the other 40 percent would be possible for anyone who bathed every day, had her hair dressed, and wore makeup. …In other words, her appearance was maintained through aristocratic privilege, and the thought made her feel a bit guilty.

The remaining 10 percent or so did make her think she might be passably attractive. However, hearing things like "What a fragile princess she is!" and "Ladylike and filled with melancholy" disillusioned her at a stroke.

I'm not "filled with melancholy," I'm just gloomy. I'm not ladylike, I just don't feel like doing anything… That's right…

As she thought these things, she slumped facedown on the table, feeling masochistic. She thought that fretting over things like this day in and day out made her a rather complicated, tiresome person, but since she couldn't stop, there was no help for it.

"Any army with a commander like yourself is truly fortunate, milord. Such power is the equal of the Eastern Knights."

"…No, our martial strength isn't that great. We still have lots of issues, particularly where our system of immediate response is concerned."

The approaching footsteps and voices seemed to belong to nobles.

One of the voices, the middle-aged one, sounded flustered. The other was younger, but it exuded a sense of calm strength.

The second she heard the voices, Reinesia sat up straight in the summerhouse.

The palace was brimming with conspiracies, and as a daughter of the House of Cowen, she mustn't show weakness. Reinesia was contrary and apathetic, but she wasn't the sort of girl who couldn't protect her family's honor.

"Please do pay a visit to my domain. Oh, and will you join me? There's some liquor from my hometown. The sun will be down before too long; let's have a drink."

"Hm. Liquor isn't really... My apologies, but..."

With a rustle, several figures appeared on the path, rounding the corner of the rosebushes.

Of the two figures in the lead, the one on the left was Marquis Kilivar of Tsukuba. He was in charge of the town of Tsukuba, where the academic guild was powerful, and he was reputed to be a man who'd seen much of life. From their clothes, the people who came after Marquis Kilivar were probably his steward and ladies-in-waiting.

The other, the one who walked beside Marquis Kilivar, was a young knight—no, he *looked* like a knight.

His close-cropped hair and glasses made him seem intelligent, but he was big and solidly built, and he carried himself with the alertness peculiar to those who live on battlefields. He was only strolling, but the overwhelming presence he exuded made him seem like a young general.

That man... I saw him yesterday.

Reinesia's memories flickered.

He was one of the Adventurers her father had told her about. She hadn't been able to greet him personally, but she remembered that her grandfather had talked to him at great length. According to her father, "For better or worse, that man will be the eye of the League's storm."

There was a good distance between the passing group and Reinesia.

To them, she probably looked like a princess from somewhere or other who was enjoying tea in a cottage on the edge of the garden. The idea relieved Reinesia slightly. As long as she bowed, she probably wouldn't get pulled into any bothersome conversations.

However, just then, although it was probably a coincidence, her eyes met those of the man who looked like a young knight. Reinesia bowed on reflex. She wore the smile her castle's young knights said was "As lovely as a flower in the rain." The expression always went over well, and Reinesia used it as a handy way to gloss over all sorts of things.

At that, the young knight stopped for a moment and smiled. ...Or she thought he had. The light had reflected off his glasses, making it hard to tell what the expression really was.

"As a matter of fact, I have a previous engagement. Marquis Kilivar. My apologies."

"An engagement? What sort of... W-well, Princess Reinesia!"

The man was heading straight toward the summerhouse where Reinesia sat. In all honesty, she wasn't happy about it. In fact, she froze up.

There was no hesitation in the knight's stride, and it seemed to make Marquis Kilivar believe his story about the promise. For a few moments, he looked from the knight to Princess Reinesia and back. Then he said, "I mustn't be boorish. We can't have that. I'll excuse myself, then, Lord Crusty. Let us continue deepening our friendship on another occasion," and left hastily.

The knight he'd called "Crusty" turned back to Marquis Kilivar in the door of the cottage and bowed politely in response. When the other man was out of sight, he entered the veranda where Reinesia sat, frozen and bewildered.

...Wow. He's really tall...

His height had to be over 190 centimeters. She'd seen well-built knights at the castle as well, but even with that physique, there was nothing coarse about this young knight, and his logical profile actually seemed refined.

"I, um. I am Reinesia, daughter of the House of Cowen of Maihama. Might I ask... What promise?"

"Ah, yes. My name is Crusty. I'm an Adventurer."

As he spoke, the knight sat down just around the corner of the table from Reinesia.

The summerhouse had several built-in marble benches that were topped with leather upholstery and down-filled cushions. The rather low table, made of the same marble, was a splendid thing meant to facilitate the elegant enjoyment of tea.

"The 'promise' was a convenient fiction. If I've made a nuisance of myself, I apologize."

The young knight spoke as if he didn't feel sorry at all.

In other words...he used me? This man really doesn't seem like a bad person, but...

Reinesia couldn't guess the man's real intentions. However, if her father's words had been correct, this young knight was "the eye of the storm." She mustn't be rude to him. Obediently, like the aristocratic daughter she was, she waited for Crusty to speak.

"You just thought *What a pain*, didn't you?"

"What—?!"

At Crusty's words, Reinesia froze up.

"Not only that, but when our eyes first met, you thought, *This is turning into a nuisance*. Am I right?"

"—!"

This time, Reinesia was completely petrified. Crusty smiled at her. His smile was intelligent and mild, but to Reinesia, there seemed to be something demonic about it.

"Wh-wh…"

"'Why'? Instinct. I have a little sister back home, you see. Her attitude is similar, so I understand," he murmured.

There wasn't anything bullying about his manner. He spoke indifferently, simply stating the facts, as if reporting research results.

…Th…Th-th-this person is *bad?!*

"No, that isn't true. Fu, fu-fu-fu." Reinesia smiled her most ladylike smile, but her movements were stilted, as though she were a machine that needed oiling.

"Don't be nervous. I'm not going to eat you."

"So you say…but…"

"The lords have been hounding me all morning. If I'm with the granddaughter of the venerable Duke Sergiad, they should hold back a bit. Would you talk with me for a while?"

"Well…"

To be honest, she didn't feel like it.

It was a pain, and a little bit scary.

This calm young man seemed to be reading not merely her intentions but her mind, and Reinesia felt as if she'd never be able to look him in the eye.

If she hadn't been a daughter of the nobility, she would have abruptly apologized: *I'm terribly sorry. I'll be more careful from now on. Please forgive me.* —She wasn't sure what she was going to be careful about, but she was beginning to want to say it.

But I haven't felt that way since the time Grandfather scolded me…

"You just thought, *I don't feel like it*, didn't you?"

"Eek—"

He'd read her again.

Reinesia was suspicious: Was this Adventurer a Brain Eater? How could he be so perceptive? It was enough to make her want to cry. However, Crusty was smiling like a perfect gentleman.

"Don't worry about it too much."

"Um, would you care for some tea...?"

"I would, thanks."

Crusty nodded. As she got out the tea items that had been placed in the summerhouse beforehand, Reinesia considered her plight. If this was how things stood, there was no help for it. Her heart was very heavy, but it wasn't because she particularly disliked this young knight. She felt this way whenever she had to meet strangers, period. Besides, even if she ran from this young Adventurer, she'd still have to talk to other people when evening came.

Lazing around in the summerhouse was probably better than going to tea parties or being dispatched to what amounted to marriage interviews with other lords' sons.

This Adventurer seemed to be abnormally quick on the uptake, and since that was the case, she'd be able to get by without being on her best ladylike behavior. If he was already on to her, then there was no need to hide anything, was there?

With that thought, Reinesia made tea for two, then slumped back down onto the marble table again. Once she dropped her polite facade, Reinesia was shameless enough to be able to do things like this without a blush.

Fu-fun... Let's see what you make of this.

The daughter of a dukedom rested her forehead against the marble, enjoying its cool. There was a gentleman present, but she was ignoring him completely, not even attempting conversation. Could there be any greater luxury? No, there could not. Reinesia was certain of that. Three cheers for solitude. Three cheers for being left alone. They could take having to make eye contact with strangers and feed it to their horses.

However, although one minute passed, then two, Crusty seemed to be doing nothing more than quietly enjoying his tea.

She could hear birdsong.

That twittering... Was it perched in a tree in the courtyard? Or was it bathing by the water?

Still, this man isn't at all attentive, is he...

If a young lady of noble birth had her head on the table in front of him, any normal knight—or rather, any *gentleman*—would have said something solicitous to her immediately. If she said she was feeling unwell, it was likely that he'd chivalrously escort her to her rooms and have her ladies-in-waiting sent for. Depending on the situation, he might call a doctor instead, or a specialist in curses.

However, the young man who called himself Crusty showed no sign of doing any such thing.

"At the moment, I'm attracting a great deal of attention at the palace. If you tell them we were having tea together, you'll have a tailor-made excuse for skipping functions and tea parties. Your parents will commend you for it, too."

At Crusty's words, Reinesia's thoughts froze for a moment.

As their meaning sank in, her cheeks flushed bright red. She was very glad she had her face pressed against the marble table. In the past few years, even her parents hadn't seen her this flustered.

Between the embarrassment, the desire to run away, and an oddly sweet sense of relief, she thought her knees would go weak.

What Crusty had just said was the very reason she'd stayed to drink tea with him.

"I'm only talking to myself. Pay no attention."

Reinesia couldn't even answer. All she could do was keep her pink face against the table.

▶ **5**

Forest Ragranda.

It was dark inside, but contrary to expectations, it wasn't cramped.

The ceilings were three to five meters high, and the corridors were easily three meters wide. The walls were made of hard stones, possibly granite, that were fitted closely together.

A faint scent of mold hung in the dry air.

"I'll call up a light."

Rundelhaus chanted the Magic Torch spell, summoning an orange-tinted light.

"Is it okay to have light? Won't it make us a target?"

Isuzu sounded worried, but Rundelhaus countered her easily: "It won't matter."

"If most of the monsters here are undead, they'll identify us with magic and by the frequencies of our souls, even in the darkness. They're the only ones who'll have an advantage in the dark, so it's actually better to have light."

With that comment, Serara also summoned a light using her Bug Light spell.

Having multiple light sources was a standard tactic. If they had only one magic light ready, and that magic user got taken out by a surprise attack, the spell's effect would abruptly break off, plunging them into darkness.

"Rrgh! Mine's brighter!"

However, Rundelhaus didn't seem to know that particular tactic. He hastily summoned another magic light, competing with her. Smiling a little wryly, Serara explained the tactic to him.

Rundelhaus had been indignant at first, but once he'd heard the explanation, he seemed quite satisfied. "Oh, well then. It wasn't that my light was weak. Of course not: I'm excellent. Ha-ha-ha-ha!" he laughed.

It made Minori think he might be surprisingly prone to getting carried away.

After following the corridor around several corners, they reached a room.

Cautiously, the group peeked into the room through the arch, searching for any sort of presence, but when nothing happened, they went in timidly.

"This is…"

Possibly because there was a gap somewhere, the stone-flagged floor was covered in fine sand. There were signs that a midsized group had walked around on the sand, and bones were scattered across it.

"It looks as if the earlier group fought Skeletons here."

Minori was examining the traces on the floor as she spoke. The scene seemed to rise up behind her eyelids.

The many scattered footprints, the marks as though something had been dragged, and the white bones showed Minori what the battle had been like. The fighting probably hadn't lasted more than a minute. It must have been a cinch. In most dungeons, the monsters near the entrance had comparatively low levels and were easily dealt with.

"I see. Well, that means we probably won't run into any enemies until that T junction, anyway."

With that, Touya started walking, taking the lead.

It was just like her little brother to sniff the air from time to time, wrinkling his nose, searching for smells.

Speaking less and less as they moved on, the party reached the first T junction. As they'd expected, the footprints that had gone ahead of them turned left.

"……"

Rundelhaus clicked his tongue in vexation. Touya nodded in agreement, staring down the left-hand corridor. Minori thought hard; she didn't get it herself, but the two of them seemed to share some understanding.

"We're going this way today. Let's go."

"Yes, but don't imagine I'll be turning right forever," Rundelhaus said, responding to Touya.

At Touya's voice, the party turned right. This probably marked the beginning of the real training. They'd entered territory where they would have to be wary.

"I'm…pretty nervous."

"Me, too."

Minori spoke quietly with Serara, who walked beside her.

In a place this quiet, there wasn't much point in keeping their voices down. Even if they were quiet, if something was around to hear them, they'd be heard.

However, maybe because of the darkness and the oppressive feeling in the dungeon, the atmosphere seemed to swallow them up, and even though they knew it wasn't necessary, their voices grew quieter and quieter, until they were whispering.

"—!"

It was Touya, walking in the lead, who noticed them first. He'd seen four Skeletons who seemed to be sentries walking toward them down the corridor.

On reflex, Touya drew his sword and prepared to leap at them.

"Touya!"

In the same moment, Minori yelled at him, urging him to restrain himself.

Leaping at them now was what the old Touya would have done.

Touya probably knew that as well. His two months of training with Log Horizon had improved him, too. Pointing his katana at his opponents' faces, he swung it once with a low yell.

A flash of light.

The deep crimson shock wave released from the sword's tip crashed into the Skeletons.

The shock wave didn't appear to have caused much damage to the Skeletons, but even so, as the writhing bones shed fine fragments, they seemed to have noticed him. They approached rapidly.

The technique was Izuna Cutter.

As a rule, Warriors weren't good at long-range attacks. This was because their job was to draw enemy attacks on the front line. However, since there were some situations which couldn't be handled that way, they did have a few long-range techniques.

Izuna Cutter, used by Samurai, was one such long-range offensive technique. Of course the damage was practically nothing compared to attacks from the true long-range attack classes—Assassin's bows or magic users' spells. However, the fact that they could attract enemies' attention without charging into their midst was convenient to Warriors in a way that had nothing to do with force.

That effect seemed to have worked well enough. Illuminated by the magic lights, the Skeletons charged down the corridor toward Touya, their movements eerily smooth.

Three of the Skeletons held axes, while one held a bow. It had looked as if all four were charging as a group, but the Skeleton Archer stopped at a point about five meters away.

Touya took a wide stance in the center of the passage, exposing himself to the three Skeletons' attacks. The ax-wielding Skeletons surrounded Touya in a C shape, then began paying out attacks one after another. It was the mechanical, emotionless action peculiar to the undead.

"Here I come!! Take *that*!!"

Touya attacked as if he meant to mow down all the Skeletons. It was Whirlwind Cutter—one of the Samurai specialties: a big technique with a long recast time.

In an instant, the Skeletons collapsed, falling on their rears.

However, they hadn't gone down without a fight. As a parting gift, each seemed to have hit Touya with a well-aimed attack. In that one instant, Touya had lost about twenty percent of his HP.

"Purification Barrier!" "Heartbeat Healing!"

Serara's and Minori's unique recovery spells flew through the air almost simultaneously.

A single-player, shock-resistant barrier that looked like a pale blue mirror formed around Touya. Minori's Damage Interception spell was a barrier that intercepted damage equal to 15 percent of Touya's maximum HP. In other words, even if he took those three attacks again, he'd get by without losing more than 5 percent of his HP.

Serara's Pulse Recovery spell was continuously recovering Touya's HP like a strong heartbeat. For fifteen seconds, it applied a continual recovery spell to the target, meting out HP nearly every second. It would take about ten seconds to recover 20 percent of his HP.

It was safe to say that these two spells guaranteed Touya's defense.

"And now it's my turn! Eat this!!"

The thing Rundelhaus's fingertips had generated was about the size of his fist…but it was still a ball of liquid lava, boiling hot.

"Orb of Lava!!"

Once unleashed, the ball of lava didn't simply travel straight ahead.

It punched through one Skeleton from the front, then made a right-angle turn, piercing the Skeletons one after another. The extreme heat carbonized the undying monsters, and the bones crumbled or blazed up in an instant.

Rundelhaus's class, Sorcerer, was one of the magic-user classes, and in a sense, it was their perfected form.

It was distinguished by ferocious attack power; just as Assassins aspired to extreme damage with weapons, the goal of the Sorcerer class was extreme damage with magic.

Unlike Summoners, they didn't use their own magic to summon and use beings from other worlds. They also weren't good at amplifying other players' power the way Enchanters did. The magic Sorcerers used was something more primitive and powerful—they converted their own magic directly into destructive force. In many cases, this destructive energy took the form of flames, ice, or lightning, and by blasting these straight at a target, they annihilated the opposition instantaneously.

Along with Assassin, the class boasted the highest attack power of all twelve classes. Many people felt that being able to choose an attack attribute put it one step ahead of Assassin, where you simply struck with weapons.

"Huh? What? …Whoa~!!"

Rundelhaus cried out in surprise.

The ball of lava had run through the enemy, and as if to follow it, a ball of rainbow light flew from the tip of his staff and inflicted additional damage.

"Yesss! It worked!"

Isuzu beamed.

Bards had many special skills geared toward support. From the other classes' perspective, Bards' distinguishing feature was their overwhelming number of special skill variations. In terms of diverse support for allies, even Enchanters were a step or two behind Bards.

The Continuous Support song Isuzu had chosen for that day's adventure was Circular Carol. Its activation key was "Ally's magic attack hits home," and it granted the ability to perform an additional attack of the same kind automatically.

"This is fantastic! This was you…? Miss Isuzu, the, erm, Bard? My spell's artistic destructive power has been raised to destructive force of mythic proportions! Ha-ha-ha-ha-ha!! *Grazie!* Nice play!"

The support seemed to have boosted Rundelhaus's mood considerably. He sent a thumbs-up in Isuzu's direction and gave a wink so huge it had its own sound effect.

Rundelhaus was blond and handsome in a Western European sort of way, and when he did these things enthusiastically, he seemed like a Hollywood actor. It looked so right it was actually a bit of a problem.

He spoke quite arrogantly, possibly because he'd grown up as a pampered rich kid, but there was absolutely no malice in his words, and deep down, he didn't seem to be a bad guy.

Besides, what incredible force…

That ability to annihilate marked him unmistakably as a Sorcerer. Touya had initially pared down their HP with a range attack, and he'd had support from a Bard, but even then, he'd managed to wipe out three Skeletons in a single attack.

In *Elder Tales*, it was very rare for battles to end this easily.

For example, if Touya fought a monster at his level one-on-one, he'd need to attack ten or more times in order to finish it off. The recovery classes were weak when it came to attacking, and Minori would have needed to attack more than twenty times.

Although these had been rather weak opponents to Rundelhaus, annihilating them at a stroke meant his attack power was truly outrageous.

…But.

"Wait, th-there's still—!"

"What's wrong, Miss Minori? You haven't fallen in love at the sight of my beautiful spell, have you?"

As Rundelhaus turned, putting on airs, one of the Skeleton Archer's arrows struck the back of his head with a *thwok!*

"Ah." "Ah." "Oh, my." "Crap."

"Wh-what's going on?!"

Quickly, Rundelhaus turned around again.

His attack had hit all four Skeletons, but Touya's initial attack hadn't reached the Archer. Thanks to the difference in the amount of damage, the Skeleton had survived.

"Grr, you blackguard!!"

"I-I'll recover you!"

Minori chanted Small Recovery as an emergency measure.

Probably not wanting to give the enemy time to attack, Touya launched himself at their foe.

However, this was a mistake. Having come farther out front, Touya was spotted by another group of Skeletons at the corner of the passage and ended up attracting enemy reinforcements.

When it came to annihilating the enemy, the Sorcerer's high attack power was a formidable weapon. However, it wasn't invincible.

Those towering offensive abilities stirred up monsters' hate. The greater the threat a player was, the more likely monsters were to see that person as a priority target that had to be destroyed. On top of that, as was the fate of all magic-user classes, Sorcerers had only paper-thin armor and meager defensive abilities.

An additional five Skeletons had appeared from around the corner. Between those five and the Skeleton Archer they hadn't been able to destroy, there were six.

Not only that, but since Touya had stretched the front, their formation was pulled into an unstable line.

This is turning into a melee! —No, stop it; times like this are when you need to stay calm. First cast an Overall Damage Interception as insurance...

But her thoughts were already far from calm.

Powerful special skills like Overall Damage Interception took a long time to chant. While this was going on, apparently unable to wait, Rundelhaus had unleashed an attack spell and pulled the enemy's attention away from Touya. Getting past Touya, who'd been building the front line, the Skeletons managed to break into Minori and the rest of the party's defensive formation.

The Skeleton Archer mounted long-range attacks, sending its arrows at Rundelhaus over and over, and the fragile Sorcerer's HP plummeted toward the red zone.

The narrow passage was now the scene of a full fledged melee

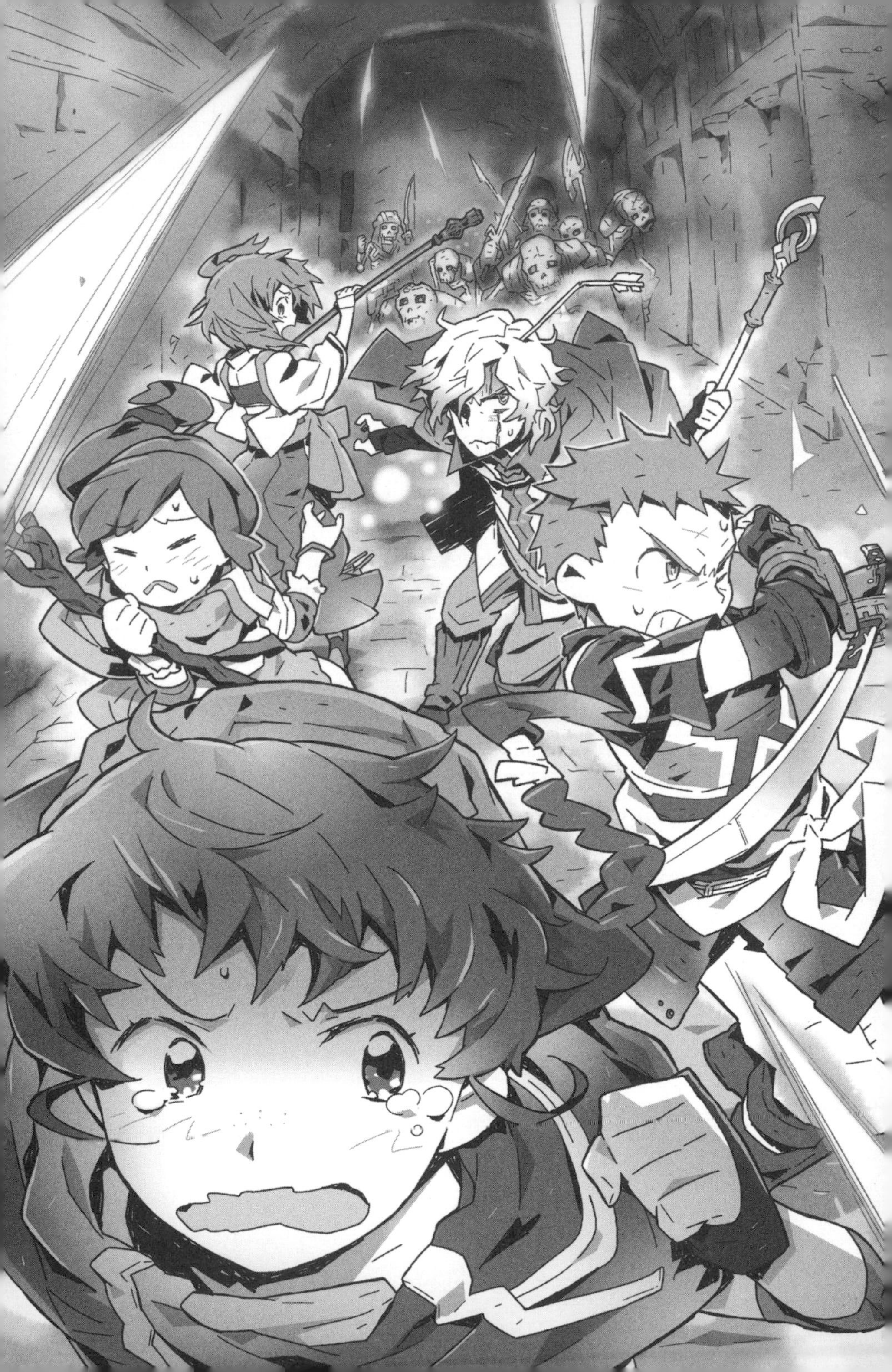

CHAPTER.
3

NEGOTIATION IN THE ANCIENT COURT

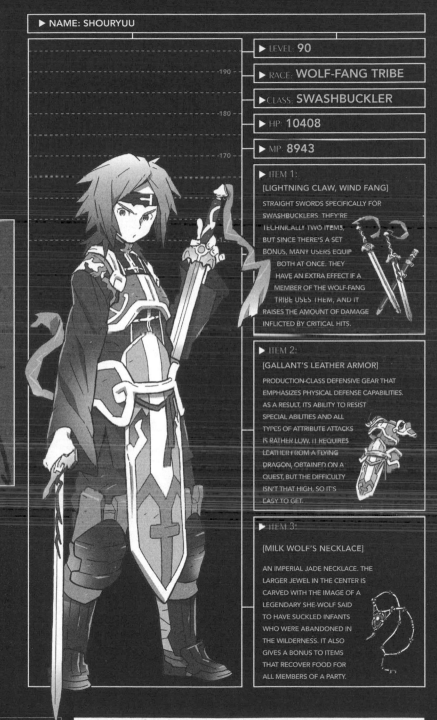

▶ NAME: SHOURYUU

▶ LEVEL: **90**

▶ RACE: **WOLF-FANG TRIBE**

▶ CLASS: **SWASHBUCKLER**

▶ HP: **10408**

▶ MP: **8943**

▶ ITEM 1:
[LIGHTNING CLAW, WIND FANG]

STRAIGHT SWORDS SPECIFICALLY FOR SWASHBUCKLERS. THEY'RE TECHNICALLY TWO ITEMS, BUT SINCE THERE'S A SET BONUS, MANY USERS EQUIP BOTH AT ONCE. THEY HAVE AN EXTRA EFFECT IF A MEMBER OF THE WOLF-FANG TRIBE USES THEM, AND IT RAISES THE AMOUNT OF DAMAGE INFLICTED BY CRITICAL HITS.

▶ ITEM 2:
[GALLANT'S LEATHER ARMOR]

PRODUCTION-CLASS DEFENSIVE GEAR THAT EMPHASIZES PHYSICAL DEFENSE CAPABILITIES. AS A RESULT, ITS ABILITY TO RESIST SPECIAL ABILITIES AND ALL TYPES OF ATTRIBUTE ATTACKS IS RATHER LOW. IT REQUIRES LEATHER FROM A FLYING DRAGON, OBTAINED ON A QUEST, BUT THE DIFFICULTY ISN'T THAT HIGH, SO IT'S EASY TO GET.

▶ ITEM 3:
[MILK WOLF'S NECKLACE]

AN IMPERIAL JADE NECKLACE. THE LARGER JEWEL IN THE CENTER IS CARVED WITH THE IMAGE OF A LEGENDARY SHE-WOLF SAID TO HAVE SUCKLED INFANTS WHO WERE ABANDONED IN THE WILDERNESS. IT ALSO GIVES A BONUS TO ITEMS THAT RECOVER FOOD FOR ALL MEMBERS OF A PARTY.

\<Abacus\>
For smart people, it's a calculator.
For dumb people, it's a roller skate.

► 1

Huhn! I see. This place's a den of wily old foxes.

Michitaka accepted a glass, all smiles, but internally, he was muttering to himself. This was the Ancient Court of Eternal Ice. However, it was the area in which Marquis Dalte was staying, not the section that had been loaned to Michitaka and the rest of the Round Table Council group.

As Shiroe had predicted, the Eastal lords' conference was moving very slowly.

According to what they'd originally heard, the conferences were generally held in the afternoon and happened irregularly. That said, in the four days since Michitaka had arrived at the Ancient Court of Eternal Ice, not a single conference had been held.

A certain noble had told him that, since the conference period was ten days, there was no need to be impatient, but in contrast to those words, furious negotiations seemed to be taking place below the surface.

As proof, day after day, invitations and requests were brought to the Round Table Council delegation. At first, Shiroe, Crusty, and Michitaka had gotten together and discussed each one, but since they'd never have managed them all in time that way, they had split up and were now acting separately.

Two things were coming in handy: The fact that they'd carefully gone over their basic policy beforehand, and the telechat function, a weapon the Adventurers had and the People of the Earth did not.

That night was just the same.

An invitation to a dinner party from Marquis Dalte of the fortified city of Mogami.

An invitation to a soirée held mainly for the young knights of Eastal, the League of Free Cities.

An invitation to a banquet from Tsukuba's Marquis Kilivar and the academic guild.

These three had overlapped.

Wouldn't attending just one of the functions be a bad move as far as the lords' power relationships were concerned? They wanted to avoid looking as though they were supporting any particular lord, and so at first they'd considered turning them all down. However, they had decided that, in the current situation, they needed to prioritize information gathering and making acquaintances, and so the delegation had split up and was acting separately.

A "soirée meant for young knights" was bound to feature orchestral music and dancing. Due to that expectation, they'd originally singled out Shiroe, but if the academic guild would be appearing at Marquis Kilivar's banquet, Michitaka and Crusty wouldn't be equal to the task.

To that end, it had been decided that Crusty would attend the gathering for young knights and princesses, or in other words, "the ones on whose shoulders the future rested." "I'm sure you'll enjoy the dancing," Shiroe had said, with a smile that seemed entertained. Unexpectedly, he appeared to be holding a grudge.

Henrietta of the Crescent Moon League seemed to have had the same worry, but Crusty had answered her calmly. "I've found a very durable defensive shield that won't wear out with use. There's a bit of a knack to putting it between myself and the enemy, but I'll be able to turn down invitations easily, so I imagine it will be all right."

Michitaka had absolutely no idea what Crusty had meant, but if that guy said it was all right, it probably was. He shrugged. Either way, the jobs Michitaka could do were limited.

Once Shiroe's and Crusty's destinations had been determined, the remainder fell to Michitaka. He ended up with the last one: Marquis Dalte's dinner party.

*　　*　　*

"Here, I've had my domain's most delicious beef brought for us. Feast to your heart's content tonight."

This welcome had come from Marquis Dalte. He was a middle-aged man whose expression was (in flattering terms) unaffected, or (if viewed spitefully) had something of the country bumpkin about it. His clothes were clean, of course, and of undeniably high quality, but they were simple, without any showy decoration. However, there was a supremely keen light in his eyes.

In real-world society, Michitaka was a mere office manager. However, in this other world, he was guild master of the Marine Organization, Akiba's largest production guild and five thousand members strong. His guild members looked up to him as an understanding, older-brother type, but it took more than that to run an enormous guild. He wasn't so dense that he couldn't see through an aura like this one.

Even so, Michitaka returned the greeting affably, and Marquis Dalte showed him to his seat. The large table was meant for luxurious feasts, and seated around it was Marquis Dalte's family.

His wife was still young; she was plump and quite a beauty. She might actually be a second wife. His oldest child was a willful-looking boy of upper elementary school age, and there was a young little sister as well.

"In these past two months, the food situation has changed, you see. We brought the foremost Chefs in our territory with us and went into this conference with enthusiasm."

As they listened to Marquis Dalte, the dinner party began.

Marquis Dalte's territory, the fortified city Mogami, seemed to be located in what would have been the Tohoku region in the old world. More accurately, in terms of the map Shiroe had drawn, it would have been in Yamagata.

The town's population was about eight thousand, and no doubt it was, to borrow Marquis Dalte's words, "the safest, most comfortable city in the region." According to the information they'd received in advance, about a dozen villages, with this city at their center, followed Marquis Dalte.

The dinner party consisted of very lavish medieval European fare.

Michitaka wasn't all that clear on the details, but it seemed a bit like French cuisine, in which the courses were brought out in small portions, one after another. However, in the fashion of this other world's nobility, large platters of food were brought out as well, as if it were quite natural.

Meat roasted with plenty of herbs was presented, and Marquis Dalte carved it himself.

"This meat is said to be the finest in my territory. What do you think?"

"Mm, yes, it's very good!"

Michitaka smacked his lips over the dish.

Calling it top-class certainly wasn't a lie. It was tougher and more sinewy than the beef he'd eaten back in Japan, but in equal measure there was a rich, distinct wildness to the flavor. It tasted the way meat really should taste.

Marquis Dalte eagerly called attention to that flavor.

I see...

By now, "delicious food" had become an important term, one that influenced this world's politics. The changes of these two months had transformed the world.

Like Marquis Dalte, all the lords seemed to have brought the best Chefs and ingredients of their regions. To them, this conference was a providential new chance. The discovery of a delicious specialty might bring even a small, weak territory wealth of a kind it had never seen before. In order to protect their power—and their honor—the great nobles had to pursue food that was a cut above anything the other nobles had.

Of course, previous Eastal conferences had probably featured this sort of ostentatious social rivalry as well, but now gourmet food had become a key strategy that was linked to imports, exports, and economics.

"There are many mountains around our town, and the terrain is rather steep. As a result, in addition to forestry and mining, our stock-farming is flourishing. Later on at tonight's dinner, our prize boar will be making an appearance."

The Marquis's son had begun to squirm with anticipation; his expression made it clear that this was quite a delicacy.

As Michitaka savored these dishes, he listened attentively to what Marquis Dalte was saying.

He spoke of the climate and geography of the northeastern area of the archipelago, and of its various customs. Sometimes his wife joined in. To Marquis Dalte, no doubt this was a preliminary to business negotiations as well as an opportunity to boast about his homeland, but to Michitaka, it was valuable information.

The northeastern area of the archipelago seemed to be a land of mountain ranges, embellished with mountains and forests. The mountains were green and lush; they held inexhaustible timber resources, and the rainfall was plentiful, which meant the land was blessed with many lakes and beautiful mountain streams.

There wasn't much level ground, and most of what there was lay along the coast or in basins in the mountains.

In these cramped flatlands, they grew wheat and rice.

The spacious area that stretched from the northeastern region to the northern Kanto region was the heartland of Eastal, the League of Free Cities, and, as expected, one of its big problems was that monsters were rampant.

According to Shiroe and Roderick's calculations, the total population of the "good" human races—the races Adventurers could choose to play as—was roughly one-hundredth the population of real-world Japan. However, this wasn't necessarily synonymous with the number of intelligent beings. This world was also occupied by goblins, orcs, and other demihumans. They weren't quite as intelligent as the human races, but they were sturdy and bred prolifically, and, most important, they were brutal and vicious.

These and other "bad" demihuman races also existed in this other world, and they had built many kingdoms and domains. On top of that, in their efforts to dominate the world, they warred and plundered endlessly, day and night.

The main force in the northeastern area of the archipelago was the goblins. Goblins were small demihumans; even when full-grown, they were only about 150 centimeters tall. They were skinny, short monsters whose roughly human shapes were stretched and twisted in ugly ways. They had a simplified tribal society, and they were divided among several roles.

The majority were Plunder Tribes who lived on the move, but some did establish main bases. This tendency was particularly common in the Tohoku region, and sometimes they built huge group meeting places which, at their largest, could have five-figure populations.

As with many demihumans, goblins' chaotic breeding had resulted in deformed, subordinate tribes. Hobgoblins were one such variety. Fiercer than goblins, they were humanoid monsters with a fanatical sense of loyalty. They could use armor and weapons, and would fight to the death for their tribe.

Then there were high-level goblin Shamans who summoned ancestral spirits, used the undead, and controlled spirits. Goblin Tamers sometimes kept Owlbears, Hippogriffs, Dire Wolves, and other animals.

Individual goblins had lower combat power than a midlevel Adventurer, but as a force with diverse abilities, it wasn't safe to take them lightly.

Naturally, these demihumans lived in slightly different areas from the human-controlled regions. Rather, in this case, it would be better to say that humans were desperately defending their territory from them. In the Tohoku region, it sounded as though they lived in the deep forests and mountains.

"But then, at that point, this— Yes, this great revolution occurred," Marquis Dalte continued.

"First, the revolution brought huge changes to the food situation. As you know, the people of my territory have been completely captivated by the charms of this new food. There's nothing to do about that."

The marquis's wife interjected, smiling wryly at her husband's solemn words.

"Even you're mad for pecorino salad and smoked boar meat, my dear. It's not fair to talk as if only the people chasing after delicacies are idlers."

As the marquis's wife gave a charming giggle, Michitaka agreed amiably. "Yes, and besides, delicious meals add richness to the day. It's a wonderful thing."

"Ahem! Well, that may be true, yes. …In fact, even in my domain, since the revolution occurred, my people have been more energetic, and the pace of all sorts of production has picked up. The effect hasn't shown in the rice yet. That particular grain takes a long time to cultivate, you know. However, the effect is already visible in livestock and vegetables. In specific terms, we've begun to raise and harvest them very carefully, to make them taste as good as we can. We also take more care not to damage them during transport.

Michitaka nodded. It made perfect sense.

"In order to purchase delicious ingredients, many of my people have developed a nose for profit. By raising something that tastes just a little bit better, then selling it at a high price, they can get various other ingredients… You see what I mean."

As a production guild member, this was something Michitaka could understand readily.

"And so: Now the problem of transportation has come up."

Michitaka considered this.

No doubt it had come up. In a region as mountainous as theirs, there were probably crops they couldn't grow even if they wanted to. In any case, there were lots of crops that grew only in the southern regions. One such crop was sugar, which Michitaka and the others also had a difficult time getting.

Sugar was a specialty of the Nine-Tails Dominion, and since the Catastrophe, its rarity had made its price skyrocket.

Things had been different before.

No matter what ingredients were used, the resulting food had been of uniform quality and taste, so differences in ingredients had influenced nothing but the food item's effect. …In other words, sugar had been treated a bit like medicine.

Well, food isn't the word. That stuff was like energy bars.

But now it was different. There was growing demand for delicious ingredients, fresh ingredients, ingredients with variety.

In this simple other world, as a rule, people ate what they grew on their own land.

Transportation cost money and time. Transporting perishable foods was even harder. Still, seasonings and indulgence items would have to be imported from distant places. Exporting was the fastest way to get the money needed for importing.

In that situation, the monsters would cause the bottleneck.

When he thought of that, he understood why this noble would want to ask the Round Table Council to send military aid.

"Well, and I don't think those of us in Mogami are the only ones hoping for this."

Marquis Dalte shrugged his shoulders.

"Still, I hear that exploring just one mountain requires the investment of a unit of more than several hundred men. The military force needed to rid the northeastern islands of goblins would be astronomical. Akiba's Round Table Council isn't powerful enough to do anything about it. Unfortunately, if it had to be constant, I'm afraid we wouldn't even have the manpower to guard the main roads," Michitaka countered.

The idea of security activities for the whole region was utter nonsense. Given the population of this world, it wouldn't be possible to secure that much territory. It was precisely because it wasn't possible that humans lived in safe zones built around cities, areas like bubbles floating on the surface of an ocean filled with danger.

On the other hand, Michitaka's words were a check as well.

He'd warned him off in advance, before the request to prioritize sending soldiers to his territory as quickly as possible, leaving the other lords' territories for later, was actually made. He'd demonstrated that their position was that, if they were going to save someone, they'd save all the areas together. Since they couldn't, they mustn't meddle pointlessly.

The dinner party had already progressed to the dessert stage.

It wasn't clear whether it was a local specialty or something they'd managed to achieve in the last two months, but the dish that was brought out to them was a type of sweet made with baked eggs. As Michitaka savored the simple, somehow nostalgic confection and strong Black Rose Tea, Marquis Dalte carefully broached the subject.

"No. We don't necessarily need to exterminate the monsters. I'd actually wanted to ask you for something else. ...Provision of the technology for marine transport."

Michitaka stared in astonishment.

Marine transport. That meant the provision of a steam-powered ship.

Marquis Dalte's proposal was to make imports and exports go smoothly without expending soldiers on monster subjugation.

▶ **2**

Inside the tent, the mood was gloomy.

To tell the truth, it was so bad it made it a bit hard to breathe.

In her sleeping bag, Isuzu stirred restlessly.

They'd been eating dinner up until a little while ago, and she could see the flames of the fire through the tent's sailcloth, so she thought it was probably still only nine PM or so. In the old world, it would have been too early for bed, but out here in the wild, even if you stayed awake, there was nothing to do.

Even if there had been, she was limp and exhausted, and she didn't feel like doing anything. That said, when she tried to sleep, sleep refused to come.

For the time being, she'd crawled into her sleeping bag, but she was just lying there worrying.

The interior of the tent was lit by a magic light, and her friends were there, organizing their packs.

"Nn..."

Isuzu turned her head toward them.

The one who was seriously working was Minori. Like Isuzu, Touya had crawled into his sleeping bag, and Serara was slumped in a corner of the tent. Rundelhaus was sitting cross-legged on top of his sleeping bag with his arms folded, looking irritated.

A heavy atmosphere hung over all of them.

This was only natural. The day's expedition had been a disaster.

Isuzu's party's battle had turned into a melee, becoming a confused, long, drawn-out fight that had attracted more Skeleton reinforcements.

Fighting with their formation in disarray had done more than simply drain the entire party's HP. It leeched away their MP, the special skills they'd been saving for later, and even their concentration. At the beginning of the battle, they'd had enough HP that they could have pushed through by brute force, but as things dragged on, they'd had to fall back on recovery spells.

However, since recovery spells were also limited by MP, it was inevitable that they would run out at some point.

Rundelhaus had complained—*I'm taking huge damage because you can't perform recovery properly!!*—but from what Isuzu had seen, she thought their two healers, Serara and Minori, had done their best.

Of course Isuzu had no idea what exactly it was they'd been doing, but since Serara looked exhausted and Minori seemed to be brooding, she could declare categorically that they hadn't been slacking off.

Isuzu was one of the newbies who had been rescued from Hamelin. Her class was Bard.

She had been friends with Minori since their time in Hamelin.

…Or rather, Minori had taken care of her.

Minori, a middle-school kid who was three years her junior, had a very good head on her shoulders.

Her level had been much lower than Isuzu's, and she'd been younger, with less experience, but Isuzu felt something very close to respect for her. Of course, some of it was because of the knowledge she constantly shared—the "things Shiroe taught me"—but more of it was due to the girl's intelligence and her strong sense of purpose.

I'm pretty dense myself… I'm afraid I've leaned on Minori a lot.

As Isuzu thought, curled up in her sleeping bag, her thoughts turned to herself. She didn't think she was the tiniest bit useful in this situation.

In high school, she was in the wind instrument club. That was her hobby: instruments. The wood bass, at that.

She was tall and gangly, but her hormones had gone off-kilter while she was growing, and she was as thin as a track athlete (not that she was particularly strong). She didn't think her face was ugly, but it was quite ordinary and far from beautiful.

She had a bit of a complex about her freckles. Her hair was on the thick side and tended to curl oddly even if she braided it, which discouraged her on a daily basis.

It wasn't that she had few friends or that she was bullied, but in the real world, she'd been no more than a country high school girl, the sort that seem mass-produced.

She'd started online gaming on a whim. Her older brother, who was a Gundam geek, had said, "I've got an extra invitation ticket that'll let you play for free. Want to try it?" and so she'd tried it.

Once she'd started playing, she'd decided it was pretty fun, and she'd been happy to settle into the music-related Bard class, even in the game. That said, if asked whether she would have played even if it hadn't been free, she probably wouldn't have. Her enthusiasm hadn't gone that far.

Then Isuzu had gotten pulled into the Catastrophe, and had gotten mixed up with the corrupt guild Hamelin.

At first, she'd panicked. She'd been so confused she hadn't known what was happening, and it had gone on and on, but soon a profound despair had caught up with her.

…And she'd caved, just like that. Her hope had been flattened, and she'd given up resisting. She'd cursed God and the world, cursed them and cursed them until she was empty, and she'd stopped thinking about anything except being fed every day.

So this is what life feels like for kids in poor countries, she'd muttered to herself, feeling terribly miserable. She hated it so much she thought she'd go crazy, but at the same time, a part of her felt that it made sense. She heard a tired murmur inside her, telling her that this was the kind of ending supporting actresses got.

Isuzu had lost to the Catastrophe.

Even at a time like that, Minori had been kind to the other new players.

True, knowledge wasn't the sort of thing that disappeared if you shared it, but that didn't mean there was no point in hoarding it. If you kept it to yourself, there was a bigger chance that when push came to shove, you'd be the only one saved.

Even so, Minori had talked to the other new players in her room every day, trying to share all the game information she knew with them.

Her little brother Touya had been like that as well.

It was impossible not to be surprised that those two were middle schoolers.

They both had a strength that was beyond exceptional. If it hadn't been for Minori, Isuzu thought she would have gotten much, much worse in Hamelin, and she might not have managed to regain her cheerfulness yet.

On the other hand, Serara was a girl her own age.

She was the one who'd first handed out hot, delicious soup and bread, minutes after they'd been saved from Hamelin. Their treatment at the cursed guild had been awful. It felt awkward to say it herself, but right after their rescue, she'd probably smelled like garbage.

Even so, Serara had hugged Isuzu, telling her, "It's all right. You're safe now."

They'd been like a group of refugees that day, in the entrance of the guild hall. As the newbies sniffled, soaked with tears, Serara had told them she was also a new player, and that her level wasn't much different from theirs.

"I was targeted by slave traders, too, in a town called Susukino, but I was rescued, and now I'm part of a proper guild," she'd told them. Those words had probably saved many of her friends.

Of the whole Crescent Moon League, she'd been one of the members who was kindest to the newbs. Isuzu had felt an affinity with her, both because their levels were similar and because their actual ages were the same. By now, she was the person she was closest to at the Crescent Moon League, and they spent almost every day together.

Because of this, to Isuzu, Minori and Serara were both trustworthy acquaintances. She thought it would probably be okay to call them "friends", but for some reason, she felt that it wouldn't be right to declare that they were friends without their permission, and the feeling made her call them "acquaintances." Still, in her heart, they were friends.

…And so there was no way the two of them had slacked off on recovery. Isuzu knew neither was the type.

Then what had caused that day's tragedy? Who had been in the wrong?

When faced with that question, Isuzu found herself at a loss.

That confused, drawn-out battle had gone on for a whole thirty minutes.

By the time they made it through the battle—a battle in which somebody could easily have died—the party was half destroyed, and every member had completely exhausted their MP and special skill recast restrictions. If the enemy had found them one more time when they were like that, they really would have been annihilated.

Desperately, the party had tried to get back to the entrance. On the way, they were spotted by the Skeletons who'd revived, and they'd ended up having to fight a gruesome running battle as they went...

Today was completely awful.

They'd had a horrendous time of it.

Isuzu and the other members' first attempt at a dungeon had set a record: They'd beat a retreat just one hour after going in.

It...wasn't Touya.

She wasn't as close to Touya as she was to Minori, but she did know him.

She thought he was a good, cheerful kid. Had they gotten into trouble because Touya was useless, or because he'd had ill will toward them? She could declare categorically that was not the case.

True, during their short expedition, he'd made a few wrong moves, like that forced charge. However, if she examined each individual case, although every one of them had certainly been a misstep, there had been some sort of idea or logic behind them on Touya's part, and they weren't the sort of things she could just arbitrarily blame him for.

She tried thinking of other causes.

For example, she had met Rundelhaus the Sorcerer for the first time at this camp. Of their current group, his personality and actual strengths were the biggest unknown.

There was nothing modest about anything Rundelhaus said. He was arrogant, and his constant bragging was annoying. True, he had the face of a handsome prince, but as far as Isuzu was concerned, he just seemed shallow.

Then was Rundelhaus behind the day's defeat? She wasn't sure about that, either.

Yes, in some ways, Rundelhaus's overconfidence and carelessness had made their situation worse. Still, when she looked at each incident separately, as with Touya, Rundelhaus's actions had been backed by intent and the idea that he could win.

More than anything, there could be no doubt that Rundelhaus loved his class and had done his best to display its true strengths. After all, Rundelhaus was a type of narcissist, and he considered annihilating the enemy a virtue, so there was no way he'd cut corners.

He isn't a bad guy...

From where she lay on her stomach, Isuzu shot a glance at Rundelhaus. With his arms crossed and his mouth set in a dissatisfied line, Rundelhaus had the air of a mountain monk sitting under a waterfall. The fact that his looks were completely Western European made this seem very strange, but there was no doubt that he was serious.

I bet he's mentally going over what went wrong today.

She also thought he might be blaming himself. Rundelhaus seemed to say whatever came into his head, and during the day's adventure, he'd roundly blamed most of the group. Still, at the same time, he was apparently hard on himself as well, and he'd seemed irritated and filled with self-reproach.

Haaaah...

In that case, when it came right down to it, was nobody to blame?

Nuh-uh. Hold it, girl. That's not quite fair, is it?

Right. There was one person she'd failed to examine: Isuzu herself. She couldn't deny the possibility that she'd had issues which had dumped them into trouble several times.

It's not as if I'm good at this stuff...

When all was said and done, Isuzu was a newbie gamer. She knew nothing about martial arts, and in the real world, she'd never even dreamed of struggling to survive. There was a decent possibility that she was bad at fighting.

Even so, it had been two months already.

Isuzu was aware that she'd fought her way through battle after battle in this world. She couldn't possibly be so unused to combat that she'd ended up this much of a mess, could she? Besides, unlike Touya, Isuzu was a rearguard class. She wasn't taking enemy attacks directly.

Still, when Isuzu thought back, all sorts of things about the day's adventure had felt off to her as well. In this case, "felt off" meant no more than actions which, in retrospect, hadn't been the best move.

She didn't know why it had ended up the way it had, but when she thought back, she felt as if several mistakes had piled up, one on another.

Bards had many types of special skills, but their Continuous Support songs were particularly noteworthy. These were musical wave patterns that were unconsciously radiated from the Bard's body.

They were convenient and powerful special skills: They were sustainable support that affected all members of the party, and they would continue to bestow their benefits indefinitely, as long as the Bard didn't end the effect. If used at the beginning of an adventure, Continuous Support songs would continue to display their effects throughout the adventure without any effort on the Bard's part, which made them the sort of special skill you'd want to use all the time.

The problem was that only two of these Continuous Support songs could be used at the same time. High-level Bards had fifteen types of Continuous Support songs, and at this point in time, even Isuzu had ten variations. The question of which two of these ten types of support to use was the first problem a Bard encountered, and it was one even high-level Bards continued to worry about.

Today, Isuzu had chosen Circular Carol and Sword-Speed Etude. The first support song added additional damage to magic attacks, while the second increased the speed of weapon attacks. Of the types of support Bards could provide, both were standard.

However, in today's combat, they had failed.

Circular Carol did increase magic damage, but as a result, the enemy's attention had been drawn to Rundelhaus. She hadn't expected that particular problem at all.

On top of that, there had been more enemy reinforcements than she'd anticipated, and the battle had turned into a melee.

At that point, although they were in the middle of a battle, Isuzu had decided to change songs. Changing a support song required a long chant, and it was generally best to avoid doing it during a battle. Even this time, she'd hesitated and put it off, but the idea that they might be wiped out if things kept on this way had stiffened her resolution to change them during battle.

She'd switched Circular Carol for Nocturne of Meditation.

Sword-Speed Etude had become Dancing Pavane.

Nocturne of Meditation was a support song that gradually recovered MP, even during battle. In *Elder Tales*, MP recovered slowly whenever players weren't fighting. Resting increased the speed of recovery. However, it didn't recover during battle. Nocturne of Meditation was used to recover MP while players fought, although the speed was a mere fraction of what it would have been if they'd been resting.

Dancing Pavane improved all party members' agility and increased their evasion rate for monster attacks.

Once enemy reinforcements had appeared, it had been inevitable that the battle would be prolonged. Actually, the battle was already chaotic by the time she'd decided to change songs. Isuzu had changed them in preparation for a long-term battle.

At the time, she'd thought there no other alternative, and even now, she didn't think the decision had been wrong.

Still, in retrospect, it hadn't changed the situation in their favor.

It had raised their evasion rate, of course, and the speed at which they expended MP had clearly slowed down. The recovery from Nocturne of Meditation was helping to buffer the amount of MP consumed by special skills and healing.

However, at the same time, Circular Carol and Sword-Speed Etude had stopped increasing damage.

Once their damage output fell, it took more time to defeat a single enemy. If defeating enemies took longer, combat time increased—and as a result, the amount of necessary HP recovery needed increased, and MP consumption grew fiercer.

It was a vicious cycle.

Still...
Yes: "Still."

Isuzu couldn't convince herself that the decision had been a bad one. It might have been a mistake, but only in that it hadn't been the best move possible. In other words, it was no worse than the mistakes Touya and Rundelhaus had made. She couldn't believe that it had been what had pushed them into the day's confused, desperate battles.

Besides, if it had been a mistake, what should she have done?

Isuzu contemplated.

...I'm not much good at thinking, either.

She wasn't good at reflecting on her mistakes and putting together strategies. Analysis and execution were her weakest fields. However, the heavy atmosphere in the tent made Isuzu even more uncomfortable than thinking did.

As a result, even though she felt as if her stomach were filled with heavy, sunken stones, there was nothing for her to do but worry.

This was probably true not just for her, but for Minori and Touya, too, and all the newbies in the tent. Worrying was the only way to pass the time.

Their first night in the mountains of Zantleaf had only just begun.

► 3

The hall was tiny—although probably still larger than a school classroom in the old world—and it echoed with a sweet melody played by beautiful women. With that chamber music in the background, many groups of people filled the room.

The Ancient Court of Eternal Ice.

The Room of Seven Maidens, in a corner of an upper story.

Young knights stood, speaking magnanimously. Young princesses had installed themselves on the sofas tastefully arranged around the room and were giving little cries of delight at bits of gossip. Young nobles behaved courteously. Fledgling scholars showed sober smiles that were almost wry. Slender bureaucrats.

Tonight's soirée was said to be a candid gathering of the young people of Eastal. About forty guests, whose ages ranged from late teens to midtwenties, were present.

＊　　＊　　＊

"…Do you intend to stay here the entire time?"

"Yes."

Crusty's answer was brief. He and Reinesia were seated across from each other at a small, round table.

Reinesia tried to smile back, but her smile was slightly strained.

It wasn't that Reinesia particularly disliked Crusty.

As a rule, the well-built knight was taciturn, and he never tried to use aristocratic flattery on her. This meant she could get by without pretending to be "a beautiful princess soaked by the rain," which was very nice.

However, she was a daughter of the Cowen dukedom.

If she spent this much time with one man, who knew what sort of rumors would spread? Things would probably be all right during the soirée. However, the thought of what might be said later depressed her.

Does this man understand that…?

In front of her, Crusty was drinking Black Rose Tea mixed with alcohol, his expression untroubled. They'd taken their seats at this table about the time the soirée began, nearly an hour ago. They hadn't made any real conversation, either.

The situation was a result of their interests aligning for the short term. For Reinesia, the advantage was that she wouldn't have to be suffocated by compliments from young nobles, knights, and civil servants. After all, she was the granddaughter of the leading lord, Duke Sergiad.

There were only two ducal families in all of Yamato. Dukes were the greatest of the great aristocrats. The title had been granted to them by ancient Westlande. Now that that ancient dynasty had fallen, in terms of the aristocratic class system, the only house that outranked the Cowen dukedom was the House of Saimiya, the grave keepers of the Westlande dynasty.

As a daughter of such a great noble family, Reinesia was courted by many knights and civil servants. Reinesia had one older sister and one younger brother, but her sister had already married someone below her station, and so when Reinesia took a husband or her brother took a wife, one of them would inherit the House of Cowen. Viewed in that light, it was no wonder that she was an object of worship, adoration, and desire to the nobles and knights of her generation.

Haaaaah…

Thinking about it made her stomach start to feel like lead, and she gave a furtive sigh. To Reinesia, "marriage" seemed like something from a distant, unknown country. Her parents' relationship seemed much too formal for what the world termed "husband and wife," and her older sister's relationship was a very soppy one. Reinesia couldn't decide which of these was really "marriage."

Personally, all she could think was that she could never live with a perfect stranger of the opposite sex, but in her position, she knew she would probably have to.

If they were married, they couldn't exactly be called "perfect" strangers, but Reinesia seemed not to have realized this.

Incidentally, upon seeing Reinesia's melancholy look, the young nobles and princesses around her whispered to each other: "How sorrowfully Lady Reinesia sighs…" and "She must be lamenting the future of this world. What purity…"

However, this had completely slipped her mind as well.

Crusty, the other much-discussed character, was also enjoying certain advantages. He was the young leader of the Round Table Council, the largest force among the Adventurers and the current focus of conversation.

In terms of soldiers, they had an army that was about ten thousand strong. Not only that, it was said that each of these soldiers was an elite no knight with lukewarm skills could measure up to. In terms of the knights the lords held, the Round Table Council's power was equal to several tens of thousands of soldiers. The scale of their economy might not be as large as that of Maihama, the largest territory in Eastal, but there were rumors that they might be nearly equal.

They were an enormous force that had appeared quite suddenly in Eastal, the League of Free Cities.

Even without these elements, when viewed as an individual, Crusty himself attracted quite a lot of attention.

His height was over 190 centimeters, and for a human, he was rather large. That said, he didn't come off as skinny and gangly. His trained, well-muscled body showed that he was a top-class warrior at first glance.

If he just sat silently, his glasses and intellectual profile made him seem aristocratic, and his sandy-colored hair suited him very well.

Even setting aside the fact that he was an Adventurer, he constantly exuded a charisma that made him the object of the aristocratic ladies' curiosity and longing.

His heavy, dark gray armor with scattered dark-blue accents—which he had worn at the goodwill match held for young knights the other day—had had scars and scorch marks all over it. That alone had been enough to make the knights who prided themselves on their beautiful armor refrain from fighting him. The experienced warriors who'd asked for a match were now completely infatuated with him.

As a result, in a different way from Reinesia, Crusty was now the focus of attention among the nobles, and being with her made it possible for him to avoid receiving unnecessary invitations or being pulled into troublesome conspiracies. That was what he'd said, at any rate.

Uuu...

Reinesia watched Crusty resentfully. Crusty completely ignored her gaze, but he did raise his head. His eyes were focused on something behind her.

"Princess Reinesia?"

"I do beg your pardon. We didn't mean to disturb your chat. Um... Would it be all right if we joined you? We've brought cookies."

The two girls were Marquis Lester's daughter Apretta and Fevel, the granddaughter of the Baron of Iwafune. They were her contemporaries, the girls who'd debuted with her at the ball.

"Yes, of course. ...You don't mind, do you, Sir Crusty?"

Reinesia answered them with a flawless smile. Crusty also smiled amiably and stood, guiding the pair toward chairs composed of graceful curves. She had no idea where he'd learned the gesture, but it was sickeningly perfect.

...Oh, I see. So he does know his etiquette... He knows how to treat ladies. ...Hmmm.

Seeming relieved, the two girls offered them cookies and began to talk about trivial things. To Reinesia, being the object of worshipful gazes was the same to her whether said gazes came from knights or princesses, but since they didn't propose to her, she felt somewhat more at ease around women.

She wasn't at all able to empathize with their private lives, though.

When they spoke of new perfumes and dresses, she couldn't actually follow the conversation.

She had a vague idea that perfume stank.

The fragrances were too strong.

Well, putting it that way, if left to herself, she would have gone without bathing for a week or so, in which case she would have smelled worse, but in reality, of course, they never left her alone. Her ladies-in-waiting dumped her into the bath every day, and they doused her with perfume.

Dresses—another favorite topic—were, on top of being uncomfortable, either too revealing or over-decorated, and she thought they were terribly hard clothes to do anything in.

Reinesia's favorites were cotton pajamas.

Thin, soft-textured, flannel pajamas were wonderful. Silk also had a nice feel to it, but it made her a bit nervous somehow. Those were the pajamas of evil.

To be perfectly honest, she would have loved to spend her entire life in her pajamas. If she could get by without ever leaving her futon, so much the better.

"—Don't you agree, Princess Reinesia?"

Fevel and Apretta were laughing, charmingly. On reflex, Reinesia smiled back. "Yes, truly."

Upon receiving Reinesia's agreement, the two girls giggled and whispered together happily. Internally, Reinesia broke out in a cold sweat. She'd agreed because it had been so sudden, but she'd been busy fantasizing, and she didn't have any idea what they'd been talking about.

"Princess Reinesia is lovely, isn't she, Master Crusty?"

"Yes, I'm honored."

At Crusty's response, the young princesses giggled. Even to Reinesia, the two girls seemed charming. They were completely different from her: They were charming on the inside.

"?"

"However... Princess Reinesia is a very compassionate lady. She spoke as she did out of consideration for me, because I am a newcomer."

"That isn't true at all. You are a gallant knight, Master Crusty."

Uh— Huh?!

Outwardly, Reinesia smiled gently, but she was panicking.

Apparently, in the course of the conversation a little while ago, the two young princesses had complimented Crusty, and that was what she'd agreed with.

Unlike Reinesia, whose ball debut had been delayed by her doting grandfather, if she recalled correctly, these girls were twelve or thirteen. To them, Crusty's age must make him the sort of knight they idolized. At their age, they could get away with that. That was probably why they'd been able to come to the table, without feeling the diffidence the other princesses felt.

Those two had praised Crusty, and she'd agreed with it—that must have been what had happened.

Please let it have been some sort of harmless compliment!

"Princess Reinesia is keeping me company this way because I am unused to palace customs, and she's helping me escape being maligned as a country bumpkin. I feel I'm quite unworthy of the honor."

The smooth tones in which Crusty spoke to the two princesses made his earlier reticence seem like a lie.

H-he's a bad person! A really bad person!

"My! Then, Master Crusty, we could introduce you to everyone..."

"Or, rather, would you join us in a game of chaturanga over there?"

The two raised startled voices.

"No, Princess Fevel, Princess Apretta. I am a barbarian who knows nothing but the battlefield. Besides, until I've repaid Lady Reinesia for the compassion she's shown me, I must not leave her side."

Even though it was likely that he just didn't want to bother dealing with the other nobles, Crusty delivered that line with a very serious, loyal expression. However, the two young princesses misread the words and assumed there was romance behind them. "A knight's pledge!" they said. "How wonderful..." It made Reinesia's head hurt.

"It's perfectly all right, Sir Crusty. Don't bother with a girl like me. Please, go admire the flowers of the palace. Won't you?"

Reinesia fixed Crusty with as ladylike a gaze as she could manage, whispering to him. Her words carried the nuance, *Isn't it about time you found some other place of refuge?*

...n an extremely bad situation. Minori was aware that she probably understood this better than anyone.

This was one of the "crises" that Shiroe had spoken of so often.

But... Even so...

Minori shut her mouth tightly. Their current circumstances certainly were critical. They matched several of the cases Shiroe had warned her about.

"Why are we this weak?"

It was Rundelhaus who'd spoken; he seemed to have gotten his wind back.

He hadn't spoken loudly, but his voice echoed strongly in the silent burial chamber.

"......"

Serara bit her lip, looking down. Isuzu couldn't raise her head.

"I'm level 24. The enemy's levels are between 17 and 21. In that case, why are the battles this hard? It shouldn't be like this, should it?"

That's...

It was probably because they weren't using their full power. That was what Minori thought. Or maybe they were being divided so that they couldn't use their full power.

...Of course, the undead didn't have that sort of intelligence. High-level undead would have been different, but undead like the Skeletons and Zombies they'd met up to this point didn't have enough sense of self or tactical intelligence.

In a manner of speaking, Minori's group was limiting their own potential.

However, she couldn't say that.

After all, Minori's level was 21. She had the lowest level in the party, and she was the one who was holding them back. Then, too, the one with the highest level—29—was her brother, Touya.

Since Minori had the least power of anyone in the group, if she said it, it would sound as if she was making excuses. If Touya said it, it would inevitably sound as if he was defending Minori.

Besides, although she knew they weren't managing to exercise their strength, even Minori didn't know how to overcome the problem.

"......"

"Will we just have to...keep training...?"

"No. My heart is frayed from battle, and the tranquility around you heals it. If you would, please grant me the opportunity to repay you for the duration of the conference."

She interpreted Crusty's words to mean, *Let me use that act of yours as a shield for the whole conference. We both benefit, you know.*

When the two princesses gave bright shrieks at their exchange and fled, the exhausted Reinesia leaned limply against the sofa.

Nearby, Crusty maintained his usual, peaceful serenity.

To a bystander, they looked like nothing more than a princess, faint from the heat of the gathering, and her faithful knight, quietly watching over her.

▶ **4**

"Haah... Hah..."

Breathing raggedly, Touya drained the contents of his canteen.

Serara, who'd seen this out of the corner of her eye, asked, "Are you all right?"

Minori's party had entered a small burial chamber on the right-hand route of Forest Ragranda. The floor was littered with the bones of countless Skeletons.

They'd just gotten through a battle in the corridor, disposed of the reinforcements, and barricaded themselves in the burial chamber, managing to survive the melee.

They all looked near exhaustion.

In this other world, their physical strength was reinforced to a great degree by their status. The fact that a mere middle-school girl like Minori was managing to hike through the mountains and explore dungeons all day was proof.

However, mental fatigue was a different matter. Fighting long battles wore away their concentration, and the more bewildering the combat situation, the worse the strain on their nerves. Even Minori had been suffering from a rather bad headache for a little while now.

Come to think of it, I haven't had any water since this morning...

Her throat didn't feel dry, but she took a swallow from her canteen anyway. If she let dehydration dull her thoughts, she'd lose everything.

This situation isn't good…

Minori looked at each of the party members.

Touya sat huddled, hugging his sword. His breathing seemed to be calming down, little by little, but he'd had a rough time during the recent battle. He'd shed a lot of blood, and there'd been a moment when his HP had dropped to 30 percent of the maximum. He'd been hit with a lot of bad status effects, and at some points his recovery hadn't been able to keep up. It must have hurt.

She thought it had to be his emotional strength that had made him camp near the door even now, when he was completely drained, securing the position that would make him the monsters' first target if another battle began.

Serara was still out of breath, but she'd begun rummaging through her bag anyway. Minori guessed she was adjusting the positions of the potions in her pack in preparation for the next battle.

It sounded funny that she and Serara, the Healers, relied on potions, but even negative-status cancellation spells had recast times. Minori's was Great Purification Prayer, and its recast time was twenty seconds. In other words, if she insisted on using Great Purification Prayer and nothing else, she'd only be able to cancel one bad status every twenty seconds.

For example, if all party members had been poisoned, in simple terms, it would be eighty seconds before she could recover the last member. In order to get the team by without that loss, Serara seemed to think it would be best to cancel her own poisoned status with a potion.

I see. That's really neat. I'll bring some next time, too.

Minori made a mental note.

Still, that did mean that Serara, a Healer whose level was higher than her own, didn't have an effective way to handle the current situation. Potions were no more than a drop in the bucket.

Rundelhaus had his eyes squeezed shut.

The position reminded Minori of something: He probabl[y] status screen open and was staring at his remaining MP.

They'd been fighting battle after battle for a while now, an[d] MP had also been driven down to 25 percent. Since they we[re] her MP was recovering at a steady pace. If they waited ten [minutes] was likely that she'd have recovered 70 or 80 percent of h[er] would be able to fight again.

However, Rundelhaus had paid out spells in rapid succ[ession] he'd used far more magic than Minori. If Minori had ke[pt accu]rate eye on his status, Rundelhaus was completely drain[ed] in every battle. To him, waiting patiently afterward to re[cover] even be part of his efforts to annihilate the enemy.

Over the past two days, Minori had heard Rundel[haus say] "Why…?" countless times. He probably meant, "Why is i[t" and] "Why can't we win?" and he probably also meant, "W[hy am I so] weak?"

It was likely his pride that made him mutter that way.

She understood. Minori was like that herself.

"Why…?" I know exactly what he's feeling. Even the [things that go] well when I was alone don't go well here. We're limiting [our own] strengths. Something's going…really wrong.

If she let those words out… If she swallowed them bac[k…]

She thought Rundelhaus wasn't just a thoughtless, p[roud] kid. It was his responsibility to crush the enemy, and he [was seri]ous about it. In fact, on that point, he hadn't compromis[ed.]

Probably… Rundelhaus is… It's hard to see it, but I thi[nk he's] for keeps.

Isuzu was silent.

Minori was a bit worried about her. Isuzu was usuall[y lively,] even a bit of a chatterbox. She was very sensitive to th[e group's] mood, and she probably couldn't be lively in a situatio[n like this.] Minori was worried that in itself might crush her.

I guess… I'm the same way…

She knew they'd made some mistake, and that it ha[d]

Rundelhaus's words sounded as if even he didn't believe them. They sounded that way to everyone else, too.

However, no one could say it, and Minori and the others only kept silent.

▶ 5

In the dark courtyard, the cool sound of water played.

Even though it was late at night, abundant water flowed smoothly from the fountain in the center of the courtyard. The water ran through beautifully carved channels, sending up spray whenever it traveled down one of the calculated steps.

The people who had designed the Ancient Court of Eternal Ice had apparently taken solid precautions against the heat of summer. To begin with, built as it was on pillars of Eternal Ice that raised it to a height of fifteen meters, the humidity in the palace was less than at ground level, and the temperature was cooler.

It wasn't clear what sort of technology had been used, but waterways like the ones in the courtyard ran all through the palace, circulating cool, clear water from the upper floors to the lower ones, as gravity dictated.

As a result, although it was August, the night air in the palace was pleasant, and almost chilly.

In this cool courtyard, a girl was silently practicing martial arts, all alone. There was nothing violent about her movements, but an observer who knew what they were looking for could have seen the extents of her efforts and knowledge through the gestures' dexterity and crisp definition.

With every move she made, her long, black hair swayed in the wind. Her body—wrapped in plain, shadow-colored clothes—was small, and she still didn't have much of a figure, but her delicate, girlish curves made her silhouette quite attractive all the same.

It was Akatsuki, Log Horizon's girl Assassin.

Lead right, slide left. One beat... Lead left, feint right, half-turn...
One beat.

The girl was running through an odd practice form.

In karate and old martial arts, although footwork is considered important, moving the upper body along with it is emphasized as well. This is the same across nearly all martial arts. However, the girl kept her arms gently curved and stationary in front of her chest, and she seemed to be training with a focus on footwork.

It seemed rather like a partial *taolu* (a sequential dance performed as training) from Chinese *kenpo*. The care she took not to drop her center of gravity and the easy use of her knees and ankles in the footwork vaguely resembled kendo, Japanese fencing, as well. It was a strange sort of dance.

Lead left, feint right, half-turn... Twist your upper body, turn again.
...Feint left, shift your body, lead right, two steps.

Akatsuki repeated the form as if in a dream.

When she'd repeated it so often she'd forgotten the passage of time, when the sequence of movements had melted together and begun to flow through her body almost like blood, she looked up, and there was Shiroe.

"My liege?!"

"Aren't you going to sleep, Akatsuki?"

"H-how long have you been..."

"Uh, not long."

Shiroe approached looking slightly troubled, and gave one of the glasses he held to Akatsuki. "Not long" had probably been a lie. If not, there would have been no reason for him to have two glasses.

How long had he been watching her? Akatsuki couldn't hold back her dismay at the thought. She worked hard, though, and managed to keep it out of her expression as she took the glass.

"Thanks."

The glass she'd accepted was filled with Garnet Tea. The taste was dull, but it was nice and cold, a good after-exercise drink.

Shiroe sat down on a carved limestone bench at the edge of the fountain. The space left next to him could have easily seated three people, but although she had the space, Akatsuki didn't have the courage to sit there.

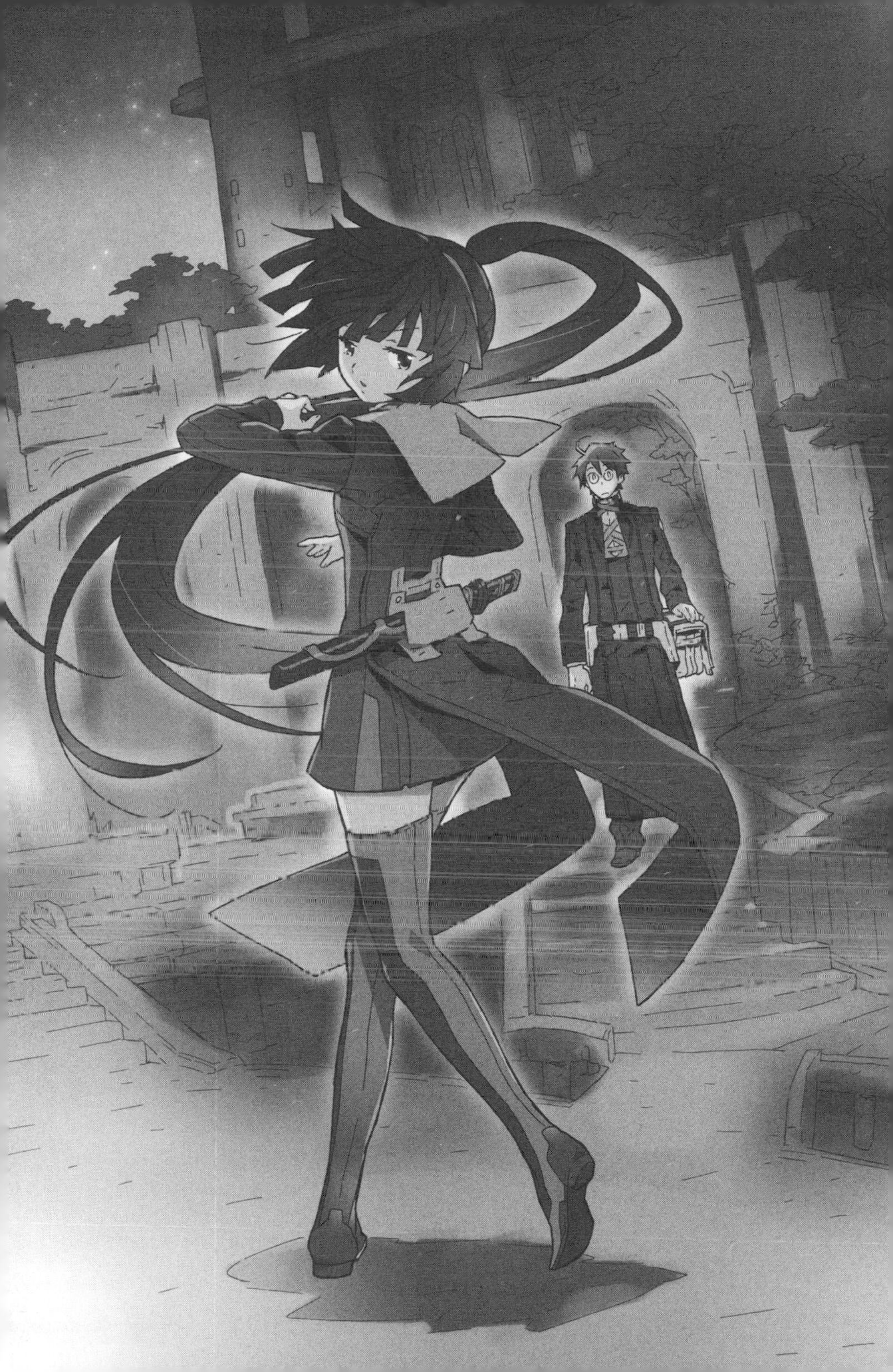

Akatsuki stood near Shiroe, drinking her tea with nothing else to do. Although she was standing close to him, she hesitated to stand directly in front of him, so she was about sixty degrees to the side.

Ninja should always be this way.

She'd muttered that to herself silently, but there was another reason: If she stood right in front of him, they'd be looking straight at each other.

It wasn't that being a ninja made her this subservient; it was only that she felt overawed, or awkward. Standing directly in front of Shiroe, face-to-face, made Akatsuki feel incredibly nervous somehow.

"……"

Still, Shiroe didn't seem to have the slightest idea that Akatsuki was thinking this way. His expression was vaguely perplexed, as though he were watching something far away. It made him look terribly mature.

Shiroe had *sanpaku* eyes, and when he stared at something, he tended to draw his eyebrows together (and he stared like nobody's business), all of which made him seem like an obstinate young man. The endearing round glasses he wore let him fool some people at first glance, but if they were around him for any length of time, they'd be startled by the depth of his thoughts and the breadth of his imagination.

In any case, it was generally hard to tell what Shiroe was thinking, but there were some things only Akatsuki knew.

When you lived together as part of the same guild, like family, you saw people in all sorts of different ways. It was like that now, when he was sitting on the bench. Even though Akatsuki was short, she noticed things.

For example, the whorl in the back of Shiroe's black hair spun clockwise.

Akatsuki thought it was really cute.

At the very least, the tuft that grew from behind that whorl and curled up like a cowlick looked like a mouse's tail in a drawing, and that was very cute.

The cowlick was sticking up now, too, and she began to want to touch it with her fingertip. Of course, in the real world, both Akatsuki and Shiroe were college students. They weren't at an age where they could make even that sort of trivial contact casually, so she shoved the urge down. ...But.

Still, my liege's whorl is cute.
That was what Akatsuki thought.

"What do you think, Akatsuki?"
"About what?"
"…The people of this palace, or their reactions…?"
Shiroe finished his sentence vaguely. Apparently this was about an impression even he couldn't explain clearly. In response, Akatsuki gave a frank report of what she'd sensed.
"I would say they're intensely interested. Goodwill and hostility. About half of each."
"I see…"
"I think the one bright spot is that, although they're hostile, they aren't malicious."
"?"
Hostility meant animosity. It was what both latent antagonists and rivals would direct at them. On the other hand, malice was a clearer intent to cause harm to the other party.
Once this was explained to him, Shiroe muttered, "Then you'd say it feels as if they don't have a specific plan yet?"
"Even if it is hostility, I think it's probably jealousy and envy."
"Right… I'd bet there's suspicion there as well."
Shiroe nodded several times, agreeing with Akatsuki's words. Shiroe had probably been observing his surroundings in his own way, searching for the meaning of those words and glances. He'd asked Akatsuki about it in order to compare their answers, to reconcile their impressions.

Over the past few days, wherever they went in the palace, Akatsuki's party had been the focus of attention.
After their dance at the ball on the first night, Henrietta and Shiroe had become the subject of rumors. Both had changed partners and danced five dances, and they'd been spoken to by many noblemen and their wives. They had taken Eastal society by storm.
At the ball, Shiroe and Henrietta, and for that matter Crusty and Michitaka, had actively interacted with people, working to make themselves known.

Petite, lovely Akatsuki had, at first, been viewed as an oddity.

Common sense told that since she had appeared in the great hall, she was either a noble herself, a family member, or an attendant. Apparently they hadn't been able to judge whether to treat her as family or as an attendant.

However, when they considered the fact that Shiroe had danced with Henrietta and the quality of the dress Akatsuki wore, they decided to treat her more as a member of a noble family than as a noble's attendant.

After that, many people had spoken to her.

Knights and the sons of provincial lords approached Akatsuki one after another. They offered her drinks, or asked her to dance. She didn't particular mind these things in and of themselves, but she was quite clearly being treated as a child, and she couldn't stand that.

Akatsuki was an adult.

Why did she have to have people doting on her and speaking to her as if she were in elementary school? The only ones in that hall who had looked at Akatsuki as an independent individual whose age equaled theirs were the sons and daughters of the nobles, and they had clearly been in their early teens.

Why do I have to have children being considerate to me, as if I'm one of them?!

Just remembering exasperated her to the point where she felt as if her stomach was on fire.

In the real world, she'd been treated like this on a daily basis.

They wouldn't let her into pubs. They'd patted her head and told her she only had to pay the child fare. Kids' brand clothing turned out to be just her size. She was sick of it. Because she was sick of it, in *Elder Tales*, she'd pretended to be a tall, silent male character, but the Catastrophe had put the kibosh on that.

She'd been so annoyed at the party she'd very nearly drawn a *kunai*, but she restrained herself and ran away instead. She hadn't wanted anyone to pay any more attention to her, so she'd used Stealth Travel and Silent Move and escaped from the hall.

After that, for the few days until today, as a rule, she'd used the same methods to prowl around the inside of the palace.

She'd hid in the shadows of carved pillars or generously draped velvet curtains, eavesdropping on the nobles' conversations. She couldn't get conspicuously close, of course. Akatsuki's excellent ninja senses told her that the People of the Earth had spies lurking in the palace as well. In this sort of secret warfare, unless there were well-laid plans, the person seeking things had an advantage over the person hiding them.

The current conditions were nothing more than members involved in the same business agreeing that, as long as no one caused mischief, they'd turn a blind eye. It was spies agreeing not to get in each other's way.

However, what she'd learned from even that sketchy surveillance was that the nobles had far more spies in Akiba than they'd assumed. They seemed to have a great interest in Akatsuki and the other Adventurers, and in the Round Table Council, too.

Moreover, it had become clear that the Catastrophe was already widely recognized in People of the Earth society, and that it was considered to be the first step in a large-scale change that would shake the world to its foundations.

"I wonder if their hostility is due to issues of military force."

"It sounded that way."

The Adventurers had great military strength. Approximately half of the fifteen thousand people in Akiba were level 90. Even if they kept their estimate conservative and assumed the average level was 70, that would mean there were fifteen thousand level-70 Adventurers.

That strength was far, far greater than any military force the lords held.

One provincial lord had let slip, "In my territory, I have fifteen level-thirty knights, plus sergeants-at-arms. There are about one hundred peasant militia members… For anything else, I have to employ mercenaries." If it was true, thirty Adventurers would be enough to subdue that force.

"I see. I don't think there was much falsehood in those numbers. That sounds about right for a minor lord in the Tohoku region."

"Do you think so?"

Shiroe seemed to have looked into the matter to a certain extent beforehand. He affirmed what Akatsuki had heard.

"Since that's the sort of force they have, when despotic Adventurers like the Briganteers act like barbarians, they aren't able to stop them. There's no help for that."

"You're right."

At present, the town of Akiba and the Round Table Council had absolutely no intention of starting a war. On the contrary: They wanted to cooperate with the People of the Earth and live in this world in peace.

Of course, if it turned out they needed to fight the People of the Earth in order to get back to their old world, for example, a different debate would probably break out. At this point in time, though, there would be no merit for the players in opening hostilities with the People of the Earth.

However, it would be too dangerous to blindly believe that the same logic applied to the People of the Earth.

First of all, Akatsuki and the other Adventurers probably saw the world differently than the People of the Earth did. The nobles lived on the taxes they collected in the course of administering their territories. The Adventurers were an element of uncertainty in these activities, and they might think of them as a blot on the landscape.

Next, and largest, was the problem of martial strength, as Shiroe had guessed.

For example, how would it make you feel if there were a man with a machine gun in the room with you? Living in that room would probably be very stressful. Whether or not you could trust the character of the gunman wouldn't be much of an issue. It wouldn't matter how virtuous he was. This would be doubly true if he were a complete stranger. If a man with a machine gun were nearby, his very presence would be disconcerting enough.

"We don't have an accurate picture of each other's abilities yet."

Shiroe's words continued beyond that point.

Even if they knew the Adventurers were powerful beings, the People of the Earth couldn't know what their true abilities were. In terms of the previous metaphor, it was as if the man who lived in the room with you had "some sort of terrible weapon," and you didn't know whether it was a machine gun or a chain saw.

It might be a trivial weapon, like a fruit knife or disposable wooden chopsticks, but in the worst-case scenario, it could even be a hand grenade or an antitank missile. In that case, the entire room would be blown to smithereens.

Since they didn't know what kind of weapon their opponents had, the nobles probably couldn't decide whether they should defeat them with a surprise attack or live so that they never, ever made them angry, no matter how humiliating it was.

"Should we stage a battle, to show them?"

"No, that would be a mistake. There's no point in spreading terror. Or rather, it would do all sorts of harm, even if it did us a little bit of good."

"I see..."

Shiroe summarily turned down Akatsuki's suggestion.

Of course, Akatsuki wasn't all that depressed by this sort of thing. This was the man Akatsuki acknowledged as her liege, and in the field in which he excelled—mental combat—she wanted him to fly so high she couldn't follow him. All Akatsuki had to do was use the special abilities only she possessed to support Shiroe, and that was enough for her.

Huh...?

It was enough. But.

It should have been enough. ...But.

She felt as if something was tugging at her, and it made her feel a bit out of sorts. Of course, since she didn't know the reason for it, it was only a slight discomfort, and ignoring it wouldn't cause any trouble.

There's no problem.

The night was growing very late.

If they stayed up any later than this, it might have a bad effect on the many plots and espionage wars that would begin once dawn broke. If it had been Akatsuki herself, it wouldn't have mattered, but Shiroe was their head counselor.

However, just as she was about to suggest he get some sleep, she felt magic, as if their surroundings had blurred slightly.

Shiroe must have felt it at almost the same instant.

He sprang up from the bench; at some point, a wand had appeared in his hand.

Akatsuki also readied her short sword. Before Akatsuki and Shiroe, a thin man appeared.

A scholar's robe. An amethyst circlet on his forehead. He seemed gaunt, as though his skin had been stretched directly over the bare minimum of muscle. If this had been all, he would have seemed sinister, but an ironic sense of humor showed in the man's expression, and it made him somehow appealing, even charming.

In a theatrical manner, the man bowed his head once, then spoke:

"Master Shiroe of Log Horizon, I presume. I am Li Gan of Miral Lake, Magician. I'd be honored if you remembered me on future occasions. ...I've come tonight because I wish to converse with you."

CHAPTER.

4

WORLD FRACTION

▶ LEVEL: **28**

▶ RACE: **ELF**

▶ CLASS: **LORE MASTER**

▶ HP: **1624**

▶ MP: **2721**

▶ ITEM 1:

[THREADBARE ROBE]

AN OLD, WORN-OUT ROBE. IT ISN'T THAT LI GAN
HAS NO SPARES, BUT—MAYBE BECAUSE HE JUST
DOESN'T WANT TO BOTHER—
HE ALMOST NEVER
WEARS ANYTHING ELSE.
LI GAN DOESN'T GET MANY
OPPORTUNITIES TO APPEAR
IN PUBLIC, SO THIS DOESN'T
SEEM TO INCONVENIENCE HIM.

▶ ITEM 2:

[GROWTH RING BOOK]

RESEARCH NOTES RECORDED OVER
GENERATIONS AT MIRAL LAKE.
IT'S WRITTEN IN A CIPHER
TAUGHT ONLY TO MIRAL
LAKE SCHOLARS, SO
ORDINARY PEOPLE
CAN'T READ IT. LI GAN'S
PREDECESSOR, JARED
GAN, ERASED A FEW NOTES,
SO THERE SEEMS TO BE SOME
LOST CONTENT.

▶ ITEM 3:

[FIREFLY CANDELABRA]

A CONVENIENT LIGHTING ITEM
THAT CHANGES ITS BRIGHTNESS
IN ACCORDANCE WITH ITS
BEARER'S WISHES. OF THE
ITEMS MADE BY PRODUCTION-
CLASS ADVENTURERS, THIS
TYPE IS COMPARATIVELY
MAJOR, BUT THERE AREN'T
MANY PEOPLE OF THE
EARTH WHO USE THEM YET.

\<Chocolates\>
If you get these from your special
someone, you'll even be able to
take down the demon king!

▶ 1

"Gyappiiiii?!"

With a huge spray of sand, a boy tumbled through the air. After executing two, three beautiful spins in midair, he dove into the water head-first with an energetic *kabloosh*.

"Oh, wow! Look at 'im go!!"

Relaxing in the shade of a beach umbrella, Marielle watched, laughing loudly.

This was Meinion Beach.

It was one of the most beautiful white sand beaches on the Zantleaf Peninsula. It was also a convenient thirty-minute trip on horseback from the school where Marielle and the others were staying.

Marielle took an iced soda out of the combination cooler and table that sat beside her and moistened her throat. She'd taken off her tank top, and the colorful bikini that had emerged from underneath was beach fashion itself.

Her equipment, consisting of a beach umbrella, deck chair, and beach blanket, was also complete.

Hawaaah. This is it. This is exactly it! Talk about paradise. Boy, could I not be luckier right now.

Marielle was often complimented on her smile, but the one she wore now was ten times better than usual—an angelic smile that could melt anything.

She didn't have suntan lotion, but bodies in this world seemed to be pretty tough. The sunburn situation would probably work itself out somehow. Also, she'd gone to great lengths to get this swimsuit.

In the days of *Elder Tales*, clothes had been nearly synonymous with equipment. *Elder Tales* had been a battle-centric RPG, and *equipment* had meant armor and weapons. Underwear hadn't been included.

Of course, if you took all the equipment off the polygon models, underwear was displayed, but it had been a game safeguard, and its purpose had been mostly to keep users from seeing the important bits. More than anything, it had been meant to keep things age-appropriate, and all you'd been able to see was solid-colored underwear that wasn't sexy at all.

This underwear was only seen on the character screen; it didn't actually exist. At this point, it wasn't even shown, so if they took off their clothes, a naked character would be displayed. …And when the character display was naked, they were naked, too.

However, underwear was important. In the first place, Japanese people who'd spent their lives in an ordinary, civilized society couldn't stand going commando.

If they could get them, they knew they'd be able to change into them, but underwear required fairly advanced sewing techniques. Just as the citizens had nearly decided that production would be impossible and were about to give up, light shone in.

That light was the existence of swimsuits.

Beautiful graphics had been one of *Elder Tales*' selling points, and it had had many special items, including items that could change your appearance. Swimsuits were one such item. In many cases, they existed as rare recipes, and specially designed swimsuits were sometimes given away at events as presents.

Of course, swimsuits and underwear weren't the same thing.

There were differences in moisture absorption, and in whether or not they chafed your skin if you wore them for long periods. However, the Catastrophe made them close their eyes to petty differences like these. As a result, the underwear crisis in Akiba had been mitigated by skilled Tailors.

Meanwhile, after the establishment of the Round Table Council, using the new item production methods Tailors were beginning to produce more "proper" underwear made of cotton and silk.

Naturally, demand was high, and underwear was one of the most popular items Tailors made. The common sense they'd cultivated in the old world was strong, and even Marielle wanted to change her underwear regularly, and thus to have several pairs. In Akiba at present, underwear was one of the Tailors' highest-earning items.

Materials like hooks, lace, and elastic could be obtained by creating a suitable accessory item from the menu and dismantling it. The trick to making a better item lay in the workarounds and careful sewing methods used at this point. Since they were hand-sewn, they cost about as much as a midrange magic item. In gold coins, the price was a solid three hundred or above.

If swimsuits were made using a previously installed recipe, it was possible to mass-produce them in a short amount of time, so they were cheap. These were, of course, plain versions that didn't use rare materials. High-level fashion items cost a moderate sum, but as a veteran player who was fond of novelty, Marielle had several suits. She had hunted this one up from among the rubbish that slept in her safe deposit box.

Marielle's swimsuit was a bikini hot enough to have provoked involuntary admiration if she'd been on a beach in the old world. It wasn't that the cloth areas were particularly scanty, but the acutely angled cut of the suit and Marielle's patently unfair figure combined to make it look suggestive.

Marielle might have been aware of this: She'd wrapped herself up in a cotton parka, but—

There's so many people here, all those eyes, and... Well, lettin' everythin' hang out seems, um... It's embarrassin' all by itself...

Even so, Marielle was sure she'd be all right if she wore her parka. In fact, the sight of her bikini bottom peeking out from under the tail of the parka was actually more of a crime, but she hadn't noticed this. Smiling away on her deck chair and enjoying her vacation to the fullest, Marielle was utterly at peace.

"Miss Marielle, Miss Marielle!!"

The boy who'd tumbled through the air a moment before came running up to her.

He held a weapon that looked like a double-pointed spear, which meant he was probably a Samurai. Even in this heat, he was wearing leather armor, but because he had been pushed into the ocean, he was dripping with water in the sunlight; he looked like a puppy who'd just gone swimming.

"Requesting treatment, please!"

Another look showed that the boy's head was bleeding heavily.

"Sure thing."

Marielle nodded energetically, then sat up and activated the spell Healing Light. White light in the shape of a six-pointed star sprang from Marielle's fingertip and was absorbed into the boy, recovering his HP in no time.

"Yesss! Healed!"

The boy put a hand to his wound, looking happy. The bleeding from his head seemed to have been cured completely as well. Healing Light was a low-ranking, instant-recovery spell; of the spells Marielle had, its chant time was relatively short, and the recovery amount was comparatively small. As a rule, it was a small recovery spell used to fill in the gaps when the recast time of a large-scale recovery spell wouldn't be over soon enough, or when reaction-activated recovery wouldn't quite cover everything. However, for a boy whose level was this low, the spell was advanced enough to completely recover his HP.

"Thank you very much, ma'am!"

"No worries."

Marielle smiled brightly.

"Never mind that, get back out there! Go bag lots of crabs! I'd try attackin' by slippin' in from the side. Make sure to ask about situations that would let you use your special skills while you're at it."

"Yes, ma'am! Understood!"

The boy ran off, energetically kicking up sand.

As Marielle watched him, he spotted a giant crab that had come up on land from the beach and changed direction. Spear at the ready, he closed the distance in one sprint. The crab was about a meter in size, and if it extended its legs to their full extent, it would probably be close to two meters. "Giant" indeed.

The boy leapt in decisively, then struck the crab's side with the spear point, as if to flip it over. This time, he managed to defeat it handily.

There were five or six similar newbies around Marielle. They were the Adventurers with the lowest levels at the summer camp.

Marielle had come down to the coast with the newbies as their leader.

In summer, countless giant crabs known as Apricots landed on Meinion Beach. If left alone, the monsters went farther and farther inland from the shore and damaged livestock and fields, so the People of the Earth weren't particularly fond of them.

That said, they weren't much of a threat, and their monster levels ranged from 4 to 8. Although there were differences among individuals, they were the perfect training partners for newbs.

If the newbies spent all day battling on the beach like this, in combination with the leg and hip training on the sand, they would get quite enough experience points. If they took too much damage, all they had to do was come to Marielle and get a recovery spell.

When MP ran out, they would take a break.

Having a dedicated healer on board made it possible to conduct intense drills.

Of course, it was a huge success as Marielle's Operation Vacation as well.

"Toryaaaaah!"

"Why you! You, you! Go *down!*"

"I'm gonna rip you a new one!"

With the vigorous voices of the newbies in her ears, Marielle lay back in her deck chair. Sweat beaded up, but her cold glass of soda cooled it right down.

This was truly time spent in paradise.

She couldn't stop her face from softening into a smile.

Most of the new players here wanted to join production classes. These particular individuals' levels were still as low as they were— even though it had already been three months since the Catastrophe— because of their aversion to battle.

That in itself wasn't a problem. The fact that Adventurers who were interested in production provided support from town made it possible for players from combat guilds to go out and earn money.

However, in this other world, being exclusively production class carried heavy risks. If you had no combat abilities whatsoever, you couldn't defend yourself when you needed to, and most important, Adventurer levels mattered to production-centered persons as well. In many cases, it was much faster to go out to a field and gather minor ingredients yourself.

Possibly, these arguments had been successful.

It was also possible that, although they'd felt these things for a while now, the production guilds hadn't had enough of a support system for combat training, and they'd given up. The low-level newbies who had gathered on the beach seemed to be enthusiastically repeating the crab-hunting drill.

There was a secret to this: They couldn't back out, no matter how badly they wanted to, because every time they came near to giving up, Marielle hit them with a recovery spell and that sunflower smile. Boys' pride is a sad thing.

As for the girls, in an atmosphere of such desperation, they had no choice but to think, *Well, there's no help for it. I'd better boost my level a bit, too.*

The only one who didn't have a clue that this reason existed was Marielle herself.

Everyone's workin' so hard… Wow, what amazin' weather.

Marielle murmured sleepily, savoring her vacation mood.

Midlevel players who had been dispatched from Keel and the West Wind Brigade were patrolling the beach as coaches and guards. Marielle's only job was to wait here as the person in charge (or, if you asked Marielle, to enjoy her vacation), and to use recovery spells to heal the wounded who came to see her every now and then.

Bored, Marielle turned over for the umpteenth time.

The air was dry, with no humidity, and although it was quite hot, it wasn't very unpleasant.

…And so it was sheer coincidence that when she happened to glance offshore, she saw a white, foaming line. Shouryuu was passing by, and on a whim, she waved him over.

"Say, Shouryuu? What do you s'pose that is?"

Marielle pointed at the white line off the coast.

"Nn. I couldn't say. ...Bubbles? Maybe it's a ship's wake. Hmm..."

However, in the end, that was as far as the conversation went.

After a little while, the white line disappeared, and nothing in particular happened afterward. The group continued to hunt crabs until the sun began to sink, ending up with a ton of meat and shells.

As Marielle and the others headed back to the abandoned school building to prepare for the evening's production-technique training, the mysterious white line had completely vanished from their minds.

▶ 2

Isuzu and the others had been trying to conquer Forest Ragranda for three days now.

Every day, their expeditions had ended in less than three hours.

The strain was tremendous, and they weren't able to stay in the dungeon.

Of course, simply managing to stay in the dungeon for long periods wouldn't be enough, but if their times were this short, it was a problem. It meant they were fighting only four or five battles.

There was nothing to do but train more.

Rundelhaus had concluded the matter that way, almost by force, but there was no way they'd be able to earn enough experience points in a mere four or five battles. Every one turned into a melee or a brawl, and they ended up wearing down their MP and their nerves and retreating with nothing to show for it. They did this over and over.

Isuzu had changed out of her leather armor into normal clothes. It was tiring to wear heavy armor all the way back to camp.

The advanced party was in the dungeon for about six hours every day, and since Isuzu and the others never lasted past morning, they had nothing to do, and they were bored.

If they rested outside the dungeon for an hour, they would recover their HP and MP.

That meant they could have gone back into the dungeon again in the afternoon and possibly earned a few more experience points, but Nyanta and Naotsugu had forbidden it. They didn't know the reason, but it had been emphasized very strongly, and they couldn't disobey.

With no help for it, Isuzu and the others did chores, gathering firewood or drawing water, and took walks to kill time.

From the angle of the sun, it was probably about three in the afternoon.

Isuzu was on her way to a nearby pond.

It wasn't a very large watering hole, but it was fed by spring water, which meant it was cool and clear, and the group drew the water they used in their daily routines from it. Drinking it might have made them sick, so they hadn't tried, but Isuzu's instincts told her it was probably safe.

Naturally, up here in the mountains, there were no baths.

Although no one in particular had suggested it, Isuzu and the others had begun coming to this pond to bathe by turns.

"——!! —Hah!!"

Compressed exhalations filtered out from the depths of the forest.

Who could that be?

Quietly, Isuzu detoured in that direction.

It was Rundelhaus; he was exercising ferociously in the woods. Over his lavender clothes, which looked like the uniform of some distinguished boarding school, he wore a mage's mantle, and he was soaked with sweat.

She didn't know how long he'd been working like that, but if the black stains on the ground were sweat, he might have been training ever since they left the dungeon.

Rundelhaus thrust out his left hand, generated an enormous ball of flames, then compressed it to the limit, turning it into a fist-sized fireball. It looked like the process took a lot of concentration: Although he usually looked like a dandy, sweat beaded up all over him, and he was gritting his teeth.

He threw the fireball, then swiftly put together a seal and stabilized it in midair before it hit the trees. Then he created a sphere of ice and cold air in the same way, launching it to destroy the flames he had released.

The magic that he had converted into flames and ice clashed among the trees, sending up fierce clouds of steam. Rundelhaus kept moving, not stopping for an instant, avoiding the sprays of hot water that sometimes came his way.

These magic attacks and violent evasions were probably a sort of drill meant to simulate a real battle.

Isuzu spotted two lines that had been drawn at Rundelhaus's feet. She couldn't think what they were for at first, but after she'd watched Rundelhaus's movements for a few minutes, she abruptly understood.

It's a dungeon corridor.

The two lines that had been drawn in the soil stood for a dungeon passage. Rundelhaus was fighting a band of unseen Skeletons that was coming down it.

He was constantly moving forward and backward, but he never crossed the lines on his left and right. He couldn't: They were the corridor walls.

How long did he drill?

It seemed like a long time, but it probably hadn't been more than five minutes. Rundelhaus knelt on the ground, exhaling hugely. In that position, he looked almost as if he were throwing up, and he made pitiful noises, desperately dragging air into his lungs.

"...Um. Are you okay?" Hesitantly, Isuzu spoke to him from behind the trees. She remembered that one of her classmates, a girl with asthma, got like this when her symptoms were at their worst.

However, her voice seemed to startle Rundelhaus to his core. He leapt to his feet in an instant as if he were on springs, turning to face Isuzu.

"Why, Miss Isuzu. ...Wh-what brings you here?" Rundelhaus smiled a princely smile, breezily combing his fingers through his bangs.

However, his sweat-soaked bangs stuck flat to his forehead.

"You don't have to push yourself, you know." As she spoke, Isuzu fought back a laugh. However, she didn't seem to have gotten through to the young man. On the contrary, he was more than a little flustered, and he tried even harder to keep up appearances.

"H-how am I pushing myself, exactly? I-I'm not. Not in the least. I was merely taking an afternoon stroll to hear the songbirds' harmony, following where the forest nymphs led..."

Simply speaking those words made Rundelhaus's face turn purple. *Well, sure, if he's going to talk like a prince when he's so low on oxygen he's gasping for air. He'll give himself cyanosis.*

That was what Isuzu thought, but even when his face had gone purple, Rundelhaus's princely smile didn't falter. Feeling sorry for him, Isuzu looked away, turning her back on him.

"I-is that right..."

When she spoke over her shoulder, she heard the sound of harsh breathing behind her.

A guy and a girl alone in the woods, with no one around, and a man's heavy breathing: Anyone would have assumed that a pervert had made an appearance, but to Isuzu, Rundelhaus seemed to be an extremely superficial guy, and she felt as if she was showing him warrior's compassion.

Hmm... Does that mean I'm weird?

When she thought about it, her level was about the same as his. She didn't know Rundelhaus's age, but he looked to be in his early twenties, so he probably wasn't younger than she was. Furthermore, he was a guy, and he wasn't delicate.

In terms of combat ability, the difference was overwhelming. Even when you considered that Isuzu was a support class and Rundelhaus was a pure attack class, his attack power was more than double hers.

However, on a completely different level from actual abilities and conditions, Isuzu seemed to feel superior. It was a state of mind even she didn't really understand.

"Miss Isuzu— Erm. What are you doing here?"

"I was going to take a bath... Oh, of course. You come too, Rundelhaus."

She didn't sweetly ask *Would you come with me?* Under ordinary circumstances, even what she *did* say would have been unthinkable. But it seemed she had lost all sense of reserve where Rundelhaus was concerned.

"To *bathe*?! I'm not in the habit of peeping on ladies' baths! I'll thank you not to misjudge me!!"

"Nobody said I was asking you go to in with me or peep on me."

Keeping her back turned, Isuzu delivered her retort in a tone that sounded both angry and amused. She heard Rundelhaus—who still hadn't caught his breath—choke. It made her feel good.

"It isn't proper to let a lady walk through the woods by herself, is it?"

Isuzu blushed a little. There was something terribly embarrassing about calling herself a lady. To be honest, it was an outrageous remark. However, once she'd said it, she couldn't unsay it.

"I suppose that's true. Yes, as a guard, you mean."

The strength was returning to Rundelhaus's voice.

"I'll escort you, then. There's a spring, you said? Which way is it?"

Isuzu turned around.

There stood Rundelhaus, looking a bit flustered; his expression seemed to say, *Yes, show me to it.* Even though it was wet with sweat, his blond hair hadn't lost its color, and when she looked at him, she saw that he really was handsome. In the real world, he could have done quite well as the protagonist of a girls' manga.

And even then, I don't feel much pressure. ...Maybe it's because we're in another dimension.

"It's over that way, Rundelhaus."

As Isuzu headed down the deer track to the pond, feeling slightly perplexed, the young man spoke to her. "Miss Isuzu. You can call me Rudy. It's what my father and mother call me."

As Isuzu listened to his voice, she felt a bit self-conscious.

▶ 3

They were taken to an area Shiroe's group wasn't familiar with, deep inside the Ancient Court of Eternal Ice.

This place was near the heart of the palace, and even though it was summer, it was filled with a cool silence. Just before the chill air went from cool to cold, the high-ceilinged corridor ended in a huge metal door with carvings on it.

"All right: This is my den. Come in, come in."

Li Gan, the self-proclaimed magician, pushed the door open, beckoning them into a study filled with thousands of books. They only knew it was a study because there was an enormous desk. The ceiling was high, and the room went deeper and deeper into the palace in a straight line, so that it looked like nothing more than a continuation of the corridor.

Around them were books piled up in small mountains.

The walls on either side of the huge corridor were fitted with bookshelves that were twice as tall as Shiroe, and the shelves were being engulfed by their own prey—the books. They overflowed with documents and scrolls to the point where tiny avalanches were occurring here and there.

This sight continued back and back, until it was lost in shadow.

Li Gan was rummaging around on the table and desk, saying, "Hm? That's funny," and "Where could it have gone to?" Shiroe and Akatsuki seated themselves on one of the sofas without being invited, although in order to do so, they had to add several books that had been on the sofa to one of the mountains on the floor.

"I'm really sorry about this. I'm sure I had a pot for drinks somewhere..." Li Gan was apologetic. Shiroe shook his head, saying, "It doesn't matter," and took several glasses and a large bottle of Black Rose Tea out of the bag he carried.

This drink, which had become a standard, tasted like a stronger version of roasted green tea, but its flavor was mild, and it was taken with honey or sugar. Shiroe was carrying around an iced type of Black Rose that had been cooled with spring water and sweetened with syrup.

Shiroe poured this into glasses for himself, Li Gan, and Akatsuki. Li Gan drank his tea and broke into a smile. He was an odd man; although he was small and gaunt, there was something charming about him.

As far as appearances went, at any rate, he seemed to be about the same age as Shiroe.

"Thank you. I'm awful at finding things. —That's Dazanek's Magic Bag, isn't it?"

"Yes. I had it made a while back."

Shiroe nodded, responding to the question frankly.

"Hm. I've done some research regarding that bag... You need a purple flame crystal and the skin of a winged dragon in order to crystallize the magic circuits, correct?"

"That's right. I got those items and had it order-made."

Shiroe was impressed. The quest "Get a magic bag" could be undertaken when players reached level 45, and Li Gan seemed to have a

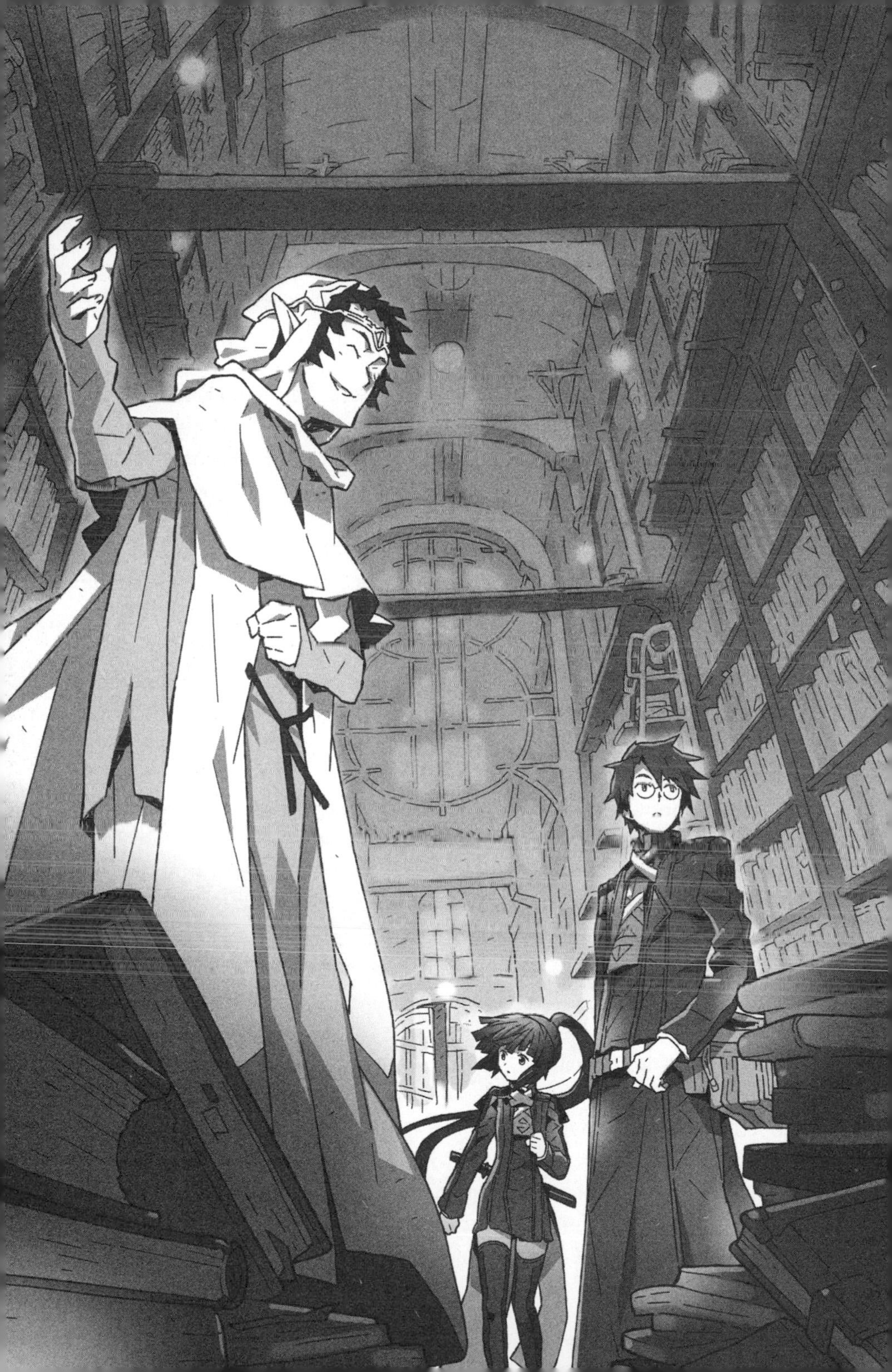

fairly accurate grasp of its content. His knowledge seemed too great for a Person of the Earth.

"Ah, pardon me. Let me introduce myself again. My name is Li Gan. I mentioned that I was a magician, and I can use magic, but it's more accurate to say that I'm a lore master."

"A lore master?"

"Yes, a researcher who studies magic. I can also teach general magic, but research is my specialty."

"Here?"

"Yes. It's been about thirty years since I settled down in the Ancient Court of Eternal Ice. This was originally my master's study, but he passed on a few years ago. After that, I inherited his responsibilities and have spent my days here, continuing his research. I apologize for my shabby appearance."

"—Miral Lake. …The Sage of Miral Lake?"

Recalling Li Gan's introduction, the name struck Shiroe.

The Sage of Miral Lake.

When *Elder Tales* was a game, that name had come up in several quests, town rumors, and various books. For example, a key item in the raid "The Nine Great Gaols of Halos" had been the Key of Eternal Darkness, made by the Sage of Miral Lake.

However, that had all been part of the game. He'd assumed it was just background information included to make the story more interesting, and he hadn't given it much thought.

"Well, yes, but honestly, I hardly ever introduce myself that way. I still feel like an apprentice, you know. When someone calls me by that name, I always think they mean my master."

"The 'Sage of Miral Lake' is a hereditary position, then?"

"Indeed it is. Please call me Li Gan."

For someone who'd inherited a name like that one, it was a very humble greeting. He had almost none of the daunting presence the word *sage* suggested.

Silence flowed between them.

As he slowly drank his Black Rose Tea, Shiroe's thoughts raced. Part of their reason for coming to the lords' conference of Eastal, the League of Free Cities, was that they'd been asked to do so, but the greater reason had been because they had prioritized gathering information on the current situation. If they attended the lords' conference, they would be able to make the acquaintance of this world's ruling class, or at least its nobles. They had predicted that doing so would give them access to a range of information so vast that town rumors couldn't compare.

He had never expected to attract someone this big.

It had been three months since the Catastrophe, and all sorts of knowledge about the world was finding its way, slowly, to Shiroe and the others. At the very least, it was probably safe to say that they had all the knowledge necessary for day-to-day life. Shiroe and the Adventurers of Akiba had acquired food, clothing, and homes in which to shelter from the rain.

However, the more of this sort of knowledge they gained, the more keenly Shiroe felt that they really knew nothing at all.

If it had been just Shiroe, on his own, this would not have been a problem.

Even if he had been living with a few companions, they could have resolved nearly all of their issues. No matter what the People of the Earth thought of them, no matter what the reality of this world was, Shiroe and the others had the combat skills they needed to survive. They could have traveled endlessly, or set up a base deep in the mountains somewhere; there would have been any number of ways to manage.

However, Shiroe wasn't in any position to think things like that now, and he didn't even want to. There were fifteen thousand Adventurers in Akiba, and nearly thirty thousand on the entire server. If he'd been able to abandon all of them, he'd never have dreamed of the Round Table Council in the first place.

There was no way thirty thousand people could live quietly, hiding from the People of the Earth. On top of that, they needed a base.

In the area administered by the Japanese server, whose total population was probably only about 1.5 million, Akiba's population of fifteen thousand was too large. Any action they took would send a ripple effect across the world. In fact, the new item production method *was* affecting the world in a big way.

Of course, even if Nyanta hadn't come across it, a trick of that level would probably have been discovered and spread by somebody within a few months. The Catastrophe had triggered a panic and everyone had been depressed, and they had managed to get in ahead of everyone else by taking advantage of that psychological vulnerability.

As a result, Shiroe didn't feel responsible for the fact that the new item production method had spread. However, they had to be aware that that knowledge had affected the world at large.

It was also likely that they would not be able to avoid causing similar situations in the future. No matter how they glossed it over, as far as this world was concerned, the Adventurers were a kind of contaminant. Guiding the situation to results that were as peaceful and nondestructive as possible would require profound knowledge. At present, Shiroe and the others had an overwhelming shortage of that.

This meeting... It just may end up being more important than the lords' conference.

Shiroe's expression had grown tense. Li Gan watched him, seeming intrigued, and began to speak.

"A moment ago, I called myself a lore master, or magic researcher, but there are a vast number of different kinds of magic, as well as broad variation in the ranges they manipulate. Of these, my research specialty is world-class magic."

"World-class?"

On hearing the unfamiliar term, Shiroe put a hand to his chin and nodded.

"That's correct. It's a way of classifying magic by the scale of its effect. The categories are action-class, battle-class, operation-class, tactical-class, strategic-class, national-defense-class, continent-class, and world-class. Of course, these categories are one-dimensional. Aside from classifying them by scale, it's possible to classify them by special features—such as magic that uses energy, magic that changes the state of matter, or summoning magic—while another frequently used method categorizes them by the caster's power."

Even as Shiroe listened, his thoughts went ahead.

It wasn't a way of thinking he was familiar with. He could understand classifying magic by type; for example, the energy Sorcerers used, or the summonings performed by Summoners. That method was easy to understand.

He also understood classifying them by the caster's power. In player terms, these would be spells acquired at different levels. That sort of thing had come up in the magic introduction section on the official *Elder Tales* website.

"Classification by scale is a method that classifies magic phenomenologically from the aspect of scale, or when examining it in combination with its objective. Action-class indicates magic of a size that could substitute for one action. Swinging a sword and wounding a demon, say. If you did this with magic, the spell would be action-class. It makes it possible to wound anything from one demon to several demons with one gesture, you see. By that definition, most of the spells magic troops use are action-class magic. Even if attack power is increased, action-class is never more than action-class."

Viewed that way, Mind Bolt, Shiroe's basic attack spell, would be action-class. It was a spell that used magic to unleash a shock wave of mental damage, and its effect was roughly equal to firing an arrow. Even if there were secondary effects or damage, they were only incidental.

"Battle-class indicates magic that can sway the outcome of a single battle. It implies being able to determine the fate of an enemy platoon, or of an ally platoon."

Apparently there was quite a lot of depth to this classification of magic by scale. For example, on its own, Shiroe's hypnotic spell, Astral Hypno, was an action-class spell. However, depending on how it was used, it held the power to push an entire platoon of enemies to the brink of death. In that case, it wouldn't be odd to classify it as battle-class.

"Operation-class is magic that can sway two or three battles at a stroke. The great magic said to have been used by the legendary combat magicians of this world would fall into this category."

Several battles at once... Would that be magic that granted powerful abilities? When Shiroe searched through all his own spells, he saw only one special skill that reached that level.

"Tactical-class is the step above that. It's magic that can sway from one day to several days—or, in terms of enemy organizations, one fortress, one tower, or one mansion—with one attack."

At this point, they were passing beyond the limits of Shiroe's imagination.

Simulation games aside, *Elder Tales* had been an RPG which gamers played by controlling individual Adventurer characters. If an individual Adventurer had had the sort of power that could destroy an entire dungeon, cooperation between players would have been completely unnecessary. It would have been overwhelming destructive power.

"Now then, we'll just skim over the rest. Strategy-class magic is an individual spell that can influence one war. National-defense-class is magic of a scale that can influence one hostile country. Continent-class is magic large enough to influence an entire continent. And world-class…"

"That would be…magic that can influence the continued existence, laws, or fate of the world?"

"That's right."

As a general idea, he understood it.

He could see it being used as a subject for research. However, did that sort of magic really exist? In the world of *Elder Tales*, Shiroe himself was an Enchanter, a petty magic user. It was ludicrous for him to talk of doubting the existence of magic, but the scale of the conversation was too big, and he couldn't seem to bring it into focus.

"I, uh… I'm sorry. I can understand the category itself, as a hypothesis, but does magic like that actually exist? Or is this purely theoretical?"

At Shiroe's question, the corners of Li Gan's mouth curved in a vaguely endearing smile, and he answered in the negative.

"It exists. In the literature and through my own senses, I've found three instances of its use. All three have been a magic known as a 'World Fraction.'"

"…You mean the Catastrophe?"

The instant he asked, he saw the answer in Li Gan's expression.

Magic of that scale was no longer the result of an individual ability.

It was possible that some sort of transcendental being had used this magic, but even the researchers weren't able to see it in its entirety.

Strategy-class. National-defense-class. Continent-class. …Why would research need classes of magic that didn't exist? They *did* exist.

It might be out of reach for both People of the Earth and Adventurers, but national-defense-class magical catastrophes could occur in the form of volcanic eruptions triggered by fire spirits' increased activity or earthquakes provoked by earth spirits.

As someone who was too familiar with *Elder Tales* as a gamer, Shiroe had seen magic as one of the techniques used by Adventurers such as himself. If considered as part of the story's background, he could accept that enormous spells did exist.

Li Gan, this gaunt researcher, had his eyes fixed on the type of magic that surpassed what individuals used. He truly was a magic researcher, not a magician. His ambition wasn't to expand his abilities but to investigate the world's mysteries. It was the same as having the ambition to figure out the structure of the world.

"Your people call the incident that occurred in May 'the Catastrophe', don't you? The People of the Earth seem to call it simply 'the Revolution' or 'the May Incident,' but I call it 'the Third World Fraction.' I invited you here to speak with you, in the hopes of obtaining any information you might have about the World Fraction. As a researcher, I want to know everything."

Li Gan's eyes shone with curiosity, but they seemed sincere.

Talking about it won't be a problem. We know almost nothing in any case. But...

"You said 'the third,' didn't you? Earlier, you mentioned that world-class magic had been used three times in this world. Could you tell us about the first and second World Fractions? The Adventurers don't have much information about the Catastrophe. I'll give you what we have; however, we also need as much information as possible regarding the Catastrophe."

▶ **4**

At Shiroe's words, Li Gan created a pause by picking up his drink.

"I don't mind at all, but it makes for a long story. Are you sure?"

"......"

"Yes, please."

After confirming that Akatsuki, seated beside him, had nodded silently, Shiroe answered Li Gan. Akatsuki was also listening to the conversation, her expression tense.

"Let's see. Where should I begin? Of course, as I've been saying, I don't know everything about the World Fractions myself… Actually, it would be better to say I know practically nothing. That makes it terribly easy to tell you, 'They're incidents that happened long ago' and leave it at that…but I expect that wouldn't be much of an explanation. Very well. I'll tell you all I know, from the roots up. …Let's begin with the oldest story."

Shiroe resettled himself on the sofa and nodded deeply.

From the beginning. That was exactly what Shiroe wanted, too.

"—About three hundred and fifty years ago, they say the world was much more prosperous than it is today. Of course, it was nothing compared to the Age of Myth, which has vanished beyond the horizon of legend, but the population seems to have been between three and five times what it is now. Their activity was mostly centered on the continent, and their territory was vast, extending to the ends of the earth."

"What do you mean by 'continent'?"

"Ah, Eured, our neighbor."

The Eurasian continent: the continent that included China, the Middle Eastern countries, and Europe. Shiroe nodded. It went without saying that it was the largest continent in this other world as well.

However, Shiroe hadn't expected the part about this not being the Age of Myth. According to the game background legend in *Elder Tales*, the Age of Myth—which had possessed a completely evolved scientific civilization—had been torn apart and rebuilt as the current world. All the official site had said was that there had been a long Dark Age after the reconstruction, so he'd gotten the impression that the Age of Myth had fallen, been reconstructed, a Dark Age passed, and then the *Elder Tales* game had begun.

However, he'd seen how far the buildings and roads from the Age of Myth had deteriorated. Now that he thought about it, all sorts of things must have happened during this so-called Dark Age. He'd assumed the Dark Age had been an empty era with no events whatsoever, so he was taken by surprise.

"The world was inhabited by four races: humans, alvs, elves, and dwarves. They were mutually prosperous, and the countries were peaceful and wealthy. Many of the high-performance magic items that are still found deep in dungeons were made in this era. Then, too, magical ruins such as this Ancient Court of Eternal Ice clearly don't belong to the Age of Myth, do they? These ruins were created during this era by the alvs. Yes, it was the alvs who invented magic and pioneered the powerful magic civilization. They are said to have created all sorts of magic implements, and to have unlocked the mysteries of the world."

Alvs... The official explanation was that they were an ancient race that had died out. As a half alv, Shiroe carried traces of their blood, but he'd never sensed any history or connection during game play. He'd thought of them only as a race with high magical abilities and an aptitude for using magic items.

"It has nothing to do with the main story, so I'll omit the details, but their abilities proved their undoing. alvs were highly intelligent and had a talent for magic, but unfortunately, as a species, their fertility was poor. Their population didn't increase, and in terms of territory, the alv kingdoms located here and there were small. Resenting the fact that such a minor tribe was monopolizing magic technology, the other races' countries formed an alliance and destroyed the alv kingdoms, one after another. —The alvs' domain was obliterated. Their glorious history ends here."

The alvs were extinct, after all. Something along those lines had to have happened.

Shiroe himself had some alv blood, but the tragedy didn't stir up any feelings of kinship with them. His only thought was, *So that was the backstory.*

"But what about me? ...I mean, there aren't many half alvs, but there are a few around."

"In other words, that reveals the fate of the alv race. What people sought to plunder from the alvs. First, they went after their knowledge of magic and their high-performance magic items, but next... They took the alv race itself. The alvs became the world's slaves. Alvs were bought and sold everywhere: in human kingdoms, elf kingdoms, dwarf kingdoms. Then they were violated, their blood diluted, and their descendants are the present half alvs. At this point, of course, they're no more than genetic throwbacks, born unexpectedly from human parents. …Ah, and I've gone off-topic. We mustn't have that. In any case, the alv kingdoms were destroyed, but there was more trouble to come. This is where the alv Ruquinjé make their appearance."

"Ruquinjé…?"
It was a word he'd never heard before. Li Gan sketched the characters it was written with on the table with his fingertip. *Six*, meaning six people? *Leaning*, and *princesses*. *Toppling princesses*.

"There are various theories regarding the identities of the Ruquinjé. In this case, when I say 'identities,' I mean their names and origins. However, what we know for certain is that they were all princesses from the alv kingdoms scattered across the continent. Parenthetically, the name Ruquinjé was bestowed on them later, by historians, and we believe they weren't even acquaintances, let alone conspirators. Like the majority of the alv people, they became slaves of the human world. Since they had been royalty, they were probably lucky simply to escape execution. According to the historical texts, 'They were admired as jewels for their overwhelming beauty.' They were taken as love slaves by various royals, rulers, and powerful families of the day, and kept as pets in six different countries. However, they didn't end as slaves. One used magic, another led fellow alvs who had been enslaved, a third beguiled a royal and controlled society from the shadows, and they launched a counterattack against all mankind."
Shiroe had been drawn into the story, but as before, emotionally, he was very close to neutral. If he'd had to say one way or the other, his sympathies leaned slightly toward the alvs, but that was all. Viewed from the standpoint of someone from modern Japan, the humans of this other world had been jealous of the alv race's magic technology and had invaded. He didn't think the alv survivors could be blamed for considering revenge, even if it had been close to terrorism.
"The humans, dwarves, and elves that had destroyed the alv kingdoms had acquired many magic technologies, but at the time, they weren't able to use them well. At this point, a terrible, confused,

drawn-out war began. It became as messy as it did because the countries all began fighting each other—humans against dwarves, humans against elves, elves against dwarves. The Ruquinjé were avengers, not heroes. They thoroughly outwitted everyone, threw society into confusion, and by leading others' hearts astray, they sowed the seeds that led the human societies into killing their own. Many people died in this war. If the chronicles are correct, the number of dead was equal to the current population of the world. However, in the meantime, the Ruquinjé were driven into a corner as well. They were alvs, after all. Their weakness was their low numbers, which stemmed from poor fertility. They could hide in the shadows of this friendly fire, but once discovered, they were fragile. Just as the Ruquinjé were about to be killed...the First World Fraction activated."

"The First..."

At the appearance of the main topic, Shiroe held his breath.

When he looked, Akatsuki, seated next to him, was also completely fascinated.

"Yes. There is a very high probability that this First World Fraction was an advanced ritual spell cast by the alvs. Many mysteries remain, of course. The technological aspects in particular are full of mysteries: Not only can it not be replicated, but even the basic principles are unclear. At any rate, a World Fraction occurred. The result was the genesis of demihumans. ...Up until roughly three hundred years ago, there were no demihumans in this world."

—The demihumans hadn't existed.

These were words he hadn't even imagined. However, if that was the case, it made sense that the human societies had been dozens of times more prosperous than they were now. The world had been theirs.

"I call it the genesis of demihumans, and I don't think it was the result of crossbreeding or a biochemical issue. This is the area my master was researching, and my current hypothesis is that souls may be involved in World Fractions. At least at the time, the world was flooded with an extraordinary amount of soul material. The repeated wars had driven the population down to nearly half of what it had been, you see. This soul material was used as raw material for the demihumans' genesis. Mankind had been weakened by the wars, and when the demihumans swarmed up from every quarter, they were driven to a cliff's edge at a single stroke. Many cities fell, and armies that had prided themselves on their invincibility were annihilated. Nearly all nations disintegrated. At present, on the Yamato Archipelago, the only remaining vestige of the countries of three centuries ago is found in the Ancient Dynasty of Westlande. The towns and cities of Eastal were no more than small country villages. The demihuman genesis worked a great change on the structure of the world, transforming it into what it is today: Mankind desperately defending tiny areas of civilization while fighting the demihumans' invasion. The world was shrouded in darkness. Humans defeated the cornered Ruquinjé, but we can probably say that their revenge succeeded."

The defeated Ruquinjé.

The activated World Fraction.

A huge outbreak of demihumans, fueled by souls.

"Next came the Steel Age. As I said before, all around the world the goblin, kobold, orc, troll, gnoll, sahuagin, and lizardman races sent up war cries. These brutal, monstrous beings eroded the remaining areas of human civilization. Gradually, human life fell into deep shadow. Our research has advanced now, and defensive magic and barriers—both relics of the alvs—have evolved. However, at the time, they didn't even have these aids. At that point, mankind planned a desperate resistance operation. Their first attempt was the creation of new warriors, using the secret arts of the alvs. As a result of this large-scale experiment—the Northtrilia Project—the felinoid, wolf-fang and foxtail beast races and the ritian race were artificially created. They began as man-made races that were sent to the front line."

Since only the human, dwarf and elf races had been mentioned, he'd been a bit worried for a while now, but apparently this was where the remaining races came in. Felinoids, wolf-fangs, foxtails, and ritians had been hybrids, created to fight.

"In addition, several countries on Eured decided that the war could not be won and gave up. They put together a huge fleet and crossed to the new continent. As it turned out, there were demihumans on the new continent as well, but they began working to build a pioneer country that would open up a new world for them. On top of that, mankind used the power of its faith to produce the Ancients."

—The new continent. That was probably the Land of Wen. In the old world, it would have been the Americas. …Which meant that, in this other world, the discovery of America had occurred during these three hundred years.

Of course, this was historic folklore from the Eurasian and Asian worlds; if they went to the place itself, the details might change. Shiroe let his imagination run very briefly to the area under the jurisdiction of the American server, but he shook his head, drawing his thoughts back.

"There are various theories regarding the birth of the Ancients, but there is no doubt that quite a few Ancient lines of descent began during this period. The Ancients… Well, we'll speak of them another time. Let me just say that it was an issue related to the Spirit Theory. However, even after investing all these technologies, mankind was unable to stop its slide toward destruction. The demihuman forces were simply too powerful. On top of that, the world seemed to retain an effect that was like the curse of the First World Fraction. It was, as I said at the beginning, a problem of souls. No matter how often they defeated the demihuman forces, their numbers did not shrink. Even when defeated, their souls reincarnated as demihumans… This is a hypothesis, but they have such an odd breeding curve that it can't be explained without thinking this way. Of course, there are immature individuals even among demihumans, so if their numbers could be decreased at a stroke, it was possible to greatly decrease their power. In other words, if a demihuman is killed, that individual is reborn, returning as a juvenile. For a period of several years, these individuals are unable to go back to war. However, in three years, they return to the battlefield. *It was impossible to wipe out the demihumans.* That meant there could be no victory."

—Well.

Shiroe began wanting to interrupt: Wasn't that issue related to the *Elder Tales* game specs? *Elder Tales* was a game, or at least it had been. If a specific player had been able to hunt the prey in a zone to extinction, and no other players could make an attempt, it would have made for a very frustrating experience.

As a result, in accordance with the game's specs, defeated monsters were replaced after a certain amount of time. The players were being provided with new prey. If it hadn't been for that, the players—who had superior combat abilities—would have hunted the monsters to extinction, and it wouldn't have taken very long.

"Humans were afraid. They despaired, and they longed for a miracle. During this period, the world seems to have been truly dark. It had already been sixty years since the defeat of the Ruquinjé and the First World Fraction. During those sixty years, mankind had sunk to the depths of despair and poverty, starvation, and terror. Most people had shut themselves up inside fortified villages or fortresses, living in fear of attacks by demihumans or magical beasts. In fact, the extinction of mankind was thought to be just a matter of time. The revenge of the Ruquinjé seemed to have succeeded. —At that point, the Second World Fraction occurred. Unlike the First World Fraction, not enough materials remain to allow a thorough examination. Mankind was in a Dark Age, and they had probably lost the energy reserves to leave such materials behind. According to the few records we have, humans, dwarves, elves, and many ritians were mobilized, and a sacred summoning was performed. A few of the scriptures clearly state 'the gods' salvation,' but… In any case, another World Fraction occurred. This was precisely two hundred and forty years ago. It marked the appearance of the Adventurers."

Two hundred and forty years ago.
The arrival of the Adventurers.

"There isn't much to tell about history from that point on. The Adventurers' powerful combat abilities became great good news for mankind. Yamato was assailed by various crises—the Hades' Breath incident, the King of the Underworld incident, the Dragon's Throne incident—but the Adventurers overcame them all. Of course, peace had not returned to the world, but it had finally gained some small stability, and gradually, it was making its way toward recovery."

Which brings us to the present…

"The Adventurers, hm? ...Come to think of it, Li Gan, you knew my name, didn't you? Why is that?" Shiroe asked, abruptly curious.

"Because you are a great magician, Master Shiroe. Even among the Adventurers, I thought you would be particularly well informed about the situation."

"A great magician...?"

Shiroe was perplexed. He didn't remember completing any quests advanced enough to earn him a reputation like that.

"You made your first appearance in history ninety-eight years ago. There are other long-lived Adventurers, of course, but in terms of frequency of activity as well, there is no doubt that you are a great magician. Isn't that so?"

Ninety-eight years?! ...Wait...

Shiroe's brain circuits activated all at once, as if his mind had caught fire. Time in this world was... The history of this world was... ...In that case, the Second World Fraction, the one that had occurred two hundred and forty years ago, was...

...the start of the open beta.

▶ 5

When she woke on the morning of the fourth day, it was raining.

The rain that had begun at midnight seemed to have continued throughout the night.

The drops were small, and they fell without much force. It was just a drizzle, unusual for summer. But the drainage in this part of the forest seemed to be good, and it didn't seem likely that there would be damage to the tents.

Either way, once they were in the dungeon, the weather outside wouldn't matter. With that in mind, Minori began the morning's equipment inspection.

She'd checked her equipment right after they had finished yesterday's dungeon expedition, but inspecting it again before going out was a habit of sorts.

I guess I'm getting nervous…

That was why she recounted the potions, over and over. On noticing her own feelings, Minori felt a bit guilty. It was like she was a little kid.

She had been as quiet as possible while she worked, but it was morning already. The other sleeping bags began to move, too.

There were four tents in all. Two of them were large: One for the advanced party, and one for the lower party. One of the remaining tents was for the three leaders, and the last, kept aside as a dressing room for the girls, was used for changing and storage.

This meant there were five people in the tent Minori and the rest of the lower party were using. Even if it was a tent, it was the sort of large pavilion tent you'd see at events in the old world, and it was roomy.

"G'mning."

Isuzu, who'd been sleeping beside her, muttered, rubbing her eyes.

Isuzu's hair was very thick, and apparently it tended to curl in all the wrong ways. Overnight, the hair at the back of her head had developed cowlicks. This bothered Isuzu, and so she always wore it in a braid, but Minori thought Isuzu's hair was adorable.

"S'morning already, huh?"

Isuzu glanced at the tent flap; her eyes were still only half open. The sailcloth around the tent's opening was roughly woven, and the light outside showed through.

"Mm-hm. It's raining, so it's gloomy, but it should be morning."

"Huh… I'm still kinda sleepy."

"Maybe it's because it's chilly."

"Nn."

Isuzu muttered something unintelligible to herself, then burrowed back into her sleeping bag again. Smiling wryly, Minori laid a blanket over the top of the sleeping bag.

Everyone else seemed to be awake as well, but no one was getting up.

It was drizzling outside, but conversely, because of the rain, the previous night had been a cool one, and it had been easy to sleep. Wrapped in the sound of the rain, the inside of the tent was as peaceful as a hideaway, and the atmosphere was drowsy.

The monotonous sound of water dripping from the tent seemed to be protecting them. It was the first quiet, relaxed time they'd had since they'd begun camping in the mountains.

She felt as if she'd seen a shadow move.

When she glanced over, Nyanta had poked his head in through the tent flap. Minori cut across the middle of the tent, making for him. The area at the center was tall enough that Minori could stand up without any trouble.

"Good morning."

"Good morning, Nyanta."

"It's technically time for breakfast, but…"

Minori nodded, agreeing with Nyanta's hushed voice.

"We can't eat outside as a group in this rain. Breakfast is sandwiches and cream of crab soup, and we've decided to eat in our tents."

"All right."

Nyanta seemed to have brought their breakfast over himself. He held it out to her: enough sandwiches for at least ten people, and a little pot full of cream soup.

"Thank you very much."

"Mm, don't worry about it. All right. See mew later."

Nyanta waggled a hand at Minori who was awkwardly trying to bow her head while she held the tray and the pot—and went back out into the drizzle. He was probably on his way to deliver breakfast to the advanced party.

Carefully, Minori carried the tray to the center of the tent. At first she wasn't sure what to do about the pot, but then she remembered she had a legged heat lamp in her pack, so she set it on that.

"Nurgh, food?"

Touya sat up; his hair was all tousled. "Uh-huh. Touya, your hair's something else," Minori pointed out, but Touya just gave a vague, "Nn."

"You're not going to eat?"

"I'll eat. Oog."

Touya got up, fumbling a little. Next to him, Rundelhaus woke as well. He didn't seem quite awake yet; muttering something cryptic like, "Good morning, Miss Minori. …You're as lovely as the sun again today," he headed for the tent flap on unsteady feet.

"It's raining, Rundelhaus!" Minori called to him, but he went out, saying, "I'm just going to change my face and wash my clothes."

At that point, Serara returned.

When did she... Minori thought, but Serara was in a good mood, and she began to set out fruit beside the unpacked sandwiches. Apparently she'd been with Nyanta. An early morning date?...

With Serara helping, Minori began to pour cream soup into cups. The reheated soup filled the tent with a fragrance like clam chowder. It looked absolutely delicious.

"It's perfect, of course."

Serara spoke to her, still in high spirits. She had probably tasted it when she was with Nyanta. It really did look good, Minori thought. The milk-colored soup had corn and crab meat in it, and even now, as she served it, it looked enticing.

"Nnuh."

Isuzu came rolling over to them like a caterpillar. Minori hugged her, helping her sit up.

As Minori took a comb out from her pack, Serara took the dishes, saying, "I'll handle this, then."

The rain fell softly, and in its midst, breakfast began.

Settling down behind Isuzu, who was only halfway out of her sleeping bag, Minori combed her hair. It really was abundant and curly. Isuzu herself grumbled that it wasn't feminine, but her hair was a bright brown, and when it was braided, Minori thought it suited her very well.

"This's really good," Touya muttered.

He was sitting cross-legged on his sleeping bag, wearing a T-shirt and shorts. It wasn't really the sort of thing to show ladies, but since this was a training camp, there was no help for it.

Immediately upon returning, Rundelhaus said, "Hullo! Something smells good this morning. What a fantastic breakfast. Don't you agree, friends?" He was scattering a breezy aura around; he'd managed to get himself dressed in a very short time and was taking things at his usual pace.

Still half in her sleeping bag, Isuzu handed Rundelhaus a sandwich, saying, "These are good, Rudy."

"Rudy"?

Rundelhaus obediently took the sandwich, then a big bite, and said, "Oho, mashed pumpkin salad, is it? Quite tasty." His manners were oddly genteel, and indicated he'd been brought up in a household with good discipline.

Breakfast quietly continued on this way.

The soft sound of the rain seemed to soothe their frazzled hearts. It was probably also true that thinking about the dungeon they would have to challenge again today discouraged them a bit, and they didn't feel like talking.

They packed the rest of their generous allotment of sandwiches into a basket, deciding to save them for lunch. There had been three different kinds of sandwich; all were masterpieces made with Nyanta's sincere good will, and they were extremely delicious. Minori's favorite was the fruit-filled omelet variety.

The fruit was still left, but they each breathed sighs of relief, hot cups in their hands. They had each descended into that blank state of mind that comes with a full belly.

"Listen…"

In the midst of that atmosphere, Touya spoke.

"Did you want seconds?" Serara asked, peeking into the small pot as she did so.

"No. It's not that."

Touya searched for words; he seemed to be thinking about something.

Finding himself the focus of questioning looks, Touya hesitated, almost beginning to speak several times. He probably couldn't find the right words—Touya wasn't a very glib talker, and Minori was used to seeing him grope around for words like this.

Their eyes met for a moment, and with that glance, Minori understood what Touya was trying to do. He wanted to do something about their situation, and he was planning to raise some sort of question. Minori even imagined that he might be trying to put himself in the line of fire, to shield her.

If Touya had made up his mind to start something, Minori couldn't possibly not be there beside him.

No. Actually, I should be the one to do this.

Listen up. If you run into trouble, step out in front. With your heart, not with your legs.

She remembered the advice she'd gotten from Naotsugu one day.

Step out in front with your heart. Now, finally, she thought she was beginning to understand what those words meant. They meant she had to summon up her courage. *Courage* didn't mean being fearless in the heat of battle. It meant the determination to overcome the cowardice inside her.

Minori realized her own heart had been frightened and holding back. For that very reason, she spoke decisively:

"Listen. Why don't we wait until this afternoon to go into the dungeon today?"

► **6**

"Huh?"

Isuzu sounded astonished.

"What are you saying, Miss Minori?! Have you forgotten we're here for a training camp? Our top priority is to get to the dungeon as soon as we can, get as much experience as possible, and boost our levels," Rundelhaus reprimanded Minori, his tone harsh.

"But you see, we've only been able to make one attempt per day. Both yesterday and the day before, we withdrew in less than three hours, remember? In that case, even if we wait until afternoon to go in, we should be able to get the same results as yesterday."

"That's...true, I suppose... But we can't just stay the same forever."

Rundelhaus seemed irritated, as if he wasn't convinced.

"This is *because* we can't just stay the same forever."

"Minori?"

Serara sounded worried. She was probably afraid that Minori and Rundelhaus were about to fight. To Minori, her tone sounded pleading: *Please don't say extreme things.*

"And so, today, for the whole morning..."

At Minori's words, both Serara and Touya tensed up.

"Let's just laze around and take it easy."

However, the last half of Minori's sentence shattered that tension at a stroke.

"Miss Minori. Are you trying to be funny?!"

Rundelhaus had risen to his knees, anger in his voice. Personality aside, with his blond hair and handsome face, when he showed naked anger like this, the impact was formidable. Inwardly, Minori felt a bit frightened.

Still, Isuzu wasn't the least bit overawed by Rundelhaus. "Calm down, Rudy," she told him, bluntly, deflecting his feelings. Minori thought this was strange: Isuzu was the type of girl who read atmospheres so well that she normally cared about them too much. It was as if she didn't feel that timidity at all as far as Rundelhaus was concerned.

"'Laze around and take it easy' was going too far, but I do think we should introduce ourselves."

Choosing her words carefully, Minori continued. As the other group members looked perplexed, she began to speak. "My name is Minori. My level is twenty-one, and I'm fourteen years old. I'm a human in this world, too. I'm Touya's older twin sister. I've got the lowest level in our party, and I feel bad about holding everyone else back."

At her words, Rundelhaus gave a quiet snort, but Minori paid no attention. More accurately, having come this far, she couldn't *afford* to pay attention.

"I'm a Kannagi. Kannagi is one of the three recovery classes."

"We *know* that."

"No, you don't know."

When Rundelhaus tried to cut her off, Minori answered back, her face serious.

"You don't. I mean it. I don't know anything about the rest of you, either. I don't know what you like and don't like, or whether you want to step out front or draw back. I know nothing about you. Since I don't know anything, even if I want to help you… I can't."

"_____"

Serara had frozen; she seemed startled. She'd probably never heard Minori contradict someone else this plainly. The only member of the group who wasn't surprised was Touya. The one reaction that was a bit unexpected was Isuzu's: Although she was startled, she soon broke into a kind smile.

"Please tell me. I'm weak, so if I don't hear these things and remember them all, I won't be of any use to you."

"What do you mean, 'all'…?"

Serara's question was hesitant.

"'All' means 'all.' …For example— That lava shell you use, Rundelhaus. What is it?"

"Hmph… That's Orb of Lava. As the name says, it's an orb made out of lava," he answered flippantly.

"But that's—if that's all I know, I might as well not know anything. For example… Why do you use that spell? That particular spell, instead of another one. I mean, you have lots of attack spells, don't you?"

"Because that spell's effective."

"Why is it effective?"

Minori peppered him with questions. Rundelhaus organized his words a bit, then answered.

"That spell is one of the most powerful spells I have. That isn't all, though. It has a short chant time; it's ready in just two seconds. For all that, its recast time is eighteen seconds, which is fairly short as well. To begin with, this balance is incredibly good. Two seconds plus eighteen seconds is twenty seconds total. The turnover isn't fast enough for me to cast it as a barrage, but being able to use it once every twenty seconds is quite excellent. I can use it several times in the same battle. On top of that, even though the spell is meant for attacking groups, it's characterized by a small orb that races through enemy ranks. That means it can pick off the enemy without involving Touya, even if Touya is on the front line. It's an outstanding spell."

Minori listened intently as he spoke, nodding several times.

"Hold it. Samurai taunting has a short range, and it takes a second and a half to chant."

Touya spoke, sounding troubled.

"What do you mean?"

"Umm… Okay, so: When the enemy gets close, I use Samurai Taunt. It's a thing called 'taunting,' and it doesn't inflict damage, but it pulls enemies' attention to me as if I'd caused massive damage."

Serara was also listening, frowning a little in concentration. She could understand the content of the conversation itself, but she didn't know much about other classes' characteristics. These were all special skills she'd never heard of before.

"Yes, I see."

However, Rundelhaus seemed to understand quite well.

—It was a very natural special skill.

If monsters' wariness was concentrated on any opponent who inflicted damage, then in order to hold the enemy, you'd need to cause greater damage—in other words, to have greater attack power—than anyone else. However, in order to take the enemy's attacks, you needed HP and defensive power.

As a tank, Touya's specialty was defense; in other words, being able to withstand enemy attacks. In terms of offensive power, Rundelhaus had more than twice Touya's ATK.

In that case, it was only natural that he would acquire a special skill that could allow him to use his insufficient ATK to draw the enemy's attention. An outstanding tank would have special skills that could focus the monsters' hate more than anyone else in the party.

These were a series of special skills known as "taunting." They didn't inflict actual damage, but they caused the monsters shock and pain, deeply impressing the tank's existence on their wary minds.

"See, though, taunting's got all sorts of different characteristics, even among the Warrior classes, and the characteristic for Samurai Taunts is that they have a short range. I think it's maybe three meters... Anyway, as far as a katana can reach. That means I have to draw 'em in before I use it. It takes two seconds for it to hit."

Isuzu was listening to them with a blank look on her face. It really was a complicated conversation.

"So here's what I'm saying. Orb of Lava and Samurai Taunt take almost the same amount of time to activate, but Orb of Lava goes way further. If we both attack as soon as they're in range, Orb of Lava's going to hit 'em that much faster. It's no wonder the Skeletons head straight for you."

In conclusion, that was it.

Touya's taunting was supposed to protect everyone, but it wasn't working.

If the enemy used projectile weapons, they'd be outside its range, and in any case, Rundelhaus's attack spell was getting to them before the taunt did.

"Then you're telling me not to use Orb of Lava?"

"No, just wait two seconds."

"But that will waste two seconds. In a magnificent battle, a loss of two seconds is fatal."

As Touya and Rundelhaus kept arguing, their voices gradually got louder and louder. They didn't seem ready to fight, not exactly, but it seemed as if heat waves rippled the air between them.

"…What if, maybe… Listen. Would Cowards' Fugue mean anything here?" Isuzu broke in hesitantly.

"What's that, Isuzu?"

Touya looked blank. Rundelhaus said, "The name sounds craven. Is it a special skill, Miss Isuzu?"

"Cowards' Fugue is a special skill I just learned; it's a Continuous Support song—Continuous Support songs are special skills that are always 'on,' and their effects are constant. I can only use two at a time, but they never stop working. So, Cowards' Fugue is… If I set that song, apparently I can make damage caused by anyone other than a Warrior look like less than it really is."

"There's actually a special skill like that?!" "Really?!"

Touya and Rundelhaus cried out in surprise.

They'd known that Bards had a wide variety of support abilities, but they'd never dreamed they had a special skill like that one.

"Uuuu, yes, there is. There really is."

Isuzu must have felt rather daunted by their intensity: She drew back a bit. She didn't seem to understand the ferocity her two interrogators had turned on her.

"I mean, the song doesn't increase damage or recover anything, and it doesn't raise the evasion rate or attack power, you know? Up until now, I'd always thought it was a pretty useless special skill…"

That was perfectly understandable.

Minori thought that if someone had suddenly started telling her about an ability that made damage caused by anyone other than Warriors look like less than it actually was, even she would have thought, *What a pointless special skill.*

However. Even knowing that was a step forward.

"We have to know more."

"Hm. Miss Minori. It seems I owe you an apology. I admit that I was ignorant and that my understanding was shallow."

Rundelhaus bowed with good grace.

"No, I didn't know any of this, either. Since that's the case, Rundelhaus, please tell me about all the spells you know. Not just their names or their capabilities. Tell me what you like about them, what you don't like, the times when you use them and the times when you want to use them. Everything."

"Everything...? That's going to take time, Miss Minori."

"That's fine. Do take your time. If there's anything I don't understand, I'll ask as many questions as I have to."

Outside, it was still drizzling, but none of them heard the rain anymore.

What they could do, and what they couldn't do.

What they were good at, and what they were bad at.

Minori and the others talked long into the afternoon.

CHAPTER. 5

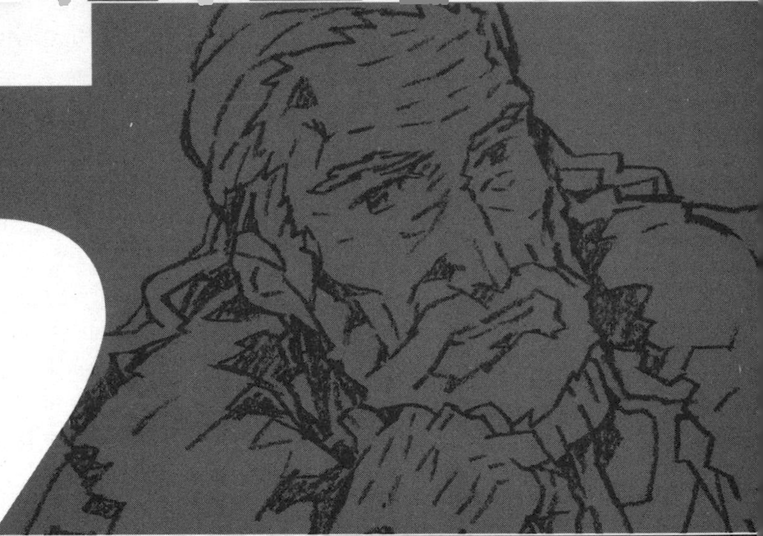

ATTACK

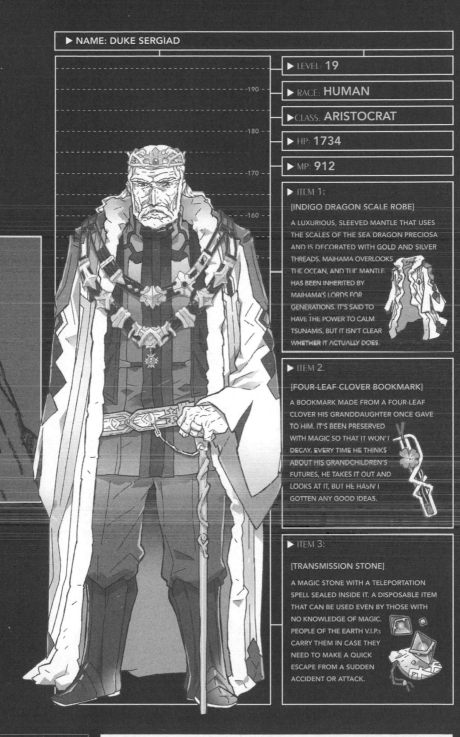

▶ NAME: DUKE SERGIAD

▶ LEVEL: **19**

▶ RACE: **HUMAN**

▶ CLASS: **ARISTOCRAT**

▶ HP: **1734**

▶ MP: **912**

▶ ITEM 1:

[INDIGO DRAGON SCALE ROBE]

A LUXURIOUS, SLEEVED MANTLE THAT USES THE SCALES OF THE SEA DRAGON PRECIOSA AND IS DECORATED WITH GOLD AND SILVER THREADS. MAIHAMA OVERLOOKS THE OCEAN, AND THE MANTLE HAS BEEN INHERITED BY MAIHAMA'S LORDS FOR GENERATIONS. IT'S SAID TO HAVE THE POWER TO CALM TSUNAMIS, BUT IT ISN'T CLEAR WHETHER IT ACTUALLY DOES.

▶ ITEM 2.

[FOUR-LEAF CLOVER BOOKMARK]

A BOOKMARK MADE FROM A FOUR-LEAF CLOVER HIS GRANDDAUGHTER ONCE GAVE TO HIM. IT'S BEEN PRESERVED WITH MAGIC SO THAT IT WON'T DECAY. EVERY TIME HE THINKS ABOUT HIS GRANDCHILDREN'S FUTURES, HE TAKES IT OUT AND LOOKS AT IT, BUT HE HASN'T GOTTEN ANY GOOD IDEAS.

▶ ITEM 3:

[TRANSMISSION STONE]

A MAGIC STONE WITH A TELEPORTATION SPELL SEALED INSIDE IT. A DISPOSABLE ITEM THAT CAN BE USED EVEN BY THOSE WITH NO KNOWLEDGE OF MAGIC. PEOPLE OF THE EARTH V.I.P.s CARRY THEM IN CASE THEY NEED TO MAKE A QUICK ESCAPE FROM A SUDDEN ACCIDENT OR ATTACK.

<Telescope>
important for reconnaissance!
No using it for naughty stuff.

▶ 1

Shiroe rolled over in bed.

It wasn't yet dawn. There wasn't the slightest sound in the dark room.

The curtains were closed, shutting out even the starlight, and the room was ruled by pitch-black. The darkness was so dense that it didn't make the least bit of difference whether his eyes were open or closed.

In that darkness, Shiroe was thinking back over the past few days.

As predicted, the nobles of Eastal, the League of Free Cities, were approaching Shiroe and the other members of the Round Table Council separately. Although their requests were varied, few places hoped to have soldiers dispatched to them. The majority wanted to be provided with technology or to form trade agreements. Shiroe's delegation had gotten the impression that they were much wilier and more intelligent than they had first imagined.

The nobles knew that dispatched Adventurer troops could easily destroy the balance of military power between cities, and that the current equilibrium could be lost. Also unexpected had been the fact that quite a few nobles had information on the magic steamship prototype that was being jointly developed by the Marine Organization, the Roderick Trading Company and Shopping District 8. He'd guessed as much from Akatsuki's report, but the town of Akiba seemed to have been infiltrated by a fair number of spies.

It spoke to the amount of attention they were attracting.

There was no gag order regarding technical information in Akiba. It probably wouldn't be that hard to extract. At present, they might as well not have any secrets at all. However, technology like steam engines required high-level Blacksmith and Mechanist subclass skills. Even if word got around that such-and-such an item was being made, it was hard to believe that they would find themselves in a situation where other countries were able to produce that item right away.

He'd spoken with Michitaka and Crusty, and with the other Round Table Council members via telechat, and there didn't seem to be any disadvantage to concluding a free trade agreement regarding food-stuffs. When it came to food, Akiba wasn't very self-sufficient at all.

The situation regarding staple foods—rice, wheat, beans, and potatoes—was particularly catastrophic. If limited to that type of food, the trade agreement would work in Akiba's favor. On the other hand, seasonings could become Akiba's main food export.

Of course they would be weak with the basic seasonings—salt, sugar, and herbs—but Brewers in the town of Akiba had knowledge from the old world regarding processed seasonings like soy sauce and other sauces, and they were good with them.

They would have to accept—with qualifications—some of the nobles' requests, or promise to consider them. There were probably several times as many requests that would have to be turned down. All were steps that would be necessary in order to clarify Akiba's stance.

However, his encounter with Li Gan had had even more of an impact than these meetings with the nobles.

I can't relax...

Shiroe turned over yet again, and thought.

Li Gan himself hadn't been an unpleasant character at all. Shiroe thought he was a rather charming researcher. He was both clever and knowledgeable. Could they trust him...? Maybe not, but Shiroe didn't think he was lying.

However, the world history that he had related had unsettled Shiroe badly.

World Fraction.
Spirit Theory.

In his research of world-scale magic, Li Gan's current interest had been narrowed down to these two points.

A problem of souls, Li Gan had called it. That was the Spirit Theory. Shiroe wasn't a specialist, and he hadn't been able to understand the technical aspects, but on the whole, the theory seemed to be as follows:

In general terms, the immaterial power that moved humans and demihumans was known as "spirit." Spirit wasn't a solid entity; instead, it was a body formed of two types of energy, yang and yin, adhered closely together.

According to Li Gan...

Yang energy was the energy that drove the mind. The human mind existed on top of this yang energy. Strong yang energy meant that the heart's power was strong, and it influenced the force of magic. MP was an expression of the yang energy's strength.

Yin energy was the energy that drove the body. The physical toughness of the human body was greatly influenced by it. If the yin energy was strong, in addition to physical toughness, it strengthened the body's spiritual energy as well. Warriors and other weapon attack classes used it in battle. It made itself apparent in HP as well, but the best expression of yin energy strength was life force.

When humans stopped being able to live, first of all, the body stopped moving. At this point in time, the mind was healthy. However, the link between body and mind was severed, and the mind became trapped in darkness. This was because the information that should have flowed through the yang energy—the consciousness— had ceased to come from the yin energy—the physical body that could feel the light of the outside world.

Then the yin energy began to disperse. As mentioned earlier, yin energy was life force, the fundamental energy of the body. As a result, the sturdier and higher-level the body, the longer this dispersion took. The yin energy of beings that were low-level or frail dispersed in minutes, but for tougher beings, the dispersion continued for half a day. This process was called "degradation."

The resurrection magic employed by the recovery classes was used on corpses in this state. It worked by gathering the yin energy that had diffused into the surrounding atmosphere, reconstructing it, and returning it to the body.

If there wasn't enough life force, the healer used their own life force to reconstruct it. The information needed for the construction was created by calculating backward from records that remained in the corpse in front of the healer. The loss of experience points was apparently due to an error during these calculations, an inevitable deterioration of information.

Now, then: If resurrection magic was not used and the yin energy dispersed completely, the body became unable to maintain its current state. In physical terms, it began to rot. For the People of the Earth, at this point, death was final. …Yes, he hadn't expected it, but resurrection magic worked on the People of the Earth as well, provided it was used directly after death.

On the other hand, when Adventurers' degradation was complete, or at the point after death when the Adventurer wished it, the body and its equipment broke down into particles. The power of their yang energy was used to transmit these particles to the temple, where their bodies were automatically reconstructed. In addition, the life force that filled the temple was used to restore their yin energy. The yang energy was then recombined with the restored body, which resurrected the ego.

As a result of this seemingly miraculous ability, although both yang and yin energy were expended to the limit, and some experience points were lost due to the deterioration of information…Adventurers came back to life. For all intents and purposes, they were immortal.

According to Li Gan's research, this was the system of death in this other world, and of the Adventurers' resurrection.

"It bears a startling resemblance to the demihumans' reincarnation system," Li Gan had said.

"When a demihuman meets its end… Or rather, when it degrades, its body rots like those of the People of the Earth, and its equipment is left behind. However, on the other hand, its yang energy is immediately given life as another being. It may take anywhere from a few years to a decade for it to reach maturity, but this is reincarnation and immortality."

In a way, it was a horrifying idea.

Of course, this was a hypothesis that Li Gan and his master had been researching, and it wasn't something the average Person of the Earth knew. However, if it was true, the demihumans might be far more troublesome enemies than they'd thought.

Shiroe had asked if, in that case, the demihumans had memories of their previous lives, memories from before they'd died.

"I can't give you any real answer about that. There are two elements involved in this matter."

Li Gan had searched for words, as if answering wasn't easy.

"First, yang energy is the seat of the mind. In demihumans and Adventurers, this is indestructible. The mind, personality, vows, temperament: Without a doubt, all these things are stored in the yang energy as information. We know that memories, or at least most of them, are stored in yang energy as well. However, on the other hand, we also know that memories are stored in the physical brain. As I'm sure you're aware, the body is the territory of yin energy. In other words, memories are an information continuum that spans both yin and yang energy. Since that's the case, we hypothesized that memories might be lost during degradation and the reconstruction of the yang energy, and in fact, this phenomenon has been confirmed. Death causes the deterioration and loss of memories.

"Yang energy is also the seat of the emotions. As that's the case, 'poisons' such as terror, despair, and weariness could circulate even in an immortal being. As a practical issue, it's possible that the yang energy in demihumans was distorted by the curse of the First World Fraction, and that it remains so. Even if minds in that state retain their memories, they've lost the power to recall them at will and recognize them as their own past. It's probably rather like schizophrenia, or as though the person is seeing their own memories as a story."

In that case, death...

In this other world, death was *not* without risk.

That was a terrifying fact as well.

Though, it was possible to say that all of this was still just a hypothesis.

However, most of Shiroe was sufficiently convinced that it was fact that he silenced that doubting voice. It was like a sense of smell, something older than logic. Life without end... It couldn't possibly be without risk.

Li Gan said that memories were stored in both yang energy and the brain...

It wasn't that he believed this magician's fantasy magic theory without hesitation, but it had reminded him of something.

It was the structure of the *Elder Tales* game, or rather, of all online games. Shiroe and the other players had sat at their computer desks at home, playing in the world of *Elder Tales*. In general, all online games were meant to be enjoyed under those conditions.

Didn't that mean that shy, real-world university student Kei Shirogane had acted as the yang energy?

Kei Shirogane the player wouldn't die, even if his character did. He had only to set the resurrected Shiroe in motion again and restart the adventure.

To borrow Li Gan's theory, the logic would be that Kei Shirogane had all the memories, and Shiroe only had a body.

However, that was when *Elder Tales* had been a game.

Although there was no telling what magic had been at work, the current Shiroe was Shiroe himself, and he existed entirely in this other world.

In other words, Shiroe's yang energy was here. It wasn't in the old world, safe and snug in front of a computer desk. The continuity of his memories was no longer protected. Death would mercilessly scar his yang energy.

Shiroe called up his status screen.

It held a counter for the number of times he'd died.

The number reflected Shiroe's long play history, and it wasn't a small one.

However, since the Catastrophe, Shiroe hadn't died once. It had seemed creepy to him, somehow. Even when he knew he'd come back, he'd felt fear and visceral dislike. Put into words, that was all it was, but... That must have been true for all the members of Log Horizon.

He didn't know how extensive the memory loss was.

He was certain it wasn't happening on a large scale.

If that had been the case, Akiba would have been in an uproar long ago. For each separate time, the loss was probably too small to notice. Alternatively, it might be selective: Unimportant memories, the sort the person wouldn't even miss, might go first.

It might be a completely insignificant amount, no different from the memory lapses that happened all the time in everyday life.

But how am I supposed to say that…?

He hadn't told Michitaka or Crusty about this.

He'd told Akatsuki to keep quiet, too.

Still, he'd have to tell them someday. It was an issue that affected all the players.

In the darkness, Shiroe turned over again.

The dark was endlessly painful.

▶ 2

"Patrol approaching. Um… Maybe five? Five of them, I think. They'll be here in about ten measures."

Isuzu made her report in a small voice, peeking out very slightly from the arch.

Um, ten measures would be… About twenty seconds?

They were in the first burial chamber on the right side of Forest Ragranda. It was a room just before the broad corridor itself began to descend in wide steps. It was about five meters square. There was no door; the arch connected it directly to the corridor.

In this ancient tomb, which held several stone caskets, Touya and the others hid, holding their breath.

Five Skeletons were slowly patrolling the passageway, according to Isuzu's report. She was the party member with the highest stealth capabilities, and so she was the one who hid and spied. Past experience told them that one Skeleton would use a projectile weapon.

"We'll do this the way we planned."

At Touya's whispered declaration, the other four nodded. As they'd planned, they scattered to various points in the room, then checked the equipment they held.

It'll be okay. We talked it through, so we should be able to do it. Besides, even if it turns out like it always does…it's not like we'll lose anything.

Touya muttered to himself, silently.

…Nah. There's no way we'll let it turn into a fight like that.

They wouldn't let today's battles be like yesterday's. Everyone held that firm resolution inside them. You could see it in their faces.

It was the fifth day of their dungeon expedition.

As it turned out, yesterday, the day it had rained, they hadn't gone into the dungeon at all.

Touya and the others had talked until past noon, asking questions and explaining their special skills. They'd quickly decided that they would have to actually see the skills to understand, and so they'd gone out into the forest. They could just as easily have gone into the dungeon and tested them in action, but if someone had had a question partway through the dungeon, the enemy would have pressed forward, and there would have been no time to explain.

In the world of *Elder Tales*, there were lots of monsters and wild animals within the fields. In particular, goblins, orcs, lizardmen, and other demihumans had built up significant forces in this ruined world, so there were quite a lot of them.

However, although there were many monsters, the fields they stalked through were vast. Even if it had been condensed to half its size, *Elder Tales* inhabited a project that replicated the entire planet, and its area was in a whole different league from ordinary MMO games or consumer RPGs.

Consequently, unless they attacked a monster settlement or had themselves followed and continually attacked, the odds of encountering a monster were pretty low. As a rule, once a battle ended, if they wanted to get a good rest before the next battle began, they could do so.

On the other hand, in dungeons, the concentration of monsters was different. They were headquarters, after all, or regional fortresses. They were also far smaller spaces than the field zones, and the fact that they might hold several hundred of the same type of monster was a possibility that couldn't be ignored.

As a result, battles in dungeons happened one after another, and the intervals between them were shorter than they would have been outside. Frequent battles with short breaks made it easy to exhaust MP, and classes such as Samurai, whose special skills all had long recast times, weren't able to recover their special skill use limits in the spaces between battles.

Dungeons also had their own unique issues with light sources and three-dimensional space restrictions.

In fields, battles generally began when there were about ten meters or more between players and the enemy. This was because, in many cases, they spotted each other at great distances.

However, in dungeons, an enemy might be waiting the instant you turned a corner or entered a room.

All sorts of factors combined to make battles in dungeons so tough that it was impossible to compare them to field battles. There was a clear difference in the skills it took to hunt enemies of a certain level in dungeons, and the skills required to do the same thing in fields.

Over the past few days, Touya and the others had seen for themselves just how formidable dungeons were.

That was why they'd confirmed each member's abilities thoroughly, one more time.

While this was true for the properties of separate special skills as well, when it came to different combinations, the numbers were vast, and countless questions arose. For example, how much damage did Circular Carol's additional magic attack damage do, and what was the probability that it would occur?

If a sword skill "mowed down the area around you," how big was the attack's range, and what sort of damage could it do? Each individual question seemed simple and unimportant, but there were many combinations, and sometimes the answers were unexpected.

By evening, they'd managed to come to a stopping point in their analysis of special techniques, but then the question of how they should use them came up.

It was after that point that Minori began to explain patrol files, for-mations, operators, and field monitors.

—Light, scraping footsteps were coming closer.

In terms of distance, the Skeletons were probably about five meters away. Silently, Touya made a hand sign to the rest of the group. Their faces were tense, but even so, they nodded in unison.

Touya scanned the group. Then, without hesitation, he leapt into the corridor. As Isuzu had reported, the approaching monsters were a patrolling platoon of five Skeletons. Touya drew his sword, unleashing Izuna Cutter on the group of Skeletons in almost the same motion. The deep crimson shock wave snaked through the air, shallowly wounding one Skeleton's arm.

Confirming this, Touya threw himself back into the burial chamber and sprinted into its depths. The dry sound of approaching bones was loud and chaotic. Up until a moment ago, the rhythm of the footfalls had been the one used for patrol. Once they'd been spotted, of course the enemy would run toward them. It wouldn't take them more than a few seconds to close the distance.

The Skeletons that rushed in were blackened in places, and a ghostly aura hung about them.

Pale flames burned in their dark eye sockets. Of the five Skeletons that had passed through the arched entry, four charged deeper into the room, making for Touya, while the archer remained by the entrance.

However, this was something everyone in the party had anticipated. "That one's yours!"

As if pushed by Touya's yell, Isuzu struck at the Skeleton Archer's hands with her two-handed spear. Minori also swung the katana she held, although she wasn't used to it.

The two girls' attacks might have done as much damage as could be expected to the undead, but they didn't stop it from moving. Unless they were completely immobilized, undead monsters didn't shrink from pain.

"...If there's only one of you, I have a spell that's more appropriate than Orb of Lava. —Take this! The magnificent magic of a Sorcerer! Lightning Chamber!"

Feeling a strange, twitching sensation, Minori and Isuzu jumped back.

In the instant the advance discharge sketched a pentagram, the Skeleton Archer was trapped by purple lightning. The Sorcerer's electrical spell ran from floor to ceiling, then back from ceiling to floor, dealing massive damage to the target and turning it to carbon.

"Awright!"

Having seen this from the depths of the room, Touya grinned. He had his back to the wall, had taken on the four Skeletons, and was fighting them without giving an inch. Serara was handling his recovery.

"Current HP at eighty-four percent. Current status sustainable!"

Through a combination of Heartbeat Healing's regular recovery effect and, when that wasn't enough, an additional Instant Heal, Touya withstood the four enemies' attacks. He was also managing to keep his HP at 80 percent.

Of course, his body hurt.

The attack power of the Skeletons' hand axes was pretty formidable, and if it hadn't been for the healing, Touya wasn't sure whether he could have lasted a minute. Now, though, Serara's recovery spells were firmly supporting him.

"Minori, check. Isuzu and Rudy, prepare to attack."

At Touya's voice, the other members responded, taking their appointed positions. Minori went to the nearby arch. Rundelhaus and Isuzu came around behind the four Skeletons, which were completely focused on Touya.

"Are these fellows completely boiled already?"

Arrogantly, Rundelhaus looked down on the Skeletons.

"Yeah, I had time, so I cast Samurai Taunt on 'em twice each. They won't go for you that easily, Rudy."

"That's good to hear. I can relax while I work, then."

Rundelhaus immediately began to chant an attack spell.

Isuzu did as well. Even though she'd started last, she was the first one to complete her spell. When she stuck the spear into the ground, the bells at the base of its head rang, and the sound waves turned into a directional, destructive shock wave that soaked into the Skeletons.

"Corridor checked! No following patrols in sight. It's all right. Go ahead, Rundelhaus!"

"Leave it to me, Miss Minori! Orb of Lava!"

At Minori's call, Rundelhaus released his spell. A lump of rock so compressed that it melted and glowed like lava floated at his fingertips.

Touya used Samurai Taunt again.

Rundelhaus's attack capabilities were off the charts. He thought he should whip up the monsters' hate even further, making sure that he was the only thing on their minds.

He'd used his special taunting skill several times over, but he needed to be careful. Touya was a Samurai. In his mind's eye, he saw Naotsugu's back.

"It's a vanguard tank's job to draw all the enemy's attacks and believe in his party, Touya. That's-a-man's-promise-city, right?!"

Touya glared at the Skeletons, his gaze strong. Behind the Skeletons, out of their line of sight, Rundelhaus's chant was changing magic into destructive power.

An incandescent ball of sizzling, roiling lava appeared in the burial room, accompanied by heat and orange shadows that wavered oddly. Released from Rundelhaus's hand, the fireball punched through the Skeleton on the far left, bounded as if it had struck something in mid-air, and pierced the second Skeleton as well.

The tiny, leaping, white-hot grim reaper pierced or shattered the Skeletons, destroying them one after another. Refusing to give them any leeway, Rundelhaus added Frigid Window, a range attack spell.

"And now you meet your end. Return to the dark world that befits your lives!"

The Skeletons, which had been writhing with intense heat just moments before, suddenly lost their strength in the freezing wind and scattered across the floor.

The sounds of battle were abruptly stilled, and the party's rough breathing echoed in the silent burial chamber.

Touya kept his katana at the ready; he hadn't dropped his guard.

Rundelhaus held up his staff, magic still crystallized in it. Working by conditioned reflex, Serara cast recovery spells at Touya, cleaning up.

From deep inside the room, everyone watched Minori.

After carefully examining the depths of the corridor, Minori turned back to her companions.

"No one's following. The battle is over."

At her words, the party's tension dissolved.

"Whew. Yes, that's how it should be."

"That went really well, didn't it!!"

"Yes, wonderful work, everyone!"

As they looked at the members' delighted smiles, Minori and Touya bumped fists, exchanging their twins' salute.

▶ 3

Everyone worked hard.

As Minori thought this, she felt her cheeks soften into a smile.

On the fifth day of their expedition, Minori's party had finally managed to explore for seven hours. They'd fought twenty-three battles. Once—and only once—they'd ended up battling two monster platoons at the same time, but she thought they'd managed to handle it far more neatly than yesterday.

After each battle, they'd taken a short break.

That break was meant to heal HP and abnormal statuses and to recover their MP to the maximum, but it had a greater significance than that.

They looked back over the battle they'd just fought, mutually recognizing what had gone well and searching for things that could be improved. During these breathers, they discussed the site and strategy for the next battle and readied their plan into action.

The very first thing they'd gone over had been formation.

Touya was a Samurai who supported the front line. That meant their tactics were built on the idea that Touya would draw all enemy attacks to himself. However, even though this was only natural, everyone had to cooperate in order to make it happen.

How could they make it so that all party members except Touya were able to move freely? If they didn't act with that in mind, Touya wouldn't be able to capture enough of the enemy's attention.

Next, they thought about the operator. Operator was a role that involved watching and keeping track of everyone's HP. In the current *Elder Tales*, it was hard to get the leeway to check everyone's status screens, particularly for the vanguard classes who were fighting in close combat.

In this other world, that was fast becoming common knowledge.

This time around, Minori's party had two healers.

Since this gave them plenty of recovery spells, it was an advantage, but at the same time, it was also a weakness.

Say two healers simultaneously healed the player who'd lost the most HP. Naturally, there was a big recovery in HP, and in many cases, the player was healed even more than necessary. That meant it went to waste.

If another casualty turned up in the meantime, both Minori's and Serara's major recovery spells would be tied up in recast time. Simultaneously casting their important recovery spells created a simultaneous vulnerability. …In other words, the wound opened further.

Minori and Serara had talked it over and decided that Serara would manage Touya's HP on her own. If she couldn't quite cover it, she'd call for help.

Since her hands were free, Minori volunteered to be the field monitor. This was a player who kept an eye on the surrounding area, even during battle. They chanted recovery and attack spells as a reserve member, but even as they did so, they watched the area and reported on enemy monster reinforcements and patrols.

By having a member perform this role, Minori's party managed to trim the possibility of getting into a melee down to the bare minimum. Even if enemy reinforcements they couldn't avoid turned up, as long as the party managed to spot them first, they could take advance measures such as increasing the amount of recovery or switching support spells.

Patrol file was a travel method that maintained their formation and the field monitor position even when they were on the move.

Touya was at the head of the file. Minori guarded the rear.

Since they were twins, by covering each other's blind spots they could quickly detect approaching enemies or the scent of battle. Isuzu, who had the best stealth and surveillance abilities in the party, kept both Minori and Touya in view. In addition to keeping an eye on the immediate area, she sometimes went on alone in places where reconnaissance was necessary.

Moving this way made it possible for Serara to concentrate on managing the party's HP and for Rundelhaus to focus on recovering his own MP, even when they were traveling. Serara was the mainstay of recovery, and Rundelhaus was at the heart of attacks that would annihilate the enemy. The core of the plan Minori and the others had come up with was letting these two concentrate on their jobs.

These four items were things Minori had learned from Shiroe: the basics of party movement in dungeons. They weren't part of the game system. They were Adventurer wisdom and workarounds.

However, even Minori didn't know what sort of nuances these basics carried. They were probably techniques that had no meaning if you only understood them in words. Because she hadn't understood them, she hadn't been able to suggest them.

What they had needed to do had been terribly simple.
They'd needed to speak to each other, to discuss things.

If they wanted help, all they'd needed to say was, "I want help."

When casting a recovery spell, they'd only had to say, "I'll handle recovery."

If the enemy was closing in: "Enemies approaching."

"Defeat the ones with projectile weapons first," or "Leave this one to me," or "I'll be out of MP in two more attacks." Anything would have been fine.

It had been such a simple thing. That alone let them defeat the enemy, as if all their trouble up until yesterday had been an illusion.

This wasn't friendship or playing at being considerate. It was a necessary survival skill.

A party in which the members couldn't work together might as well

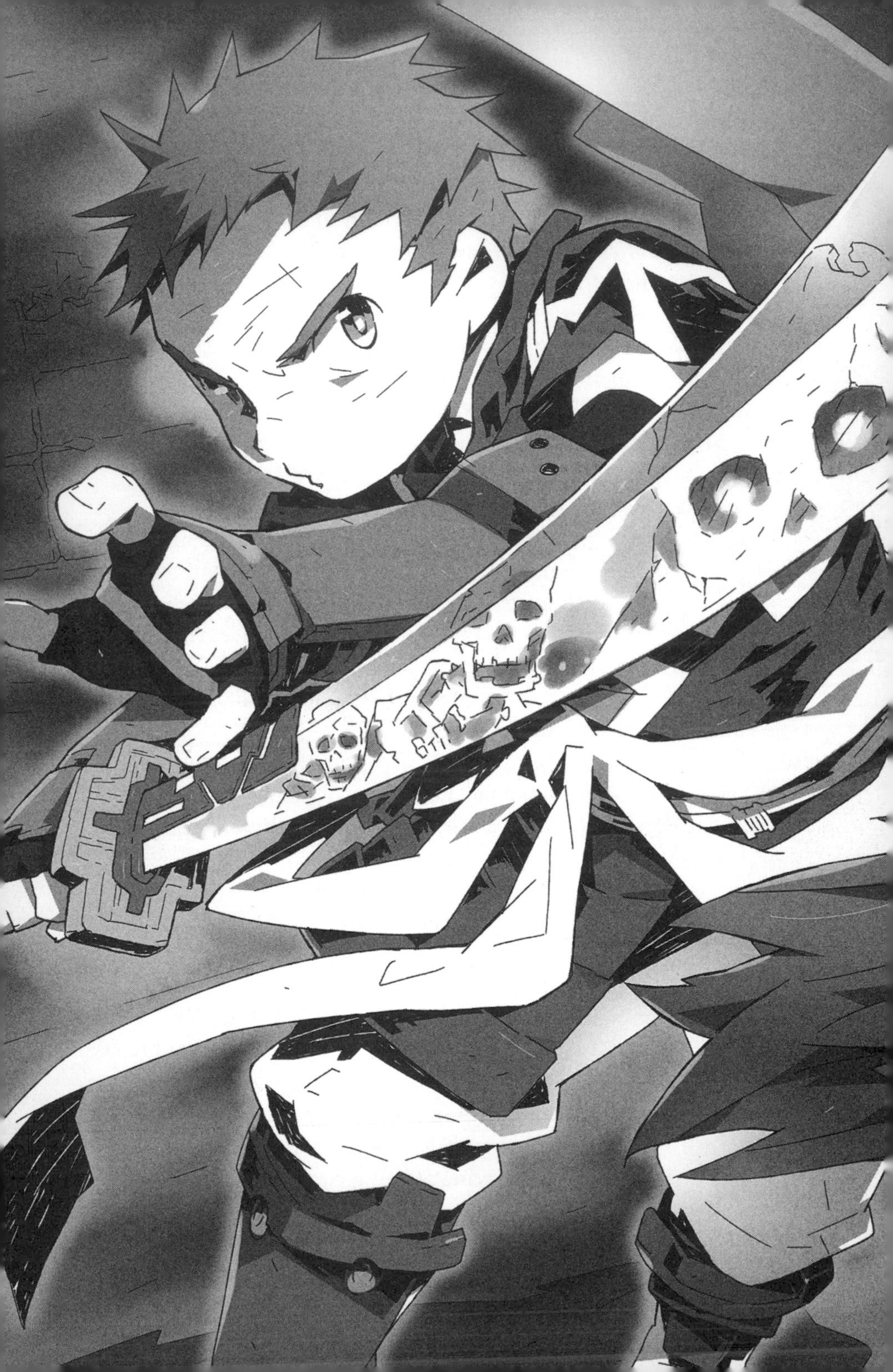

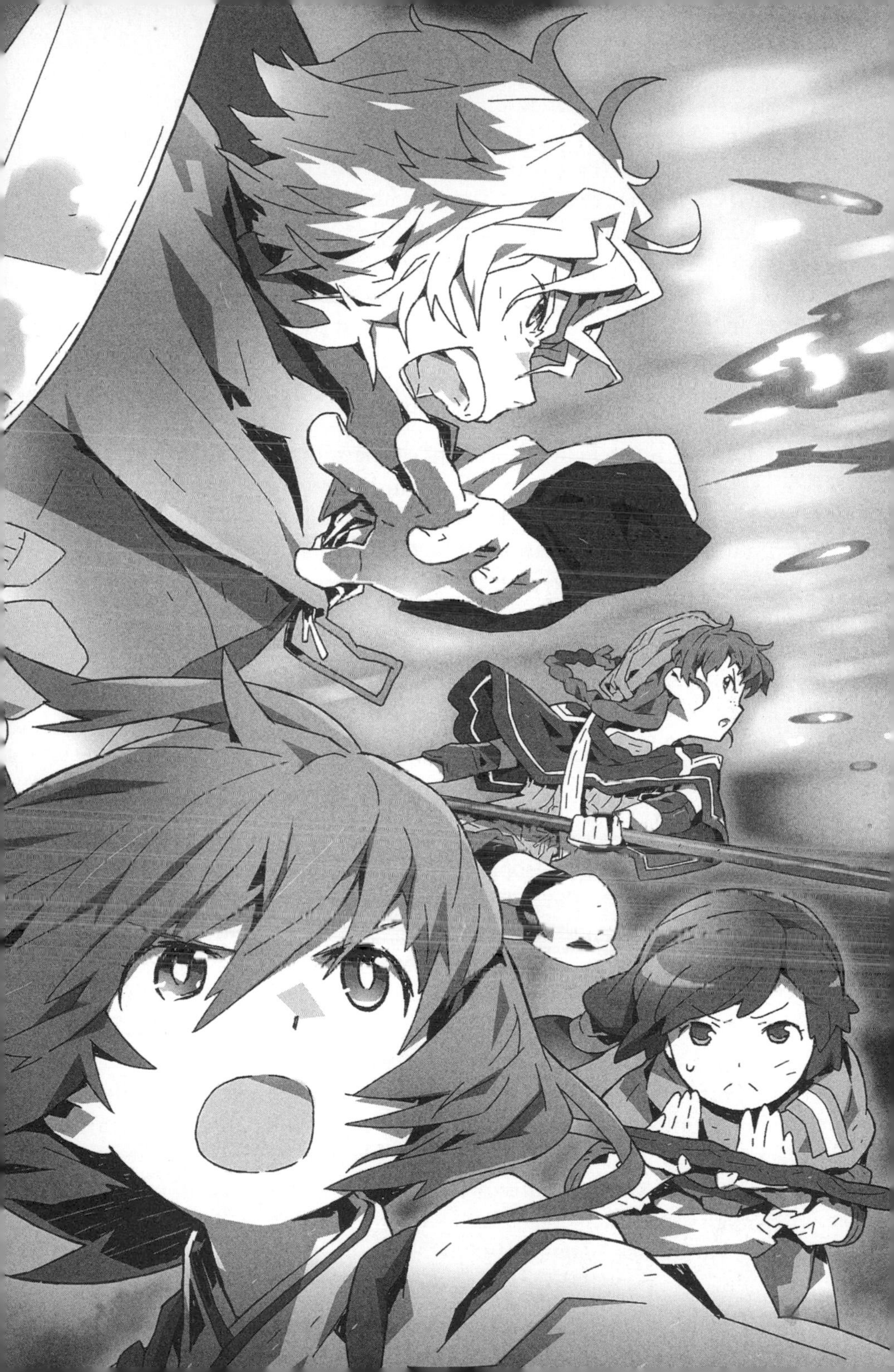

be sealing its members' abilities. Only when they combined their abilities did Adventurers like Minori's group begin to be able to oppose monsters. That was the way this other world worked.

However, on the other hand, these techniques were a terribly warm and sacred thing, something that went far beyond friendship or superficial consideration. On a battlefield where each instant meant the difference between life and death, in order to genuinely ask for the help you needed or stretch out a helping hand that the other person probably needed right now, in addition to knowledge of the other person's techniques and the abilities they held, you had to have deep mutual understanding.

Did they want to fight at the front of the room? Did they want to draw the enemies deep inside the room before they fought? Should they begin the battle with a charge? Should they lure the monsters in instead? Did they have a vision for victory in this battle? What was it? Was it all right to leave something to someone, or not?

The members of Minori's party gave each other the answers to all sorts of questions.

It was also a harsh test in how well they understood each other, and as Minori and the others began to pass this test, for the first time, they went from being "five Adventurers" to "a party."

"Ah ha! Minori, your nose is all black."

Isuzu laughed.

When they left the dungeon, the last light of evening was streaming into the forest. It was the peaceful time just before sunset; in another thirty minutes, everything would be dyed madder red. Under that light, Isuzu was pointing at Minori's nose.

"Is it dust? Maybe it's a cobweb…"

As Minori spoke, Isuzu giggled at her. But even Isuzu had blotches of mingled sweat and dust on her forehead and leather armor.

Still, when she laughs, her eyes are wonderful. They're perfectly clear.

Minori smiled, handing her a little cloth from her pack. "You, too," she said, laughing. Isuzu hastily wiped at her face, and when she'd finished and looked at the mini-towel, her expression was mortified.

"Nnugh. Am I pitch-black, too?"

"Not *pitch*-black. Should we go to the spring, though?"

"Probably. Ahh. Want to invite Sera?"

Isuzu called to Serara, who was walking in front of them.

"What? You guys are going to the spring, too, Minori?"

Touya, who was at the head of the line, heard them and looked back. Apparently Touya and Rundelhaus, who walked beside him, had also been discussing visiting the spring.

"Grr. We're all sweaty, too, you know."

"The fairer sex takes precedence. Tough it out, Touya, my lad," Rundelhaus admonished Touya.

Rundelhaus himself was so sooty that not a trace of his usual dandyish self remained. Even his glossy tunic was dull and dingy.

On today's expedition, they'd made great progress.

They'd reached the underground workshop that was thought to be the innermost area of the right-hand route.

There, coke blazed with magic flames, and in the midst of the rising black smoke, ghosts that harbored grudges were becoming Skeletons and being put to work.

The one forcing the Skeletons to work had been a Burning Dead. Unlike ordinary Skeletons, the specter had had the blue-black flames of the Underworld blazing from every one of its joints, and it had been a powerful enemy that could even use magic. However, having defeated each of the patrols, Minori's party had used a lightning suppression operation and smashed through this formidable foe.

Thanks to that battle, though, the soot that filled the room had clung to them, and they still wore the results.

"Why not just go together?"

"I-Isuzu!"

Isuzu had spoken nonchalantly, but Serara flapped her hands frantically in refusal. Registering this and realizing what it meant, Isuzu grew abruptly flustered as well and amended her statement.

"When I said 'go together,' I didn't mean 'go *in* together'!! I just meant we could wash at the spring in the bushes, and Touya and Rudy could wash their faces or bodies or whatever in the pond!!"

As Isuzu hastily made excuses, Serara said, "Oh. Oh, yes, you're right," and smiled awkwardly.

"What about it, Minori?"

"If you two are okay with that, Touya."

The twins agreed quite easily, and they got fresh clothes from the tent. The five of them headed toward the spring, chattering noisily as they went.

They talked about the day's battle and conquest.

The Burning Dead had been level 24. It had probably been the toughest enemy on the right-hand route. From what Shiroe had told them, in an atmosphere like the one in that battle, the only enemies they could safely beat were enemies "five or more levels below your party's average level." Their current average level was a bit over 24. This meant the only enemies they could fight safely were level 19 or below, and they'd defeated an enemy who was far stronger than that.

Just knowing this made them all a little excited.

Defeating an enemy on their level with a party of only five was a considerable achievement. They'd also gotten their first magic items, which had startled them.

What made them even happier, though, was the fact that the ordinary battles along the way had gone so incredibly well. The importance of drawing the enemy in, or charging them, and fighting from an advantageous position had been beyond imagining.

More than anything, they'd learned how vital it was to talk to each other.

We've become a party.

Minori smiled quietly to herself.

She was happy that the meaning of Shiroe's words had settled firmly into place in her heart.

It hadn't simply been about level.

Level hadn't been the key to getting stronger.

In order to fight in this world, they needed companions.

In order to make these companions, they had to talk and act, over and over. They were a treasure you couldn't get with special skills or level, no matter how powerful.

Her days at Hamelin were melting away.

At the very least, those days of forcibly boosting her level couldn't have brought her here. There was something certain here, something that couldn't be reached by simply leveling up.

"Minori~~~? Hurry u~~p!"

Deep in the brush in the forest, she could see Isuzu bouncing up and down, waving to her. Minori responded energetically, then broke into a run, making for the spring with the reddening sunset at her back.

▶4

Whew...

Shiroe slipped the papers he'd bundled together into a leather document case.

The papers he'd been organizing were documents of all sorts.

Briefings, surveys, reports... There were many different names for them, but they were papers filled with miscellaneous information. Among them were notes that Akatsuki and the members of the Round Table Council had put together for him. This sort of information had to be collected and organized daily.

After all, in their negotiations with the People of the Earth, there was no telling where an ambush might appear.

On the other hand, the papers filed in the larger, more severe document case were, as their name stated, "documents." Notifications from guilds, balance sheets, contracts, promissory notes, and title deeds...

Shiroe was a Scribe. His role was to copy books and documents, and to transcribe written incantations, technical books, and maps.

No matter how complicated the object was, if he knew the item's production method, he could make it in under ten seconds.

However, he couldn't state positively that there were no new possibilities for Scribes, as there had been for Chefs. It was an area Shiroe wanted to study, but he kept getting distracted by his Round Table Council work, and he'd made almost no progress in his research.

Shiroe stretched hugely. He was sitting at the big table in the living room he'd been given at the Ancient Court of Eternal Ice. The sun had set, but all the rooms in the palace were illuminated with magic lights, and it wasn't yet time for bed.

From a different document case, he took out a map of Eastal. By now, it wasn't simply a beautiful copy of a map: Shiroe had nearly filled it with handwritten annotations here and there.

He felt that his Scribe subclass was helping him out a lot. The greatest assist it gave him was probably in paper quality.

In this other world, the quality of paper was pretty poor. On journeys and adventures, he'd seen parchment frequently, and some places used paper that might as well have been tree bark. Fortunately, Shiroe was a Scribe, and Scribes' functions included copying and creating maps, documents, and magic primers. As far as the game system was concerned, these were magic items, and they couldn't just be written on any old paper. While it depended on the level of the item, if he wanted to create a high-level item, he needed suitable materials—in this case, paper and ink. Scribes' duties included creating special paper and ink, and Shiroe had the magic materials in abundance.

Just making notepaper this way didn't require very high-class magic materials. It only had to be easy to write on and of high quality.

In terms of paper, this meant thin, light, uniform and white. Ink had to be light resistant, quick-drying, nonrunny, and have bold colors.

Shiroe had mass-produced ink and easy-to-use paper, and it was a great help in his clerical work.

Shiroe gazed at the hand-drawn map.

He ran his fingertip along mountain ranges and coastlines, thinking about the connections; he knit his brow and jotted down questions in his notebook.

For a while, the only noise in the room was the *scritch* of his pen skimming over paper, but suddenly, as if to cut if off, the sound of a bell rang in Shiroe's ears alone.

"Hello?"

"That's Shiroe, isn't it? It's me. It's Minori."

A notification from his friend list made this clear whenever a call came in, but Minori always began her telechats this way. It was probably her well-mannered nature showing through. It was completely different from the energetic way Touya started his conversations: *"Hey, mister, it's me!"*

"Good evening. Have you finished training over there?"

"*Yes!*"

Minori's voice was cheerful, although her reports had been gloomy for the past few days. Shiroe guessed that they must have gotten over a wall.

Minori and the others were at a training camp, attempting to explore a dungeon for beginners. That said, in this case, "for beginners" didn't mean "easy to conquer." Quite the opposite, in fact: It was a difficult dungeon that gave beginners a rough welcome.

In other words, it meant that all the obstacles beginners needed to overcome were crammed into one place.

Corridors that intersected in three dimensions. Rooms that could be looked down into. Open stairwells. Monsters that appeared regularly in patrolling groups. Nearly inexhaustible hordes of undead.

This was a strong citadel, and it thwarted brute-force captures that relied on class abilities. In particular, since undead monsters welled up endlessly due to malicious underground energy, if players broke through without thinking first, they'd probably be tormented by infinite enemy reinforcements.

"Did you make any progress on your capture?"

"*Yes! I'll report it now. During today's invasion, we went in at seven thirty in the morning. We spent about seven hours exploring, then withdrew at fifteen hundred. During that time, we went to the end of the right-hand corridor route and vanquished a Burning Dead in the smelting furnace!*"

"Whoa, that's amazing!"

If Shiroe's memory served him right, the levels of Burning Dead varied between 23 and 25. That was about the same as the average level of Minori's group. Defeating a monster that was almost on their level—with five people, no less—would have been one thing in the former *Elder Tales*, but in the current setup, it wouldn't be easy even for a veteran party.

Compatibility with the enemy monster had probably come into it, too, but he thought they must have fought extremely well. Considering how depressed she'd sounded up until the other day, it had to have been a brilliant achievement.

"Yes, sir!"

He could understand the cheer in Minori's voice now: It was a huge victory.

Even though she'd sounded so discouraged the day before yesterday. Shiroe felt something warm fill his heart.

Since yesterday, he'd felt emotionally cornered. The ominous premonition within the Spirit Theory. The *creepiness* he'd sensed in the history of this world, a feeling even he couldn't explain. These had become a pressure he couldn't talk about, and it sat heavily in his chest.

It could probably have been called uneasiness. A feeling of anxiety, as if he couldn't do anything, didn't know anything. ...And yet the situation was being swept along with irresistible force. Shiroe had been fighting that premonition all alone.

However, on hearing the voice of this young, brave companion, a Log Horizon member, he felt that darkness dispersing as though blown by a light-infused wind.

That was the blessing of comrades.

If he'd put it into words, it would have sounded trite, but that was what Shiroe felt.

"How was everyone?"

"*They're fine!*"

"Not that."

Shiroe asked her again, laughing a little. Minori seemed to be in very high spirits tonight. Her speech was as courteous as always, of course, but when she answered instantly in a voice this lively, in addition to giving Shiroe a bit of trouble, it made him happy.

"*Hm?*"

He could almost see Minori tilting her head to one side, politely, on the other end of the telechat.

"How did everyone do? How did you pull off the capture?"

"*Oh, well, you see, Touya was the vanguard; he kept the enemies together and drew them to him. That was the same as before, but this time we changed our strategy. We calculated our battle locations before we started, moved between safe rooms and split the enemy into small groups.*"

That was a technique known as "pulling." The trick to fighting back-to-back battles lay in figuring out a way to maintain the advantage of numbers. In simple terms, your chances of victory were higher if you fought one-on-one a hundred times than if you fought a hundred enemies at once.

"We dealt with monsters that used projectile weapons first. After that, I kept an eye on the area and acted as an assistant healer. We cut down the enemy's combat power with concentrated victories as we fought. ...Um, does that make sense?"

"Yes, I understand."

Minori's strategy had been correct.

She was observing the basics Shiroe had taught her.

However, those basics weren't the sort of things you could carry out just by having heard them. Recovery or attack? During battles, all actions acquired a priority. Who decided the order of priority, and how? How were these decisions shared?

He could understand why Minori would be worried that he hadn't understood her explanation—she probably couldn't wait to know whether what she was talking about was getting through or not.

We defeated individual enemies while watching the area.

Said out loud, that was all it was, but just how many detailed tricks and processes had they needed in order to make that happen? They'd have to grasp the layout of the surrounding area, and the distances at which they could provide support for each other. All members would need to know the ranges of attack spells and recovery spells by heart. They would also need to understand and train to cover for other party members whenever one of them got into trouble.

When Minori was in trouble, Serara would provide backup.

When Rundelhaus was in trouble, Minori would use a damage interception spell.

When Isuzu was in trouble, Serara would cast Instant Recovery while Isuzu fell back. The teamwork of combat actions was formed by an accumulation of countless subtle team plays like these.

Would that delicate accumulation come through in this explanation? Shiroe knew Minori's unease stemmed from that sort of impatience as clearly as if it were his own.

It's all right. I know. You're getting through. I know how trivial it is, and how important. ...How many small tricks you have to accumulate in order to protect your safety and reach your goal.

"It's all right. You're getting through. Everyone else played their part, too?"

"Of course! Serara's recovery magic is amazing, isn't it?! She recovers HP several times faster than I can! It makes it hard to stay confident. She has lots of spell variations, too."

When it came to sheer recovery, a Kannagi (Minori) couldn't compare to a Druid (Serara). Their approaches to healing allies were different, to begin with. Kannagi, Minori's class, wasn't a class that recovered damage. The recovery class's unique spells *intercepted* damage, reducing the damage itself to zero.

In terms of recovery performed after damage had been inflicted, Druid would win hands down.

"As you level up, you'll catch up in terms of spell variations."

"Will I? …Isuzu is really fantastic. I'm not sure whether you'd call it variations or a repertoire, but she has so many special skills it's hard to remember them all."

Isuzu was a Bard, he remembered. In that case, it was no wonder her special skills had so much variation. In fact, it wouldn't do for Minori to compare the two of them: Having a wide variety of special skills was what set Bards apart. Shiroe chuckled.

"Touya worked hard, too. He held the enemy right on the spot, and he's learned how to keep from using big moves… Shiroe? Oh, honestly! Are you laughing?!"

"I'm sorry. I'm not laughing. I mean it," Shiroe answered, laughing a little.

On the other end of the telechat, Minori's voice was also laughing a bit shyly, so it was probably okay.

"Everyone calls Rundelhaus 'Rudy.' Sorcerers really are amazing, aren't they?"

"He's unaffiliated, isn't he?"

"That's right. He's handsome, but…a bit silly. He's also really stubborn and uncool but fun. He's friends with Isuzu, and he uses incredible magic. On top of that, he won't give an inch until he's defeated the enemy. I think he might be the most dedicated member of our group."

Handsome and silly and uncool and fun and dedicated?

What Minori had said didn't make much sense, but somehow he understood that he must be a likable guy.

Minori went on to report several other things. That they'd fought with Skeletons. That they'd kept them from pursuing them.

About Touya's brave combat. Serara's devotion. Isuzu's perseverance. Rundelhaus's daring. ...And just a little bit about what Minori herself had done.

Shiroe nodded in response to everything her happy, lively voice said.

The party members laughing at a dumb joke Touya had told, and Isuzu with the tip of her nose all black. The way Serara was head-over heels for Nyanta, as usual. How Nyanta completely failed to notice it. How when Rundelhaus ate sandwiches, he politely used both hands, for some reason. She made him feel almost as if he'd been there in person.

Time flies when you're having fun.

After reminding Minori to avoid putting her life in danger, Shiroe ended the telechat. Since Naotsugu and Nyanta were there, he thought it would be all right, but he didn't feel like taking risks yet.

In the quiet room, after the telechat had ended, it felt as if he could still hear Minori's bright, happy voice.

There was something terribly strange about this world. At this point, he couldn't tell anyone that there were risks to dying, but he'd probably have to someday.

Still, even so, they had to get by in this world, and when he listened to Minori's cheerful voice, it felt as if that would be possible.

▶ **5**

Sparks crackled and danced.

These were the mountains at the center of Zantleaf.

An open space cleared in the forest. It was the base camp from which Isuzu and the rest were working to capture Forest Ragranda.

Isuzu and Rundelhaus sat by the fire.

There had been more people up until a short while ago, but the others had all gone back to the tents in twos and threes.

They were a week into their invasion. Today was the last day of their first expedition, and they planned to return to the group camp at the abandoned school after noon tomorrow. That meant they'd only be going into the dungeon briefly tomorrow morning.

Isuzu and the others had gotten good at working together, and they'd sat around the fire a little earlier, drinking after-dinner Black Rose Tea with honey. As they cleaned their weapons and armor, they'd chatted with each other. The conversation had wandered, but it had been fun. Nyanta had patted Serara's head, and Minori had stealthily made a telechat to somebody yet again.

Isuzu had taken her lute out of her pack and strummed it. The lute was a stringed instrument from medieval Europe. It was shaped like a cross between a guitar and a Japanese *biwa*, and it fit perfectly in Isuzu's too-skinny arms.

The lute's tones were flatter than those of a guitar, but there was something elegant about its sound, and it lent an atmosphere of supreme luxury to the camp. Apparently, lutes were a typical portable instrument in this other world. When you strummed it gently—not with a pick, but with your fingertips—the tremulous notes unique to string instruments flowed out.

Wow... Lutes aren't bad at all, are they...?

She'd taken part in the conversation up until a moment ago, and that had been fun as well, but, Isuzu thought, she really did *need* music.

Just strumming the strings this way filled her heart with nostalgia and yearning until it nearly overflowed.

Isuzu liked music. She liked instruments in general.

She was a perfectly ordinary country high school girl, and her "like" didn't mean she had a passion for them, or that she was determined to make a living with them in the future. Conversely, though, precisely because of this, the feeling was simple and sincere.

If she had to say one way or the other, she thought, *Oh, it feels wonderful to have an instrument in my hands. I never want to stop playing.* She'd felt this way since she was in elementary school.

"You're quite elegant, Miss Isuzu."

"Nn. Well, I am a Bard, technically."

Isuzu raised her eyes, smiling.

Now that everyone had gone, Isuzu and Rundelhaus were the only ones left near the fire.

She didn't have any particular score in mind; she just strummed chords.

Isuzu had never touched a lute before this. She seemed to remember reading an article in a music magazine that had said it was a European instrument that was the ancestor of the guitar, and that it had been used in the Middle Ages...but until she came to this world, she'd never played one. *The basics are the same as a guitar or violin, though.*

At Isuzu's house, they had a guitar and a cheap wood bass, but no violin.

What had given her the most trouble was the fact that the lute had fifteen strings.

Even so, in two months, she'd learned how to play chords. Single-note melodies weren't a problem, either.

Tin cup in hand, Rundelhaus listened quietly to this session, which couldn't even be called a performance. His gaze didn't make Isuzu uncomfortable, and he didn't interrupt.

The music was like waves that rolled in and receded, over and over.

She hadn't been playing with a clear song in mind in the first place, so the performance wandered here and there, meandering off on detour after detour. Pop songs Isuzu knew from the old world appeared unexpectedly, then disappeared back into the sea of chords. Classical melodies and the sort of children's songs that were printed in textbooks surfaced, then dissolved.

There wasn't any real need for her to stop, but she'd reached a good place for it, so she struck a chord and rested for a bit. Seeming impressed, Rundelhaus began to clap.

"Oh, quit. It wasn't anything that great."

"No, it was good. It was as if the notes spilled out and melted into the air."

Isuzu thought that might have been the case, in a literal sense.

Still, if the sound of the lute had been that pleasant, it was probably due more to the situation than to anything Isuzu herself had done.

In a forest on a night of twinkling stars, seated by a fire, with a slightly cool mountain wind that still held the scents of summer. Under those circumstances, any instrument was bound to sound heavenly.

Isuzu was about to say so, but Rundelhaus's eyes held nothing but genuine admiration. It didn't seem right to find fault with that emotion. "Thank you," Isuzu said, briefly, and let the matter rest.

After that, they returned to idle chitchat.

From time to time, she strummed the lute she held in her arms, as if she was playing with it.

The droplets of sound floated up into the night air, and it made her happy.

"What do you usually eat, Rudy?"

"Toasted sandwiches, or toasted sandwiches, or toasted sandwiches."

"So, *just* toasted sandwiches. Do you mean the ones with fish eggs?"

"That's right, Miss Isuzu."

These were sold from a mobile shop on the grounds of the train station in Akiba, run by a guild called Ray Parker (abbreviated on menus as RP.jr). They were a small guild, but they prominently displayed the super-popular menu item Mentaiko Toasted Sandwich, and they were making a killing with it. The secret of its popularity was probably the delicious bread they were rumored to bake six times a day.

Isuzu liked them, too; they had items like Mentaiko Potato Salad that focused on ingredients that cost less than meat-based dishes, and they were good at business.

"Those really are good, aren't they?"

"Mm-hm. The way the fish eggs pop is superb."

For a while, they talked enthusiastically about food.

As far as drinks went, they both liked the Black Rose Tea that was currently all the rage in Akiba.

Crush Sherbet—made by adding a little honey and lemon juice to water, then having the spirits freeze it—was also delicious. When you wanted a bit of a feast, the breaded pork cutlets from Kitchen Buu were the best.

Isuzu felt unusually talkative.

She knew that she was a plain girl, and she had very few memories of ever having talked with a boy for this long.

Was it because the boy was Rundelhaus?

She took another look at the young man. His eyelashes were long, he was good-looking, and he had the face of an Anglo-Saxon model. In other words, he looked like a prince, and if he'd come to the country school Isuzu attended, there would have been such an uproar that it would have been impossible to hold classes for a week.

However, even when she looked at that face, Isuzu didn't feel the least bit romantic.

"Hmmmm," Isuzu murmured.

That's it! A golden retriever!!

The big, smart, handsome dog that seemed linked to the English aristocracy—Rundelhaus bore a strong resemblance to that sort of canine. His intelligence, elegance, and arrogance fit, too. The way his eyes tilted down at the outer corners, the way he was really kind of dumb when you got to know him, and his friendliness toward people all matched perfectly.

Isuzu's mind had placed Rundelhaus solidly in the spot meant for golden retrievers.

I see… That's why Rudy isn't the least bit scary.

Isuzu loved dogs, and she thought they loved her back.

Being with Rundelhaus felt exactly like taking care of a big dog. That was why she didn't get nervous, Isuzu thought, and she felt oddly satisfied with the answer.

The conversation turned to regular lodgings. Isuzu slept at her guild house, but Rundelhaus didn't belong to a guild.

"Fu-fuuuhn. I always stay in the royal suite on the second floor of Siden's Tavern."

His conceited manner of speaking sounded just like a puppy's woofing to Isuzu, and she didn't mind a bit. Besides, where the taverns of Akiba were concerned, Siden's Tavern was a bit below average. Its good location made it popular, but its prices and status were only so-so.

Um, no. That's not really the sort of place you can brag about.

Although the name sounded good, the "royal suite" on the second floor of the inn was perfectly ordinary lodgings for Adventurers, nothing more.

It was quite like a golden retriever to brag about a place like that, Isuzu thought.

Of course that was cute, too.

"I see. By the way, why aren't you in a guild, Rudy? Aren't you going to join one?"

"Tying my brilliant talent to one place would be sin itself, wouldn't it?" Rudy answered, posturing, then gave her a casual wink.

I've never met anyone who could wink that naturally before. Rudy's amazing. ...Well, amazing and dumb.

Rudy was dumb, but the decision of whether or not to join a guild was up to individual players.

It wasn't something for other people to find fault with.

"I see..."

"But you have natural beauty, Miss Isuzu. I've never heard such a moving solo performance. You really do seem to love music. ...You're reliable in battle as well. I'd never seen a Bard with a two-handed spear before."

"G-geez, Rudy. Shut up..." Isuzu shot back.

She'd chosen the two-handed spear only because it seemed to go with something she'd seen in her father's collection: a rock star smashing his guitar on his amp.

It was a fairly heavy weapon, and even she was surprised at how oddly easy it was for her to use. Wood basses might not look it, but even they weighed about fifteen kilos, so maybe it was only natural that she could swing a two-handed spear around. In other words, she thought, anything was possible with practice.

"Ha-ha-ha-ha! I like your spirit, Miss Isuzu! You're a rare companion; it's relaxing to be around you. We both live in Akiba, you know. We'll run into each other even after the training camp. I hope you'll keep an eye out for me!"

"Mm. Me, too."

Isuzu nodded, simply.

They weren't likely to get out of this world anytime soon.

Battles were scary. Sometimes memories of the pitch-black emotions she'd felt when she was in Hamelin came back to her, and it felt as if her chest would be crushed.

Even so, Isuzu had music right there with her, and she had friends. If she couldn't go home yet, she'd just have to make the present as nice as possible. Isuzu had learned that determination from Minori, and because of it, she was able to accept Rundelhaus's words at face value.

"Oh. In that case, I'll add you to my friend list, Rudy. If I hear about any good money-making opportunities, I'll call you. We also need to go get Mentaiko Toasted Sandwiches sometime. Fu-fu-fu! Okay, adding, adding..."

"Uh—"

Rundelhaus's face clouded.

It was the expression of someone regretting a mistake.

Of someone reproaching his own naïveté.

Isuzu's menu screen wouldn't let her add Rundelhaus to her friend list.

▶ 6

The sound of violently clashing swords echoed through the forest.

Sword striking shield.

Ax and spear, each seeking out the other's weakness.

In one sprint, Shouryuu closed the distance between himself and the Kannagi he was fighting. The young player was level 38, and he'd just taken some distance and begun to chant, preparing to unleash Sword's Mystic Spell.

Shouryuu added a follow-up attack with Razor Edge, a fundamental Swashbuckler sword skill, blocking the chant as he closed the gap between them.

Coughing, the young player fell. Shouryuu lent him a hand, helping him to his feet.

"I know you want to get some distance before you chant, but if your opponent picks up on your intentions, he'll stop you. You won't have to worry about things like that if you're up against regular monsters, but enemies get stronger, too, you know. You'll have to get better at teamwork."

"So I really was too slow?"

"Not too slow, exactly. More like too honest. I'd think about picking up more action patterns."

The young man nodded meekly in response to Shouryuu's advice.

By level 40, players were in the *Elder Tales* middle class. In order to acquire the practical skills needed to reach this level, it was necessary to make it through a considerable number of battles. His level was probably good enough for artisan's self-defense, but if he was going to get by as a fighting Adventurer in the future, he'd need combat abilities that were more than just window dressing.

Now that *Elder Tales* was no longer a game, this was an important point that made the difference between life and death.

Adventurers in this world might be deathless, but they did feel pain.

According to players who'd died, the pain was quite possible to endure. They said it was about like breaking a bone, for example, or being hit by a car (although these things hurt far more than enough), but even without the pain, the disadvantages were significant.

For one thing, there was the problem of time.

When *Elder Tales* was a game, time in this world had moved twelve times as fast. For every two hours that passed in the real world, a day had passed in this world.

This had been a measure taken because of the game's quests. Some quests had events that only happened at night. If the real world and the *Elder Tales* world had run on the exact same time, when it was night in the *Elder Tales* world, it would have been night in the real world as well.

If the system had been run that way, users who could only ever play *Elder Tales* during the day could never have cleared these quests. Players were humans who lived their lives in the real world, and naturally, there was a regular rhythm to the times at which they played the game.

To accommodate these players, time had been adjusted to run twelve times as fast in the game world, so that one day would pass roughly every two hours.

However, now that *Elder Tales* had become another world, the players—in other words, the Adventurers—existed inside it. Unlike when it had been a game, they needed to take breaks, and they needed to sleep.

For that reason, they found themselves in a situation where destinations that could have been reached with an hour's journey when playing the game—in other words, destinations that were twelve hours away—now took a full two days to reach, since the journey included breaks and camping.

Under the current circumstances, with the Fairy Rings and all other methods of travel greatly restricted, that trend was even more noticeable.

Whether they were going to a dungeon or to a zone where high-level enemies appeared, simply getting there was hard.

The upshot was that experience points meant more than they had in the game. The number of experience points required to level up hadn't increased, but the number of points that could be earned per hour had shrunk considerably. Naturally, it also took more trouble to recoup the property and experience points lost through death.

Considered this way, you could say that battles themselves had become more difficult to approach. Since death didn't exist, in a pinch, every player was guaranteed the bare minimum of physical safety, but Adventurers who put themselves in combat on a daily basis needed to acquire skills with considerable determination.

The young Kannagi probably understood this. He raised his katana and began running through a sequence of moves, over and over, his expression serious.

Of the recovery classes, the Kannagi class was based on an Asian concept, and it was possible for its members to carry katana.

It wasn't clear how it worked for the rest of the world, but on the Japanese server, male Kannagi were often called *negi*—a term for a senior Shinto priest—while female Kannagi were known as *miko*. The *suikan* shirt and red *hakama* appropriate to those names were dedicated equipment that could be used only by players at or above level 40, and they must have been a goal for many players.

Many items in *Elder Tales* had been added by subcontracting companies, and the Japanese server had lots of exclusive equipment for Kannagi and Samurai in particular. Some—like Sacred Sword—were items that boosted magic abilities, and these were popular with Kannagi who played solo, like this young player.

Shouryuu looked at the young man and grinned.

His form wasn't bad. Fundamentally, Kannagi was a recovery class; save for a few exceptions, he wouldn't be able to learn special skills that involved close-combat weapons, but the training itself wouldn't be a waste. Being able to use both long-range spells and close-range weapon attacks dramatically increased the variety of combat maneuvers. Even among other Kannagi, this could become an advantage.

Just as Shouryuu was about to show the Kannagi one more thing—a practical method of walking—he whirled around as if he'd been stung.

Bad premonitions are always correct.

The gloomy sound of the bell that rang just then was something Shouryuu would probably never forget. It wasn't a sound from reality. It was a signal sent from the menu.

The ominous sound signaled an incoming telechat.

"Shouryuu?! Come to the beach, quick!"

"What's wrong, Miss Mari?"

"Sahuagins are comin' up out of the ocean! The newbies are— ghk. ... Hurry!!"

Leaving the telechat connected, Shouryuu yelled to the nearby, young Kannagi: "Get everyone together! It's an emergency!"

He didn't know what things were like on the beach.

He didn't know the sahuagins' numbers, or their military force.

However, the telechat audio was grainy, Marielle's breathing was harsh, and he could hear the sounds of battle. The players at the coast were low-level newbies. That meant there were lots of high-level Adventurers there with them, but depending on the enemy's numbers, there was no telling what the situation was.

What's going on?! Do sahuagins even appear here?!

"When you get everyone assembled, contact me by telechat. — Check in with me every ten minutes, too!"

Flinging those words over his shoulder, Shouryuu broke into a run. Quickly, he blew his summoning whistle, racing through the grove as if he couldn't wait for the horse.

Of course, it was important for someone to be here with the midrange players as well. However, the newbies at the coast were thirty levels lower.

Sahuagins were a species of monster.

As their name meaning "green water-dwelling demons" suggested, they were demihumans who lived in oceans and lakes. They looked like fish that had sprouted arms and legs, and their bodies ranged from pale gray to dark blue all over. Most of them had brown spots.

Their heights could be anywhere from 160 centimeters to—for the biggest—over two meters. They probably weighed a hundred kilos, give or take.

They had webs between the fingers of their thick forelimbs, and because they breathed with gills, they were able to live underwater. On top of that, possibly because they could also use their lungs to breathe, they sometimes came up on land.

It wasn't clear whether the problem was with their skin or the way their bodies were built, but they never went far from the water, which meant this type of monster was very rarely seen in ordinary wastelands or dungeons.

In terms of intelligence, they were on par with goblins, and they often used throwing spears or tridents as weapons. However, that was all Shouryuu knew about them.

He hadn't fought them very often.

Their levels were...from 20 to about 30, I think...

A chestnut horse had come galloping up beside Shouryuu, and he leapt from his run up onto its back, then spurred it straight for the coast at full speed.

The horse ran.

Through groves bursting with greenery. Through gooseberry bushes hung with berries.

Down field roads through hill country that was marked off like tiles.

Cumulonimbus clouds, the symbol of summer, floated in the blue sky.

What a beautiful sight.

That was what Shouryuu felt, even at a time like this.

Even though the summer was so calm and beautiful...

In his ears, from the open telechat transmission, he heard harsh breathing, clashing swords, and the shrill sound of magic splitting the sky.

Beyond it were the sahuagin's roars, like gnashing teeth, and the chaos of battle.

He could hear the quiet sound of something dripping… Was Marielle bleeding?

Shouryuu was assailed by a sense of urgency, as though he had a stone stuck in his throat.

The horse raced through the grounds of the abandoned school, now empty, and then made a beeline for the coast. This wide hill road was probably a farm road from the Age of Myth. The rotted utility poles on either side were buried like useless signposts. Leaping over fields of rapeseed blossoms and ridges of greens, Shouryuu's horse ran hard.

When he reached the coast, passing fleeing newbies as he did so, it was the front line of a battle. There, among members of the Knights of the Black Sword and Keel, Marielle was fighting to protect her companions.

Shouryuu drove his horse in among the sahuagins, kicking down a few that had held tridents at the ready. The high level–exclusive warhorse fought freely, responding to Shouryuu's expectations.

"Miss Mari!"

"Shouryuu!"

Shouryuu barred the way, shielding the pale Marielle. Shouryuu himself was the leader of the Crescent Moon League's combat team, so it was his job to fight to protect her. He was up against sahuagins, whose levels were low, but their numbers were so great they buried the coast.

"Miss Mari, get back!! We need to call back the groups that are scattered at area camps. Hurry!!"

Drawing his twin swords, Shouryuu leapt at the sahuagins—whose hideous forms were neither fish nor reptile—with movements as splendid as those of a young classical Chinese opera actor.

He turned himself into a gust of wind, charging again and again, not even avoiding the blue-black sprays of blood. There was no strategy or deliberation here. He only ran at them, threw himself into the melee and cut them down recklessly, striking at anything within reach.

Shouryuu didn't know yet.

He didn't know the sahuagins were coming up on land one after another, flooding the coast. He didn't know this wasn't an isolated battle, triggered by chance, but the beginning of a crisis like a dark cloud that was assailing the Zantleaf peninsula.

Wielding his twin swords, the boy scattered sparks into the air, fighting simply to protect his companions.

< Log Horizon 3—Game's End (Part 1)—The End >

[ELDER TALES]

MONSTE[

AN IN-DEPTH INTRODUCTION TO MONSTERS,
THE SHADOW PROTAGONISTS OF *ELDER TALES*!!

Illustration: Mochichi Hashimoto

| 600 |
| 500 |
| 400 |
| 300 |
| 200 |
| 100 |
| 0 |

▲ SHIROE ▲ BRIER WEASEL ▲ ASCOT CRAB ▲ SAHUAGIN ▲ SKELETON ▲ SKELETON ARCHER

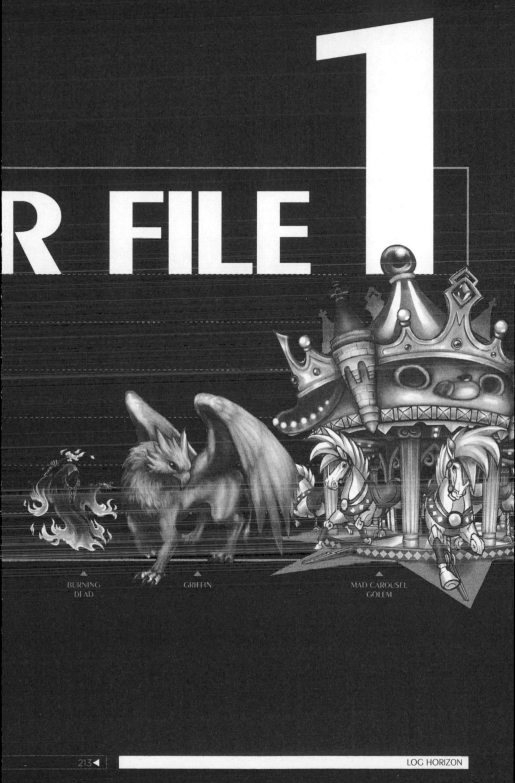

R FILE 1

BURNING
DEAD

GRIFFIN

MAD CAROUSEL
GOLEM

ASCOT CRAB

▶ LEVEL: **4–8**

▶ RANK: **NORMAL**

▶ APPEARS IN: **COASTAL AREAS**

GIANT CRABS THAT RANGE FROM **ONE TO TWO METERS IN SIZE**. THE COLOR OF THEIR BRIGHT SHELLS HAS EARNED THEM THE NICKNAME **APRICOTS**. THEIR BODIES ARE LARGE, AND THEY HAVE HIGH DEFENSE, BUT SINCE THEY AREN'T VERY INTELLIGENT AND THEIR ACTIONS ARE EASY TO READ, THEY'RE **GOOD PRACTICE OPPONENTS FOR COMBAT BEGINNERS**.

DEPENDING ON THE SEASON, THEY APPEAR ON THE SEASHORE LIKE FOAM AND DAMAGE NEARBY FIELDS, SO FARMERS HATE THEM. INCIDENTALLY, **THEIR MEAT IS PRETTY TASTY**.

BRIER WEASEL

▶ LEVEL: **8–46**

▶ RANK: **NORMAL**

▶ APPEARS IN: **PLAINS & FORESTS**

SMALL, MAGICAL BEASTS WHOSE BODIES RESEMBLE ERMINES. THEY POSSESS MAGIC THAT CAN CONTROL PLANT SPIRITS, AND THEY HAVE **MAGICAL BRIERS** WRAPPED AROUND THEIR TAILS. DURING BATTLE, THEY **USE THESE BRIERS LIKE WHIPS** TO ATTACK. THE WILD SPECIES ARE DISTRIBUTED ACROSS A WIDE RANGE OF LEVELS, AND THEY'RE **A VERY FAMILIAR MONSTER** TO ADVENTURERS WHO TRAVEL SOLO. THEIR CUTE APPEARANCE HAS MADE THEM **A SORT OF MASCOT** FOR *ELDER TALES*.

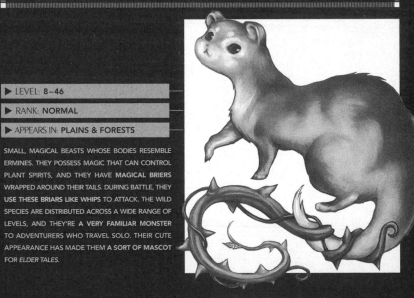

SKELETON

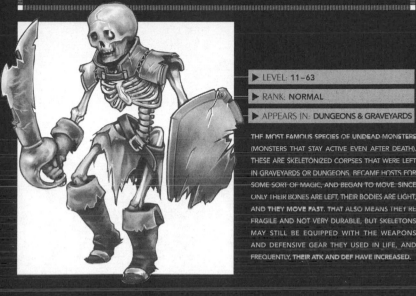

▶ LEVEL: **11-63**

▶ RANK: **NORMAL**

▶ APPEARS IN: **DUNGEONS & GRAVEYARDS**

THE MOST FAMOUS SPECIES OF UNDEAD MONSTERS (MONSTERS THAT STAY ACTIVE EVEN AFTER DEATH). THESE ARE SKELETONIZED CORPSES THAT WERE LEFT IN GRAVEYARDS OR DUNGEONS, BECAME HOSTS FOR SOME SORT OF MAGIC, AND BEGAN TO MOVE. SINCE ONLY THEIR BONES ARE LEFT, THEIR BODIES ARE LIGHT, AND **THEY MOVE FAST.** THAT ALSO MEANS THEY'RE FRAGILE AND NOT VERY DURABLE, BUT SKELETONS MAY STILL BE EQUIPPED WITH THE WEAPONS AND DEFENSIVE GEAR THEY USED IN LIFE, AND FREQUENTLY, **THEIR ATK AND DEF HAVE INCREASED.**

SKELETON ARCHER

▶ LEVEL: **12-67**

▶ RANK: **NORMAL**

▶ APPEARS IN: **DUNGEONS & GRAVEYARDS**

SKELETONS **EQUIPPED WITH BOWS** ARE CALLED SKELETON ARCHERS. DUE TO THEIR PHYSICAL COMPOSITION, SKELETONS ARE FULL OF HOLES, AND PIERCING ATTACKS THAT TARGET A SMALL AREA ARE VERY LIKELY TO SLIP RIGHT THROUGH THEM. THIS MEANS **ATTACKS WITH BOWS AND ARROWS ARE NEGATED** TO A CERTAIN EXTENT. SKELETON ARCHERS ARE **TROUBLESOME** MONSTERS THAT ATTACK BY FIRING WHILE **NEGATING ADVENTURERS' BOW-AND-ARROW ATTACKS.**

▶ LEVEL: **23–25**

▶ RANK: **PARTY**

▶ APPEARS IN: **DUNGEONS**

ONE OF THE MONSTERS **LURKING IN FOREST RAGRANDA**. IN THIS AREA, IT HAS POWERFUL ABILITIES AND **ACTS AS A BOSS**. IT LOOKS LIKE A HUMAN SKELETON, BUT ITS BODY RADIATES AN AURA OF **MALICIOUS FLAMES**. IT **LURKS IN THE FORGE** DEEP INSIDE THE DUNGEON AND USES FIRE MAGIC. THIS STRONG ENEMY HAS MANY WALKING CORPSES AS ITS UNDERLINGS, AND IT CAN EVEN **RAISE ITS IMMORTAL UNDERLINGS' COMBAT ABILITIES**. LONG-RANGE ATTACKS ARE TOUGH ON BEGINNING PARTIES, SO BE CAREFUL.

▶ LEVEL: **22–48**

▶ RANK: **NORMAL**

▶ APPEARS IN: **WATER AND COASTAL AREAS, SUBMERGED DUNGEONS**

A HUMANOID SPECIES THAT LIVES IN OCEANS AND LAKES. THEY LOOK LIKE FISH THAT WALK UPRIGHT, AND THEY CAN BE ANYWHERE FROM 120 TO 170 CENTIMETERS TALL. THEIR COLOR RANGES FROM PALE BLUE TO DARK BLUE, AND IN MANY CASES, THEIR BELLIES ARE PALE. THEY **LIVE IN THE WATER,** AND THEY'RE NORMALLY ACTIVE ON THE OCEAN FLOOR OR LAKE BEDS, BUT THEY'RE ALSO ABLE TO COME UP ON LAND FOR SEVERAL HOURS. THEY OFTEN USE THEIR **FORELIMBS TO HOLD KNIVES OR TRIDENTS** WHEN THEY FIGHT. BY NATURE, THEY'RE VERY CURIOUS AND **INHUMAN.** DURING COMBAT, THEY'RE **BRUTAL.**

▶ LEVEL: **41–69**

▶ RANK: **PARTY**

▶ APPEARS IN: **MOUNTAINS**

A FLYING SPECIES WITH THE BODY OF AN ENORMOUS LION AND THE HEAD, WINGS, AND FORELEGS OF AN EAGLE. THEIR BODIES RANGE FROM TWO TO FOUR METERS IN LENGTH, AND BECAUSE THEY CAN FLY WHILE CARRYING ONE OR TWO HUMAN-SIZED BEINGS, SOME ARE **TRAINED TO BE USED AS MOUNTS.** GRIFFINS HAVE **ADVANCED COMBAT ABILITIES,** AND AMONG FLYING MONSTERS, THEY RIVAL WYVERNS. HOWEVER, **WYVERNS** TEND TO BAND TOGETHER, WHILE MOST GRIFFINS ARE ENCOUNTERED **ALONE OR AS MATED PAIRS.**

MAD CAROUSEL GOLEM

▶ LEVEL: **82**

▶ RANK: **RAID 1**

▶ APPEARS IN: **ANCIENT RUINS**

A POWERFUL MONSTER THAT APPEARS IN THE MAIHAMA UNDERGROUND RUINS, RAID CONTENT ADDED WITH THE CENDRILLON'S LEGACY EXPANSION PACK. IT'S AN ANCIENT AMUSEMENT ATTRACTION THAT WAS MODDED INTO A GOLEM. IT WAS ERODED BY A CURSE THAT SENT THE SURROUNDING FACILITIES MAD, AND NOW IT'S **OUT OF CONTROL**. ITS MAIN METHODS OF ATTACK ARE DARKNESS CURTAIN, AN ATTACK SPELL THAT LOOKS LIKE **BLACK MIST**, AND A **TORRENT OF SPINNING WOODEN HORSES**. IT ATTACKS ADVENTURERS WHILE SWITCHING BETWEEN THE MANY TELEPORTERS INSTALLED IN THE AMUSEMENT FACILITY.

►*ELDER TALES*

A "SWORD AND SORCERY"—THEMED ONLINE GAME AND ONE OF THE LARGEST IN THE WORLD. AN MMORPG FAVORED BY SERIOUS GAMERS, IT BOASTS A TWENTY-YEAR HISTORY.

►THE CATASTROPHE

A TERM FOR THE INCIDENT IN WHICH USERS WERE TRAPPED INSIDE THE *ELDER TALES* GAME WORLD. IT AFFECTED THE THIRTY THOUSAND JAPANESE USERS WHO WERE ONLINE WHEN HOMESTEADING THE NOOSPHERE, THE GAME'S TWELFTH EXPANSION PACK, WAS INTRODUCED.

►ADVENTURER

THE GENERAL TERM FOR A GAMER WHO IS PLAYING *ELDER TALES*. WHEN BEGINNING THE GAME, PLAYERS SELECT HEIGHT, CLASS, AND RACE FOR THESE IN-GAME DOUBLES. THE TERM IS MAINLY USED BY NON-PLAYER CHARACTERS TO REFER TO PLAYERS.

►PEOPLE OF THE EARTH

THE NAME NON-PLAYER CHARACTERS USE FOR THEMSELVES. THE CATASTROPHE DRASTICALLY INCREASED THEIR NUMBERS FROM WHAT THEY WERE IN THE GAME. THEY NEED TO SLEEP AND EAT REGULARLY, SO IT'S HARD TO TELL THEM APART FROM PLAYERS WITHOUT CHECKING THE STATUS SCREEN.

►THE HALF-GAIA PROJECT

A PROJECT TO CREATE A HALF-SIZED EARTH INSIDE *ELDER TALES*. ALTHOUGH IT'S NEARLY THE SAME SHAPE AS EARTH, THE DISTANCES ARE HALVED AND IT HAS ONLY ONE-FOURTH THE AREA.

►AGE OF MYTH

A GENERAL TERM FOR THE ERA SAID TO HAVE BEEN DESTROYED IN THE OFFICIAL BACKSTORY OF THE *ELDER TALES* ONLINE GAME. IT WAS BASED ON THE CULTURE AND CIVILIZATION OF THE REAL WORLD. SUBWAYS AND BUILDINGS ARE THE RUINED RELICS OF THIS ERA.

►THE OLD WORLD

THE WORLD WHERE SHIROE AND THE OTHERS LIVED BEFORE *ELDER TALES* BECAME ANOTHER WORLD AND TRAPPED THEM. A TERM FOR EARTH, THE REAL WORLD, ETC.

►GUILDS

TEAMS COMPOSED OF MULTIPLE PLAYERS. SINCE IT'S EASIER TO CONTACT AFFILIATED MEMBERS AND INVITE THEM ON ADVENTURES AND BECAUSE GUILDS ALSO PROVIDE CONVENIENT SERVICES (SUCH AS MAKING IT EASIER TO RECEIVE AND SEND ITEMS), MANY PLAYERS BELONG TO THEM.

▶THE ROUND TABLE COUNCIL

THE TOWN OF AKIBA'S SELF-GOVERNMENT ORGANIZATION, FORMED AT SHIROE'S PROPOSAL. COMPOSED OF ELEVEN GUILDS, INCLUDING MAJOR COMBAT AND PRODUCTION GUILDS AND GUILDS THAT COLLECTIVELY REPRESENT SMALL AND MIDSIZE GUILDS, IT'S IN A POSITION TO LEAD THE REFORMATION IN AKIBA.

▶LOG HORIZON

THE NAME OF THE GUILD SHIROE FORMED AFTER THE CATASTROPHE. ITS FOUNDING MEMBERS—AKATSUKI, NAOTSUGU, AND NYANTA—HAVE BEEN JOINED BY THE TWINS MINORI AND TOUYA. THEIR HEADQUARTERS IS IN A RUINED BUILDING PIERCED BY A GIANT ANCIENT TREE ON THE OUTSKIRTS OF AKIBA.

▶THE CRESCENT MOON LEAGUE

THE NAME OF THE GUILD MARI LEADS. ITS PRIMARY PURPOSE IS TO SUPPORT MIDLEVEL PLAYERS. HENRIETTA, MARI'S FRIEND SINCE THEIR DAYS AT A GIRLS' HIGH SCHOOL, ACTS AS ITS ACCOUNTANT.

▶THE DEBAUCHERY TEA PARTY

THE NAME OF A GROUP OF PLAYERS THAT SHIROE, NAOTSUGU, AND NYANTA BELONGED TO AT ONE TIME. IT WAS ACTIVE FOR ABOUT TWO YEARS, AND ALTHOUGH IT WASN'T A GUILD, IT'S STILL REMEMBERED IN *ELDER TALES* AS A LEGENDARY BAND OF PLAYERS.

▶MAIN CLASS

THESE GOVERN COMBAT ABILITIES IN *ELDER TALES*, AND PLAYERS CHOOSE ONE WHEN BEGINNING THE GAME. THERE ARE TWELVE TYPES, THREE EACH IN FOUR CATEGORIES: WARRIOR, WEAPON ATTACK, RECOVERY, AND MAGIC ATTACK.

▶SUBCLASS

ABILITIES THAT AREN'T DIRECTLY INVOLVED IN COMBAT BUT COME IN HANDY DURING GAME PLAY. ALTHOUGH THERE ARE ONLY TWELVE MAIN CLASSES, THERE ARE OVER FIFTY SUBCLASSES, AND THEY'RE A JUMBLED MIX OF EVERYTHING FROM CONVENIENT SKILL SETS TO JOKE ELEMENTS.

▶FAIRY RINGS

TRANSPORTATION DEVICES LOCATED IN FIELDS. THE DESTINATIONS ARE TIED TO THE PHASES OF THE MOON, AND IF PLAYERS USE THEM AT THE WRONG TIME, THERE'S NO TELLING WHERE THEY'LL END UP. AFTER THE CATASTROPHE, SINCE STRATEGY WEBSITES ARE INACCESSIBLE, ALMOST NO ONE USES THEM.

▶ZONE

A UNIT THAT DESCRIBES RANGE AND AREA IN *ELDER TALES*. IN ADDITION TO FIELDS, DUNGEONS, AND TOWNS, THERE ARE ZONES AS SMALL AS SINGLE HOTEL ROOMS. DEPENDING ON THE PRICE, IT'S SOMETIMES POSSIBLE TO BUY THEM.

AFTERWORD

Hello! It's been two months since we last met. I'm Mamare Touno.

Thank you very much for buying *Log Horizon 3: Game's End, Part 1*. There are two parts to this one, and *Log Horizon 4: Game's End, Part 2* will be in stores next month. *Log Horizon*: brought to you on a monthly basis. I'm deeply indebted to everyone involved. To those of you whose allowance won't stretch far enough, I'm really sorry! Still, as with Part 1, Part 2 is scheduled to be jam-packed with content.

......

....

And now that I've role-played as a responsible adult, I'll talk about the Bon Festival dance.

The weather here is hot one day and cool the next, but where I live, it's almost Bon Festival dance season. I live in Katsushika Ward, one of Tokyo's leading Shitamachi neighborhoods, and this means it's one of the greatest Bon dance towns in the world. How amazing is it, you ask? When this season rolls around, to keep the schedule staggered, the neighborhood association schedules Bon dances every weekend, and the Tokyo Ondo song is in heavy rotation. Women's associations that have trained hard all year for this head out to nearby neighborhood associations' Bon dances and show their stuff in a type of diplomacy.

The streets are alive with the *boom ba-boom* and *tak-takalak* of drums, and the sounds are more a part of everyday life than at the Samba Carnivals of Rio or Asakusa.

And why are festival food stalls so absurdly alluring, anyway?

The scent of scorched sauce, the color of synthetic-looking sweeteners… It's obvious they can't be good for you, but I can't get enough of 'em.

So, when I happened to run across a Bon dance venue, I e-mailed my little sister Touno a photo of yakisoba, and she replied, "Now I'm mad." I had no idea what she was talking about, so I sent her a photo of grilled squid, and got a "You're annoying." Since there was no help for it, I sent a photo of a chocolate-covered banana, and her response was, "Curl up and die." When I got carried away and sent a photo of roasted corn, I got a phone call.

If she wanted to eat some, she could have just said so.

Come to think of it, when we were kids, I told my sister, "The Bon dance food stalls are run by guys from the neighborhood association. They're volunteering for the sole purpose of making kids happy, so every time a food stall sells something, they run a huge deficit." Maybe because our family was in business, Young Touno was an unpleasant kid who talked about profit and loss starting in elementary school.

In connection with that, I seem to remember Little Sister Touno making a terribly sad face when she bought yakisoba that year.

Of course, that's all in the past now.

I brought her some, and we scarfed it down messily.

It's not that I really want to eat like a pig, but with festival fast food, the image of devouring it greedily is important. Eating that way makes you feel like you're spending extravagantly.

After Sister Touno had eaten for a while and had a full belly, I started telling her the "Bon dance food stalls are run by guys from the neighborhood association" story, and she got super mad at me. Apparently she remembers. Tch.

Since there was no help for it, I made up random stuff: "These days, food stalls are becoming standardized, and they're run by franchises. Food stall placement is increasingly being done electronically, and a group based in eastern Japan sends ingredients out to food stall proprietors from a central kitchen, so their gross margin ratio is several times that of regular restaurants."

I told her this while handing her a convenience store ice cream (the expensive kind), so she was terribly impressed, and I felt kinda guilty.

Little sister, don't say, "If I get a lot of money, maybe I'll invest in Bon dance food stalls." No such financial product exists.

A group run by the Charlatan Family manages franchisees? What kind of cyberpunk worldview is that? Is this Neo-Saitama? I'll buy you as much roasted corn as you want, so spare me the business about ethanol futures.

You're won over by things like frozen yogurt, and your big brother's really worried that you'll buy some silk screen thing in Akiba or somewhere and come home looking terribly pleased with yourself.

Even so, seeing her get that worked up over ice cream made me think that Little Sister Touno is really eas… I mean, really something. Although she's dumb.

And now for the sequel.

When it happened to cross my mind and I looked into it, I discovered that the business about standardizing festival stalls and the central kitchen and IT and gross margin ratios was actually pretty close to the truth, and I'm not sure how that makes me feel. If this keeps up, I wouldn't be surprised if they did introduce a financial product. The world's a scary place!

(Let's call the fact that Would you believe it?!—the Log Horizon manga project is moving forward proof that the world is indeed a scary place.)

All right. Regardless of the modern Bon Dance economy, Log Horizon is being published in both August and September. The twins, Touya and Minori, and Serara of the Crescent Moon League appear in this volume, as do new characters like Isuzu and Rundelhaus. A party made up of these newbies works to capture a dungeon without Shiroe and the other veterans.

"The best laid plans…" In other words, the world is full of things that don't go the way you want them to. The majority of what happens in this world doesn't go at all the way you'd like. Since that's true, at the very least, I'd like to make myself go the way I want me to, but there are lots of times when even my own attitude and growth and efforts don't go as planned. I'd like people who are going through times like that, and people who've been through times like that, to read this. That's the sort of hard, desperate battle Minori and the others fight in this volume.

The items listed on the character status screens at the beginning of each chapter in this volume were collected on Twitter again, in June 2011. I used items from 545454248, FroisL, IGM_masamune, Mrtyin, RyosukeKadoh, ebius1, gontan_, hige_mg, hpsuke, makiwasabi, roki_a, sig_cat and x_unizou_x. Thank you very much!! I can't list all your names here, but I'm grateful to everyone who submitted entries. Maybe I'll find some kind of opportunity to use this item data...

For details and the latest news, visit http://www.mamare.net. You'll find all sorts of other non–*Log Horizon* Mamare Touno information there, too, as well as info on the comic version!

Finally, let me thank Shoji Masuda, who produced this book, too; Kazuhiro Hara, who drew Marielle's swimsuit (crucial!); Mochichi Hashimoto, who designed the monsters; Tsubakiya Design, who handled the design work (and we even had them make the map!); little F_ta of the editorial department! And Ohasama, whom Touno practically considers his master when it comes to text! Thank you very much!

Now all that's left is for you to savor this book. Bon appétit!

Mamare "Squid legs are way better than
the bodies, don't you think?" Touno

MAOYUU HERO DEMON KING × LOG HORIZON

Illustration: toi8

Illustration: Kazuhiro Hara

A LITTLE SOMETHING TO HELP YOU BEAT THE LATE SUMMER HEAT.

HARA

▶LOG HORIZON, VOLUME 3
MAMARE TOUNO
ILLUSTRATION BY KAZUHIRO HARA

▶TRANSLATION BY TAYLOR ENGEL

▶LOG HORIZON, VOLUME 3:
GAME'S END, PART I

▶©2011 TOUNO MAMARE
ALL RIGHTS RESERVED.

▶FIRST PUBLISHED IN JAPAN IN 2011 BY
KADOKAWA CORPORATION ENTERBRAIN.
ENGLISH TRANSLATION RIGHTS ARRANGED
WITH KADOKAWA CORPORATION ENTERBRAIN
THROUGH TUTTLE-MORI AGENCY, INC., TOKYO.
ENGLISH TRANSLATION © 2015 HACHETTE
BOOK GROUP, INC.

▶YEN ON
HACHETTE BOOK GROUP
1290 AVENUE OF THE AMERICAS
NEW YORK, NY 10104
WWW.HACHETTEBOOKGROUP.COM
WWW.YENPRESS.COM

▶YEN ON IS AN IMPRINT OF
HACHETTE BOOK GROUP, INC.

▶THE YEN ON NAME AND LOGO ARE
TRADEMARKS OF
HACHETTE BOOK GROUP, INC.

▶THE PUBLISHER IS NOT RESPONSIBLE
FOR WEBSITES (OR THEIR CONTENT) THAT
ARE NOT OWNED BY THE PUBLISHER.

▶FIRST YEN ON EDITION: NOVEMBER 2015

▶ISBN: 978-0-316-26384-9

10 9 8 7 6 5 4 3 2 1

▶RRD-C

▶PRINTED IN THE UNITED STATES OF AMERICA

▶AUTHOR: **MAMARE TOUNO**

▶SUPERVISION: **SHOJI MASUDA**

▶ILLUSTRATION: **KAZUHIRO HARA**

▶AUTHOR: MAMARE TOUNO

A STRANGE LIFE-FORM THAT INHABITS THE TOKYO BOKUTOU SHITAMACHI AREA. IT'S BEEN TOSSING HALF-BAKED TEXT INTO A CORNER OF THE INTERNET SINCE THE YEAR 2000 OR SO. IT'S A FULLY AUTOMATIC, TEXT-LOVING MACRO THAT EATS AND DISCHARGES TEXT. IT DEBUTED AT THE END OF 2010 WITH *MAOYUU: MAOU YUUSHA (MAOYUU: DEMON KING AND HERO)*. *LOG HORIZON* IS A RESTRUCTURED VERSION OF A NOVEL THAT RAN ON THE WEBSITE *SHOUSETSUKA NI NAROU (SO YOU WANT TO BE A NOVELIST)*.

WEBSITE: HTTP://WWW.MAMARE.NET

▶SUPERVISION: SHOJI MASUDA

AS A GAME DESIGNER, HE'S WORKED ON *RINDA KYUUBU (RINDA CUBE)* AND *ORE NO SHIKABANE WO KOETE YUKE (STEP OVER MY DEAD BODY)*, AMONG OTHERS. ALSO ACTIVE AS A NOVELIST, HE'S RELEASED THE *ONIGIRI NUEKO (ONI KILLER NUEKO)* SERIES, THE *HARUKA* SERIES, *JOHN & MARY: FUTARITTA SHOUKIN KASEGI (JOHN & MARY: BOUNTY HUNTERS)*, *KIZUDARAKE NO DIINA (BEENA, COVERED IN WOUNDS)*, AND MORE. HIS LATEST EFFORT IS HIS FIRST CHILDREN'S BOOK, *TOUMEI NO NEKO TO TOSHI UE NO IMOUTO (THE TRANSPARENT CAT AND THE OLDER LITTLE SISTER)*. HE HAS ALSO WRITTEN *GEEMU DEZAIN NOU MASUDA SHINJI NO HASSOU TO WAZA (GAME DESIGN BRAIN: SHINJI MASUDA'S IDEAS AND TECHNIQUES)*.

TWITTER ACCOUNT: SHOJIMASUDA

▶ILLUSTRATION: KAZUHIRO HARA

AN ILLUSTRATOR WHO LIVES IN ZUSHI. ORIGINALLY A HOME GAME DEVELOPER. IN ADDITION TO ILLUSTRATING BOOKS, HE'S ALSO ACTIVE IN MANGA AND DESIGN. LATELY, HE'S BEEN HAVING FUN FLYING A BIOKITE WHEN HE GOES ON WALKS.

WEBSITE: HTTP://WWW.NINEFIVE95.COM/IG/

Fragrant green winds blow across this new, yet somehow old land. The imaginary world of Theldesia is home to dragons and giants, monsters and demihumans. With a burden weighing upon your soul, go forth, O winged nine <Adventurers>! This land spreads out before you like a blank page: make your mark on it!

LOG HORIZON

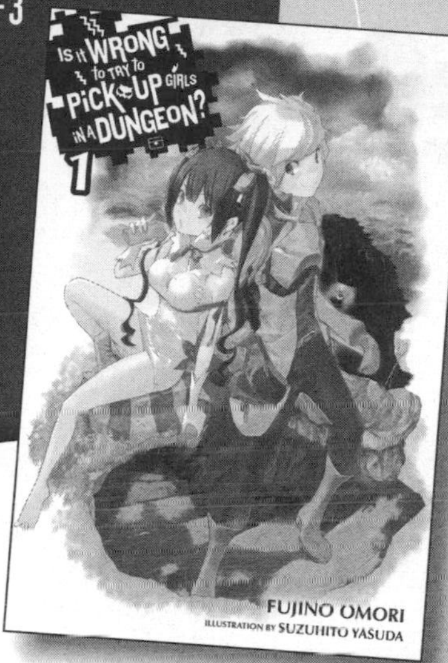

Is It WRONG to Try to PICK UP GIRLS in a DUNGEON?
1
FUJINO OMORI
ILLUSTRATION BY SUZUHITO YASUDA

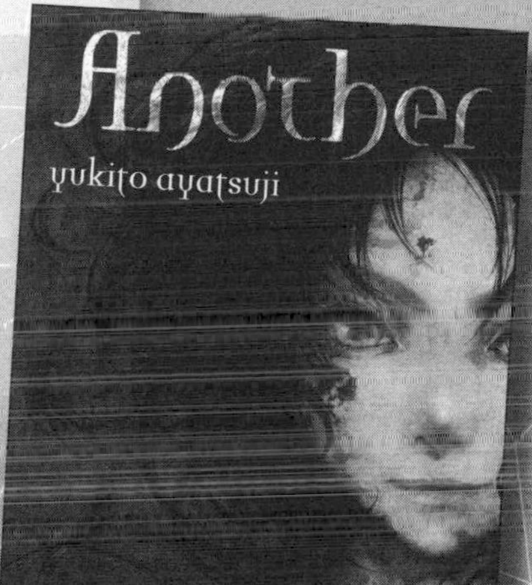

Another
yukito ayatsuji

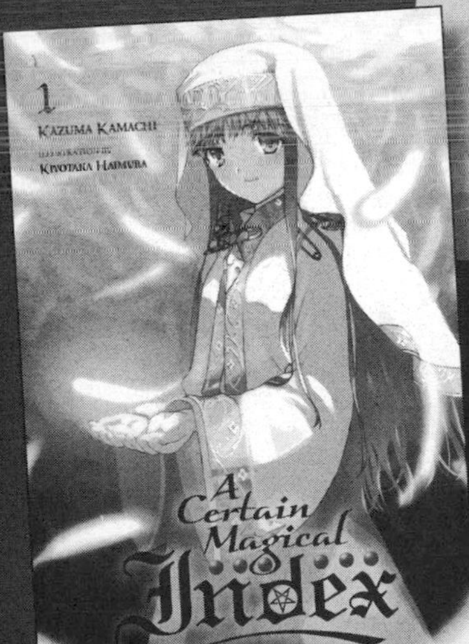

1
KAZUMA KAMACHI
KIYOTAKA HAIMURA
A Certain Magical Index